I0628175

VIA Folios 172

Collegiate Gothic

COLLEGIATE GOTHIC

Matthew Meduri

BORDIGHERA PRESS

All rights reserved. Parts of this book may be reprinted only by written permission from the author, and may not be reproduced for publication in book, magazine, or electronic media of any kind, except in quotations for purposes of literary reviews by critics.

© 2024, Matthew Meduri

Cover art and design by Korey Kunze.

Library of Congress Control Number: 2024942092

Published by
BORDIGHERA PRESS
John D. Calandra Italian American Institute
25 W. 43rd Street, 17th Floor
New York, NY 10036

VIA Folios 172
ISBN 978-1-59954-220-1

Table of Contents

For Amber, Lil, and Milo

Where does [our] investigation get its importance from, since it seems only to destroy everything interesting, that is, all that is great and important? (As it were all the buildings, leaving behind only bits of stone and rubble). What we are destroying is nothing but houses of cards and we are clearing up the ground of language on which they stand.

—LUDWIG WITTGENSTEIN

It's clear we love the Dead Girl, enough to rehash and reproduce her story, to kill her again and again, but not enough to see a pattern. She is always singular, an anomaly, the juicy new mystery.

—ALICE BOLIN

The Dead Girl Show

Come and see the dead girl whose body lies motionless in a rented room at the old Athens Motor Inn. Barefoot and dressed in a pair of faded blue jeans and a grey sweatshirt, she is simple and plain; her long, dark hair splayed on the cheap and dirty carpet. Marvel at her pale and ashen skin painted violet by the bruising on her neck and throat, little silhouettes of her assailant's hands, so pronounced, so cartoonish. Be amazed by the broken blood vessels in her eyes, which were open upon discovery, beautiful azure eyes that watched her perpetrator squeeze the life from her.

Come and see the dead girl whose cause of death was strangulation on this chilly afternoon in late October 2009. Of course, there were signs of a struggle: the disheveled comforter, the bed's mattress askew, the faint patterns in the carpet around her legs paired with the bruising on her heels. Watch the thrill (disturbance?) of the investigators as they examine her room, her belongings, her body, her life: the text messages and phone calls, the relationships, the broken hyoid bone, the DNA under her fingernails. Isn't she idyllic? One-of-a-kind? She's not just another Jane Doe. She has a name, an age, a place of residence, a time of death. Do those details even matter? The dead girl is your obsession, an American artifact.

Feast your eyes on Lily Zephyr, 28, from New York City. The lead investigator holds the victim's driver's license like an advertisement for an event. The owner of the complex, an old hippie in a faded army jacket, confirms the name on the lease, though the man who found her seems perplexed by this information. According to him, she went by another name, and they had a meaningful relationship, the details of which are sensitive, an affair perhaps. Delight in this man's confusion as he's escorted to the police station for further questioning. He doesn't yet realize what he's a part of, what this is.

These events don't happen all the time, folks, not in a small college town like Athens, Ohio. A place where outsiders go for an education and insiders stay for the insulation. A quaint Midwest suburb, a good place to raise children. Where crime rates are low, and boredom is at an all-time high. Where you can try to escape your past, but your future will deny it. Welcome to The Dead Girl Show.

Part I

A College upon a Hill

Chapter 1

It was another pointless late Friday afternoon meeting—unnecessary, unrequired, and largely unproductive. William Thierry sat in an old, paisley armchair in the Buchanans' living room, stomach growling from the aroma of garlic sautéing in the kitchen, mind elsewhere as he feigned concern for Dr. Harvey Buchanan's complaints about the typical academic woes. What had begun as the occasional get-together with drinks and casual philosophizing had quickly devolved into a weekly supper club and shop talk. As Harvey paced the room and ranted about the current university drama, Will emptied his glass of beer and watched Harvey's wife Anne prepare dinner. He didn't watch her for the way she used a knife to delicately cube the tofu after pressing it, or julienned the vegetables for the stir fry, or even how she dressed the kale salad with a pesto of walnuts, lemon juice, and herbs. Will witnessed her every movement solely by way of the position of his chair.

Angled more toward the kitchen's doorway, the chair provided Will a perfectly framed view of Anne's body, making it difficult to give Harvey his full attention, which was compounded by the man's relentless pacing. Maybe if Will discreetly rotated the chair back to where he thought it had been, he'd feel less like an awkward spectator.

"Do you hear what I'm saying, Will?"

"Sure, but is it me, or is this chair in a different spot?"

"What? No. It's always been there." He paused long enough to sip his bourbon. "The predicted university budget cuts are giving me a goddamn ulcer."

Will returned his gaze to Anne. The way she moved or stood

or did absolutely anything was enough. Her slender physique in teal yoga pants and a Guided By Voices T-shirt, her shoulder-length auburn hair yanked back in a ponytail. She had taught her morning and noon Power Vinyasa but didn't bother to change. *And now,* Will thought, *she's choreographed a dance that Harvey is too preoccupied to notice.* His eyes followed her each time she pivoted slightly to the left or right, opening a cupboard or pulling out a drawer for a utensil. And his thoughts stripped her naked as she stretched for something slightly out of reach in a cupboard. She stood on her tiptoes to grasp it, and in his mind, she returned to downward facing dog, and now he's behind her—

"Will."

Will jerked his head in Harvey's direction.

"If you want to help her in the kitchen, be my guest. I'll tell someone who actually gives a damn about the department's future."

For a moment, Will thought Harvey could read his mind. "I care about the department, but my thoughts are on the conference and Laroche. Is he going to rip me a new asshole like he did with the book review?" Will downed the last gulp of beer and set his glass on the coffee table.

"With the money we're paying him, he should be your best friend for the whole weekend." Another sip. "What I was trying to tell you is I met with the Dean of Humanities yesterday. He's certain the university and board of trustees will vote unanimously on its 'restructuring' plan, and, as you know, we are on the list for proposed cuts."

"Jesus, we're one of the least-funded departments in the most neglected building on campus. They'd be saving pennies."

Harvey sat on the couch facing Will. "They don't care that we have the oldest philosophy program in Ohio or an increase in enrollment. It's all about STEM and business now. That's where the money is." He emptied his glass with a final gulp and hunched forward, resting his forearms on his knees. "They'll make it public when they vote November 1. I guess that gives them two weeks to prepare for the backlash from the other targeted departments. You know those fuckers at the Office of Institutional Advancement only care about numbers and appearances."

"So, what now?" Will shifted in his chair and crossed his legs.

"I'm hoping for a good turnout at the conference. That might help our case. Some national recognition wouldn't hurt. Maybe we could find someone to cover the conference in *Philosophy Now*? I also have a few other ideas, but we need a refill first." Harvey stood. "You want another beer?"

"Sure."

Harvey walked to the kitchen as Will leaned his head back and looked at the ceiling, the upholstery rough on his neck. Not even halfway through his third year at Athens and his position was in jeopardy, an unanticipated consequence of taking the first job thrown at him during a recession. If only his circumstances had been different in New York, then he wouldn't be biding his time in this purgatory of strip malls, cornfields, and the perpetual noise machine of residential landscaping. But it gave him the headspace he needed to write another book. Isn't that why most people from the East or West Coast moved to the Midwest, as a kind of detoxified, affordable living? Still, he committed a second term to an underfunded, largely unknown university in Ohio whose philosophy studies might be heading to the list of defunct programs. Will sighed. *What a joke?*

Harvey returned with a refreshed glass of bourbon in his right hand and a can of Genesee Cream Ale in his left. He handed Will the beer. "I still don't know how you can stomach this stuff?"

"Where I come from, this stuff is sacred." Will poured the can's liquid into his glass.

Harvey sat in his spot on the couch. "At this point, the conference means everything this year. Our biggest attraction is Laroche. There are two hundred people officially registered for the weekend, twice as many as last year. We have all the expenses covered. If this goes well, it might give us some leverage. Show the bastards philosophy matters." Harvey shook his head and set his glass on the coffee table. "I hope this leads to possible partnerships."

"Like what exactly?"

"A study abroad program with the Sorbonne. What student wouldn't want to travel to Paris, walk the streets of Voltaire, Diderot, and Sartre, and study with world-class philosophers and faculty?"

"We don't have the caliber of student for the Sorbonne. They wouldn't last a week in one of those courses. Plus, I don't speak French. Do you?"

"That's not the point. We could bounce the idea off Laroche over drinks. Make it is a six-week program. Really sell it to him. Try to get a few contacts. If we could offer an option like that, I have no doubt we'd increase our enrollment. The Global Education Department would love us. But we need a strategy."

"It couldn't hurt to try."

"If we get our shit together, we could have this up and running by next year. Make it a summer opportunity."

"I don't think it's really up to him."

"No, I know. But it wouldn't hurt to get Laroche's seal of approval."

"Shit," said Anne.

"What is it?" asked Harvey.

"Nothing. I just burned myself. I'm fine."

"That's what she gets for trying to be Rachel Ray." Harvey grinned. "She's always cutting or burning herself. I tell her to throw some burgers on the grill or get a pizza, and what do I get? Homemade turkey or black bean patties and pizza that tastes like salad and cardboard. She even once tried to make a cauliflower crust." Harvey shook his and pointed to his bourbon. "Most of the time I'd rather just drink my dinner."

"Are you kidding? I'd gladly take Anne's cooking over my limited takeout options."

"Thank you, Will," said Anne. "At least someone appreciates me."

Harvey continued talking for talking's sake, but Will failed to comprehend. Again, he stared at Anne, and she glanced back, catching eyes with him, and smiled. Will's attention landed on Harvey. *What the hell did she ever see in him?* Harvey didn't appreciate her, not to mention his irritability and obnoxiousness were at an all-time high, and he practically sprinted to empty that bottle of Knob Creek he kept in the kitchen. The man seemed off.

"Food's almost ready," said Anne.

"Mind if I use the restroom?" asked Will.

"Knock yourself out," said Harvey.

Will walked to the bathroom on the first floor and shut the door behind him. He unzipped his pants. A stream of urine hit bull's-eye in the still water. He stared at a small, framed, eight-by-ten black and white photograph centered mid-wall over the tank. Aside from the mirror above the sink, it was the only object hanging on the narrow, sage walls, like a single stain on a blouse. A print of some path or walkway in Central Park. Will knew the area. At the furthest point of the path, a person stood out of focus. That part of the photo always mesmerized him, even as he stood there relieving himself. He could never distinguish as to whether the person was approaching or retreating. Every time he studied the picture he came to the same conclusion: he didn't know. And after nearly every visit to the Buchanans' bathroom, he only thought of Lily walking away as he lay on the ground, barely conscious. Her face had worn a combination of fear and detachment. His last view of her, the image so vivid in his mind he felt like she was next to him looking at the photo.

This time, however, he forced himself to picture Anne squeezing his hand as they walked along the path parallel to West Drive, past the Strawberry Fields, and onto the lake's shore. They sat on the ground in a spot hidden by small trees and tall grass. He kissed her, and she kissed him back. He ran his hand through her hair, warm and red from the sun. They looked out at the water under Bow Bridge. His arm wrapped around her. She was real, and she felt just right. On the bridge was a figure of a woman he couldn't quite distinguish. Her back turned to them, her dark hair pouring over her shoulders. The sky darkened. Will shook himself out of the trance and looked at the photo once more. *If only I could take Anne to New York*, he thought. But New York would never be home again. He finished, zipped up his pants, and washed his hands. The soap didn't smell like it normally did, less flowery, sweeter, and slightly familiar. A strange feeling lingered.

Harvey Buchanan
In an interrogation room,
Athens Police Station

OCTOBER 2009

I'm not being defensive. I know this is your job and all, but how about some goddamn sensitivity? I just lost someone very special to me, and all you keep saying is you think I killed her. And why? Because you have a hunch? You say you want information, but when I give you everything I know, you disagree with my facts and try to implicate me. I can walk you through it again: I entered the apartment, which was unlocked; she was on the floor, unconscious; and I immediately called the police. Why would I do something like this? I loved her. Yes, I know it sounds ridiculous to love a woman you barely know, but I did. I've never felt anything like this in all my life. But to you, I just look like a philanderer and a liar. I have yet to process what happened no thanks to your theater of detective work—the leading questions, the coercion, your sad excuse for the Reid technique, the whole good cop, bad cop routine. It's complete horseshit.

Because I show up at the scene of the crime, and I had an intimate relationship with the victim, all signs point to me as the main suspect, right? Signs are signs, but some of them are lies. It was the husband or the boyfriend or the lover every single time. Every crime show tells us that, but we watch anyway. Do I consider myself a suspect? Of course, not. I know the truth. But I don't determine guilt—you do. I reported the murder of a woman who told me many lies about herself. I don't know why she did, but the facts were concealed or distorted in ways I couldn't confirm. And why should I have to? My reality was predicated on the appearance she presented me. I took it at face value.

The reason I sit here relates to your hunch about how I fit into all of this, a hunch that I killed her to cover up the affair. Cheating on one's spouse isn't anything new, and to think people of certain ideologies, religious beliefs, or intellectual leanings are exempted from it is absurd. All people are motivated by the same basic things: competition, acceptance, eating, sleeping, and fucking—and may I add the general angst of existence. Everything they do is a response to that. Sure, what I did was wrong. I'm not about to argue morality at this point, but by no means was it justification for killing her. Had she not come into my life, I'd likely be having an affair with someone else. There are very few people who haven't done it or at the very least entertained the idea. Hell, academia is a swarming cesspool of sex, even in the smallest departments or with the ugliest of people. Humans are strange and disgusting, and even when something isn't happening, rumors spread out of jealousy or boredom or the desire for an appealing narrative. What could be a lighthearted encounter, like a lunch date or casual cup of coffee, becomes a story of scandal and debauchery. People just love rolling around in each other's shit, real or imagined, and that's what turns these minor affairs into exaggerated tales of gossip. We all act like what we're doing is important, but all we're doing is talking about other people in the past tense. As academics, we research great minds and people from history in hope that we can somehow live vicariously through their accounts. Or when a faculty member or student takes notice of us, we have a choice, and most of the time, we relegate ourselves to affairs with these people because humans want attention and acceptance. So when this woman approached me at Moe's that evening in late July, there was something that detonated inside of me. I had to go home with her. It wasn't the only choice I had, but I chose it.

I will never be a great philosopher like Sartre or Camus, but when I was with Elli, I was the closest to feeling like one of the existentialists. I don't care how pathetic or delusional that sounds. She made me want to retire and move to Paris where we could sit in cafes all day, drink wine, and talk about life. Instead, we spent most of our time together either in her room or driving an hour away to get a sense of anonymity. You may think it pathetic, but that time was electric. We'd spend the day in the city, sitting outside of these quiet bars, unlike the dive bars in Athens full of college students and reeking of vomit and stale beer. She'd smoke her clove cigarettes and drink red wine, smiling at me while touching my leg. I would drink bourbon and talk about literally anything. I never experienced anything like it. I swear if she hadn't died, I would have left my wife.

Instead, here I am in this room talking about a dead woman I barely knew. My marriage is over, and very shortly the media is going to paste this story all over the goddamn place. My job and department are likely done, over. I'm sure if the affair had come out, there wouldn't be any issues. I'd still be chair of the department, people would talk about the incident behind my back, and I would take it in stride. Life as usual. A dead body in a college town is always a story for the national news, the next bestseller, or a true crime drama. Do I claim responsibility for my actions or pretend like none of this is my fault? At this point, I have legally done nothing wrong, so whatever hunch you think have, you can forget about it.

Chapter 2

Will handed a small stack of flyers to the first person of each row. "You must attend either a panel discussion or a paper reading and then type a one-page summary about it," he said loudly, competing with the rattle of the classroom's old heater. "Because the conference's theme this year is 'Hello, Philosophy. Are you there?'—not my idea—and our seminar topic is 'Death of Philosophy,' you'll get a firsthand look at what contemporary academics and theorists—"

"Like Laroche," Stephanie Green interrupted from the back of the room.

"Yes, Stephanie. French Philosopher Jacques Laroche is our keynote speaker and one of the many talented academics at this year's event. He and I will take part in a panel discussion Saturday night. I encourage everyone to attend the conference in its entirety."

Stephanie raised her hand as expected.

"Yes, Stephanie?"

"Will there be extra credit for those attending the whole conference? I mean, it is homecoming weekend and all. This sort of takes away from our normative college experience."

"It's my understanding that attending the conference is a requirement for the president of the philosophy club." Some students laughed. "In life, sometimes you must choose between what you want to do and what's required." She wasn't wrong. It was a terrible idea to have the conference the same weekend as homecoming. The surrounding hotels were fully booked, and both alumni and conference goers were scrambling to find accommodations that didn't necessitate an hour plus commute.

Stephanie appeared unamused. "I know, I'm going to be there. I was just seeing if there was an incentive for the rest of the class."

"How considerate. It's an easy way to network and scope out graduate programs. But also, homecoming is once a year and the university does a great job. If you go to a panel or a speaker early Friday, then you can enjoy the rest of the weekend's events. You won't have to worry about missing our dear Argonauts losing to the Spartans on Sunday. Again, the conference is only Friday and Saturday." He surveyed the classroom. "If that's it, then I'll hopefully see you all this weekend."

While the students gathered their bags, they talked about where they'd party for the weekend and tailgate on Sunday. Will quickly packed his folders of papers and notes into a brown leather messenger bag, intent on a swift departure. With peripherals, he noticed his student Jack taking an exceptionally long time to gather his things and exit the classroom. The classic sign for "I need to talk." Will hesitated, feeling an inherent need to guide his pupils, a sentiment much like Catholic guilt. Year after year, they came with the same problems via after class chats, random office drop-ins instead of scheduled office hours, and the ambiguous and unpunctuated emails. Will replied to most with the same answers using a copy-and-paste strategy. Once they left his course, he'd think they were better off with a business or communications degree—no doubt the university would prefer it. *What I wouldn't give for a senior seminar full of NYU students.*

Will grabbed a cheap eraser and proceeded to smudge his chalk scribblings, rather than erase the blackboard. He slung his bag over his shoulder and walked to the door, feeling relief: another innocuous conversation avoided. Before he could get his foot out the door, he heard, "Hey, Will," and turned around to Jack's awkward half smile.

"I need to talk to you about something."

"I know I said calling me Will was fine outside of class, and class is over, but could you wait until we're physically out of the classroom to do it?" *One beer with the guy, and he thinks we're best friends.*

"Yeah, sorry. I just, I don't know. Sorry."

"What's up?" Will glanced at the clock. Eight minutes after eleven.

"It's about Dr. Buchanan."

"What about him?"

"I'm worried he might have a drinking problem."

Will sighed. "I would avoid accusations about a professor without any evidence?"

"He came to our eight a.m. Existentialism class drunk and rambled about Sartre and Simone de Beauvoir's sex life the entire time."

"I mean, their lives and relationships were very pivotal in the Existentialism philosophy and movement. Are you sure he was drunk?"

"He smelled like whiskey, and he literally staggered into class."

"Are you sure it was whiskey?"

"I'm twenty-seven, Will. I know what whiskey smells like, especially at eight o'clock in the morning. He kept talking about apricot cocktails and orgies. He tried to show us some sex scene from the movie *Henry and June*, but he couldn't find it on *YouTube*. And because it was too beautiful to miss, he's bringing the movie next class. I'm pretty sure it's making students uncomfortable, but no one wants to say anything because they're not sure if that's part of the curriculum or not. The whole Existentialism subject is kind of confusing, you know. Like we don't know if what he's doing in class is like a public display of Existentialism and is going to be part of the final or whatever. But he talks a lot about the philosophers' sex lives."

"I see what you're saying. Why don't we talk more about this in private? Say my office, twenty minutes?"

"That works. I have to grab my pass for the conference. See you in twenty."

"And avoid mentioning anymore of this to anyone else. We don't want rumors circulating."

"For sure."

Will exited, making a left out of the classroom. At this time of day, the hallways of James A. Gordon Hall were empty. Without the people to fill the void, the florescent lighting only made the space look longer and narrower than it really was, especially since the summer paint job. The plaster walls layered with coats of lead paint were now an antique white, and the once dark oak trim was light gray. The place screamed lifeless office building rather than historical monument.

They were nearing midterms, and the maintenance workers had yet to rehang Dr. Buchanan's curated collection of philosopher portraits, another of Harvey's complaints.

Will continued down the hall, turning at every corner like he was walking in a circle. He worried that Jack's concern was real, and Harvey's behavior had progressed well past inappropriate. Were the cutbacks and conference planning finally too much to handle? There had to be something else. Will climbed a set of stairs to the second floor. The situation had Will thinking about a professor in grad school at NYU who would come to every class drunk, practically the stereotype of the troubled and lubricated college professor whose unorthodox instruction offended more than educated. The professor rarely accepted the students' responses in discussion, and that was true of any class he taught. The man would laugh at those who stumbled through an explanation of Hegelian Phenomenology. He would argue with stubborn students until he was purple in the face. He would often rant nonsensically for an entire class, and the students wouldn't know what the hell he was talking about. There was one time, and Will remembered it so vividly, when the professor staggered into class. He never came with any notes or a briefcase, but merely walked into the room, beginning a lecture in mid-thought. This time he looked like he had been wearing the same clothes for days: wrinkled tan trousers with indistinguishable stains, a shirt buttoned in the wrong places, and a tweed jacket that appeared like it had been balled up and used for a pillow (who knew tweed could look so bad?). He hadn't shaved, and his hair was greasy and matted, eyes bloodshot. As he talked, he kind of stumbled along the aisle between rows of desks, lost his footing, and fell ass-over-teakettle into a couple of empty desks, which horrified the students. A few tried to help him to his feet, but he had split his head open, and blood poured down his face and onto his shirt. Embarrassed, disoriented, and likely concussed, the professor yelled a string of profanities and shuffled out of the room. The students immediately reported it to the department and the custodial staff. Consequently, the professor took a leave of absence for the remainder of the semester. Will feared Harvey would not have it so easy if a similar situation occurred.

When Will entered the department, Sylvie the administrative assistant wasn't at her desk. Instead, there was a young girl staring inquisitively at Will.

"Can I help you?"

"Is Sylvie off today?" he asked, looking confused.

"Sylvie Shepard? She's in the philosophy department across the hall."

"Jesus. I walked through the wrong door." Will turned to leave. "Sorry."

The girl giggled to herself. He left the history department and saw the small, black plastic sign with white lettering at eye level on the door across the hall that read:

PHILOSOPHY DEPT.
CLASSICS DEPT.

Two years, he thought, *and I still walk into the wrong side if I'm not paying attention.* He hated the thought of having to do this two more years. The place was no longer a novelty.

"Good morning," said Sylvie from behind her desk. She stopped typing and looked at Will, practically gushing. She brushed aside the bangs of her short blonde bob. Her hair, although cute in its own right, wasn't very flattering, drawing too much attention to her crooked nose and not enough attention away from the horrid floral print blazer she wore. "You're looking as handsome as always, Will. If I were single and a little younger."

"You're too sweet, Sylvie," said Will whose consistent monochrome attire gave him the appeal of television static. He didn't enjoy being the object of attention, felt uncomfortable even at the thought, but he appreciated Sylvie's routine flirting. Her advances seemed sincere but were perfectly harmless coming from the committed, married woman she was. It felt more like an aunt's flattery. Will reciprocated with small compliments. "As long as you're the first person I see in the morning, I know it'll be a good day." The comment sounded so stupid, but it made her smile. And being in Sylvie's good graces was crucial to getting what you needed in this department, though there was very little Will desired. "Is Harvey around?"

"No. He went to lunch. Didn't say where. Shall I leave him a note?"

"Don't bother. I'll catch up with him later. I'll just be in my office."

Will walked down the short hallway to the faculty offices, thinking of ways to diffuse the Harvey situation. He was just relieved to not have to teach another student until Monday.

Will passed several offices as he made his way around the corner and down, yet again, another hallway. The building was just a series of meandering vacancies. He passed Dr. Seymour Rausch's office, the Nietzsche scholar and resident asshole. The man sat at his desk as if posed, appearing scholarly with a book in hand, but managed to glance up. Will raised a hand, feigning a greeting, but Seymour looked away. *Good to know he hasn't changed.* Will took out his keys and fumbled for the right one. He opened his office door and set his bag on the desk.

Depending on whom you'd ask, Will's office wasn't a typical humanities faculty office. It was sterile and lacked character. Most professors, even the adjuncts, had pictures, posters, books, junk, or something that signified "my space." It was an extension of who they were or, at least, who they thought they were. Hell, even some had the maintenance workers paint their offices specific colors. One of the tenured English professors had her office painted a deep purple, which would have been lovely and warm in a study with a fireplace, an armchair, and an ottoman. However, it was a little overwhelming in an eight-by-eight cell with the fluorescent lighting and a tiny window. Will's space was more a negation. The bookshelves held only a dozen books or so, mostly the texts he currently taught. There was a book about the romance of Sartre and Simone de Beauvoir a present from Harvey for Will's birthday—a book he had yet to read but assumed contained something similar to what Jack had mentioned this morning—and the faculty handbook. Aside from a few personal items and, of course, his name on the outside of the door, no one would suspect his residence. On a few occasions, colleagues had even asked if he were leaving to teach at another university just from the lack of flair.

Will sat in the black swivel chair behind his desk, opened his laptop, and clicked on the university email. There was a message in his inbox from Jacques Laroche with the subject *RE: Concerning a position at your university.* He clicked the email. Laroche's response wasn't clear about an open position at his institution, but he was interested in reading Thierry's next book.

There was a knock at the door.

Jack already? "Come in."

The door opened, and Seymour poked his head in. "I need to speak with you."

Great. "Just a moment." Will closed the laptop as Seymour shut the door. The unannounced visit was odd since Seymour had not only disliked Will from the moment he arrived but had avoided him for the better part of two years. The two academics had only three formal exchanges since Will's arrival at Athens, all of which were less than desirable. The first time, at a faculty meet and greet, Harvey had asked if anyone would like to say a few words to welcome the young visiting philosopher. Seymour had stood and said, "Yeah, I have something to say. This is the best you could get? I think it's a mistake," and was silent for the rest of the party. The second time, Harvey and Seymour were having a conversation about a painting of Nietzsche Harvey had purchased for the department. Will had walked out of his office, and Harvey had asked him what he thought of the painting. Will had replied it was a better likeness than Munch's painting. Seymour had screamed, "You don't know a goddamn thing about the likeness of Nietzsche," and had stomped away. It just so happened Munch's painting was one of Seymour's favorites. The third time, Will had asked Seymour if he would join him for lunch, a gesture Sylvie had suggested in order to soften the beast. She had warned him not to stare at Seymour's unusually long fingers; he was self-conscious about it. Seymour had agreed to the lunch, but Will could not stop stealing glances at Seymour's hands as the man ate a pastrami Reuben, occasionally licking Russian dressing from his fingers. Since then, their interactions have been brief.

"What's up, Seymour?"

"I know what's been going on, Thierry." He grasped the back of the armchair facing Will's desk, his grotesquely long fingers looked like vulture talons. He leaned towards Will.

"What are you talking about, Seymour?"

"Don't act like you don't know. You've been planning it since you got here."

"What have I been planning? I really don't—"

"I know you're hiding something, actions and situations that could scandalize you and this department. Maybe involving Harvey or even Laroche. Some people think that others won't notice when they're sneaking around, but I notice."

Will's heart rate quickened. "I, well, I really don't know what you're talking about."

"Yes, you do. But that's who you are, Thierry, intent on undermining the system. Your ideas, your being here, and the conference—you come in and pretend to have all the answers. You may have them fooled, but you don't fool me. You might be able to manipulate them, but I see right through you."

Will we ever have a normal conversation? Will wondered.

"I know you're weaseling your way into a tenured position."

"A tenured position?"

"You're just aligning yourself, what with finishing the PhD this summer and co-planning the conference with Harvey. Trying to be the star of the show. What else are you hiding?"

"Seymour, this is absurd. How is that even possible?"

"What's absurd is that I've worked too goddamn hard for this position. You come in here with your NYU degree and your Oxford University published book, and you're just going to solve all of philosophy's problems, the university's problems? You can't. I'm going to expose you. Whatever it takes. I will make sure you're gone by the end of the year."

"Seymour, I assure you, there's no way I'm trying for a tenured position. I hate this place so much. When my renewal is up, I'm gone, just like this department."

Seymour seemed caught off guard. "There's no way the university would vote in favor of that."

"They wouldn't? Have you ever read your contract? Firing tenured faculty and dissolving a department isn't as impossible as it sounds. Ever heard of 'financial exigency'? We are in the Great Recession, Seymour."

"Don't change the subject, Thierry. You're a liar and a manipulator. I'm watching you."

Before Will could tell him to leave, Seymour was gone.

Tenure? Will thought. The chance that Seymour would watch him and potentially mess with his life was due cause for a mild stomach ulcer. He didn't need the nosey fuck rifling through his belongings or surveilling his home. Will tried to shake the notion, but if the guy was going to do what he said he would, then maybe he should file a formal complaint. But, ugh, the paperwork alone wasn't worth it. He opened his laptop to finally read Laroche's email. Again, there was a knock at his door. He looked up. It was Jack. Of course, the meeting.

"Hey, Jack," Will said, closing his computer. "Did you happen to hear any of that?"

"Hear what?"

"Nothing. Shut the door and have a seat."

Jack closed the door and sat in the chair Seymour had been clutching. He held his bag on his lap and looked a little nervous. Will leaned back in his chair and crossed his arms. He didn't want to take it any further than this, but Jack clearly had a concern.

"So, Jack, walk me through this again?"

Seymour Rausch
In his office in the Department of Philosophy, James A. Gordon Hall

JANUARY 2010

To be completely unambiguous, I've hated Thierry since the day I met him in March 2007. I was curious as to why Harvey overwhelmingly endorsed this no-name kid from New York, though I had no desire to hear him speak. I understand the excitement that comes from a renowned visiting philosopher. At Princeton, I was involved with organizing a lecture series where people like Saul Kripke, Noam Chomsky, and even Foucault spoke. Those were intellectuals for whom no introductions were needed. But Thierry? What the hell had he done to deserve any of this?

Although the event was free, the turnout at the Burns Theatre was much larger than I anticipated. There were familiar faces from nearby university philosophy departments. Clearly, I had missed something. So, I made my way to the reserved faculty seating near the front. Within minutes, Harvey introduced Thierry as "the man who would save philosophy by killing it." People applauded. If he was so brilliant and innovative, then why had I not heard of him? Harvey rattled off some accolades, which were few. I was still perplexed as to why so many were excited to see him. Then again, just because he was popular didn't mean what he wrote was of any value. The public largely neglected most great writers and thinkers during their lifetime.

I would guess Thierry's popularity hinged on his provocation.

When Thierry spoke, he began by listing all the universities in the U.S. and England that had defunded, closed, or consolidated their philosophy programs. He read a few excerpts from different chapters of his book, *The Death of Philosophy*. He quoted Heidegger, Rorty, and Derrida. Nothing he said was original. From what I gathered, he had composed an anthology, a themed history of philosophy. His premise was that our field needed a transformation, that it was no longer relevant to a postmodern society. He treated these theorists and philosophers like Old Testament prophets foreseeing doom and the destruction of our Israel. It was as if by taking the old and modifying it, he made himself to be the Christ figure of our discipline. Everyone loved it, but I felt nauseated by the whole charade.

The next week Harvey circulated an email to the faculty:

Dear Faculty Members:

If we are to be a competitive program that produces work of the highest quality and provides a curriculum that prepares and encourages students to move further in their careers of philosophy, then we must become more dynamic and offer something that other universities don't. What I'm alluding to is the area of study soon to be known as the Decline or Death of Philosophy. Although it is not an official subfield like Phenomenology or Ethics, it soon will be. This is where Mr. Thierry will be of great importance and value to our institution and program. He is a pioneer in this field and will provide the credibility we need. In short, I am proposing a two-year Visiting Lecturer/Philosopher position with the option of renewal beginning next fall 2007.

I realize we do not currently have funding for permanent faculty positions, but Thierry is essential for us to be at the forefront of this research. With the full support of Dean Murphy and outside funding from private donors, this addition will be possible. With his book gaining national and international recognition, other individuals and institutions will begin studying and developing philosophy on this subject. This is going to be a very exciting endeavor. Anyone wanting to discuss this matter is free to do so. I encourage you all to welcome Thierry with open arms.

Cheers,

Harvey J. Buchanan, Ph.D.
Professor and Chair
Department of Philosophy
Athens University
(xxx)xxx-xxxx

The correspondence was merely a matter of formality. Harvey had put everything in place long before Thierry visited the university. I wish Harvey would focus that kind of energy on our program all the time and provide more for the current faculty rather than setting his sights elsewhere. I considered responding to the email in writing but thought better of it and, instead, resorted to a meeting in his office to discuss the issue.

When we met, I wanted to approach the matter as levelheaded as possible, but I didn't have it in me. I didn't shout in the beginning but made my case against hiring Thierry. He was a fad and a poor use of department resources. And if anything, he would only use this place as a means for advancement. As I spoke, I could see Harvey had already formulated a speech, undoubtedly disregarding everything I said. He began with something about our longstanding friendship and my loyalty and importance to the department. This went without saying. I stopped him mid-sentence, pointed my finger right in his face, and told him to drop the diplomatic bullshit. He was throwing money at the traveling snake oil salesman, not investing in our program, and I wouldn't support it.

He tried to pacify me, ease my mind by being "honest." He broke into rhetoric about tough decisions and gambling on something that could yield a large return for the department and university, the jargon of a businessman. He acknowledged the move was sudden and not the usual protocol, but it was important to lock Thierry into a contract before he received other more lucrative offers. And he would. Harvey was convinced that Thierry's work was important, reached a larger audience, and would get people to read philosophy again. I felt that same sense of nausea much like the night of the reading. So what if he was a twenty-eight-year-old "sensation." Our department did not need some wonderboy. Maybe he had promise, but this was a discipline not an industry. If we treated it like an industry—as many universities have—only few would benefit. Do you know what follows an industrial boom? Decline. A wasteland, barren and uninhabitable. I didn't want to be a part of that, nor did I want to be part of his theory. People like him are always mining their experiences for their writing. But Harvey showed very little concern for my apprehension. He forecasted the next two years. If Thierry is at the forefront of this movement, if that's what this is, then he'll receive more attention. The attention he receives would provide our program with more exposure, and in turn, our program enrollment would increase as well as our funding, practically unheard of in the humanities. He tried to bait me by promising me only courses in Continental Philosophy and Nietzsche. And then Harvey paralleled Wittgenstein's work with Thierry's. Comparing this inexperienced hack whose work reeks of plagiarism to one of the greatest minds of the twentieth century was absurd and laughable. If Wittgenstein couldn't solve all of philosophy's problems, there was no way in hell Thierry would. He said the department wouldn't lose money or be greatly impacted if Thierry was a bust. No matter how anyone felt, this was going to happen. I left his office wanting people to know I didn't support it. So, I did the only thing that seemed reasonable at the time. I slammed my door as hard as I could and shattered its glass. I know it seemed like an overreaction, but passivity is suicide in academia. Needless to say, I had to pay for a new pane of glass.

That next fall Thierry joined our faculty with a 3/3 load, completely unheard of for a non-tenure-track faculty member, especially one without a PhD. He taught two entry-level courses and a course he developed on the death of philosophy. Although the teaching load was objectionable, his office was small and his salary modest, so I didn't further involve myself with the matter. I did keep a close eye on him though. Each day after class, he went home to one of the university-owned faculty housing. He didn't appear to do much outside of that.

Harvey began a department newsletter, charging Sylvie with

the task of writing it. Professor Harlowe, who advises the student philosophy club, seemed to present them with more opportunities for involvement and growth, and eventually they started a small student publication for philosophy-themed writing. By the end of his first semester, Thierry had three articles on his subject forthcoming from well-known journals. I could hardly believe it. He had published more that first semester than I had in the last two years. Thierry was interviewed and mentioned Athens University as "an overlooked but beautiful institution, teeming with world-class professors and excited, hungry minds." He even mused that the Midwest was the new incubator for philosophical thought. I read all about it in the new newsletter. Everything seemed to be coming together as Harvey said it would. As more attention centered on Thierry and his pseudo-philosophy, I tried to adapt.

I researched and wrote more, but what did I have to say about the death of philosophy? As a Nietzsche scholar who studied under the esteemed Walter Kaufmann, I, too, know about the death of philosophy. When Nietzsche proposed God was dead, he also claimed that metaphysics had died. Philosophy was dead because at the time metaphysics and philosophy were one and the same. What now do I have to say about it? I don't give a damn whether or not people see philosophy as something that will end or die. People have been proclaiming the death of one thing or another throughout most of the 20th century. The rise of film and later television proclaimed the death of the novel, though novels are created and produced in rather large quantities every year. The rise of college graduates is supposedly leading to the death of the factory worker and manual labor, yet the U.S. still leads in manufacturing output. There are myriad examples.

Life is a constant transformation of phenomena. Ideas, concepts, structures, people, society, etc. Even death is often looked at as being a kind of transition in existence into something else rather than an end. Philosophy is among them—it is not dying, nor will it ever. Thierry is merely taking an incident, a hypothetical expression long discussed and writing a fable about it. People believe this fable as truth, though I imagine he doesn't even believe it himself. How could he? It's like turning your back on those who taught you everything. However, we write about our obsessions, our own experiences. Our own perspectives of the world are the lenses for our life's work.

Perhaps I am putting myself in an awkward position refusing this ideology, but stubbornness and pride are in my blood. I refuse to succumb to something because of its popularity. In many ways I suppose I am my father, a man whose stubbornness forced him out of his career. My father, a German-born citizen, left his plastering company and hometown of Leipzig as the Third Reich came into power. When he arrived in the United States, he joined the German Trade Union of Plasterers and was able to make a living. Plastering was thriving at this moment in time, but as the 1940s came to a close, drywall had all but replaced plaster. The product was new, inexpensive, easier to use, and less time consuming to install. I promise, my story has a point. In my father's stubbornness, he would not accept what seemed cheap and fake, a fad and a poor substitute, an invention some idealistic person created to make money. He refused to learn that trade, and when the plasterers' union disbanded for lack of membership, he didn't receive his pension. He spent the rest of his life working odd jobs just to support us.

Am I bitter? Yes, I'm bitter. Imagine working your whole life on something, building a legacy, and in the process, not only is your work neglected but also destroyed. Thierry is demolishing what I've built, what many of us have built, to replace it with something cheap, fake. No, better yet, he is taking a Polaroid picture of our well-built structure and then setting the photograph on fire in front of an audience. He hasn't destroyed the structure but only an imitation of it. Thierry doesn't have the ability to negate philosophy, because when all his work has finally lost the interest of everyone, philosophy will again rise out of the ashes like a phoenix. And his books will be placed back on the shelf of postmodern thought. To an extent, I feel as though I am part of Thierry's ideology, a fable about death and the obsession with the finite. It is a story in which a man is not only killing ideas but also destroying people's lives in the process. He is by far the worst thing to have happened to Athens in years.

Chapter 3

As a favor to Harvey, Dr. Elizabeth Harlowe volunteered to pick up Jacques Laroche from the airport. She obliged Harvey's request as a consolation for not participating in this year's conference: the male-dominated speaking schedule and "death" theme were huge turnoffs. Harvey promised her a course release in the spring if she committed to this task, and a course release was the *raison d'etre* of academia. Although it was a rather large repayment, even ethically questionable, it was also a no-brainer: she needed that time to research for the NEH grant she'd received. But course release or not, sharing an hour-long car ride with Laroche while Harvey drank himself stupid in his office was not the way she wanted to spend her afternoon.

Elizabeth took the airport exit ramp off the highway. A few turns and she arrived at the parking deck entrance, grabbing a ticket from the automated machine and pulling into a space close to the skywalk, a small victory for some. This provided Elizabeth with the least amount of distance for necessitating conversation on the walk back. As she crossed the skywalk, she stopped to view traffic below in its manic state during the arrivals, cars pulling up to different airline entrances, some double or triple parked, and people scurrying out of the building with cell phones in one hand and luggage in the other, searching yet again for their transportation. She continued down the escalator to the lobby of the airport.

The time was two thirty, which put Laroche's arrival at fifteen minutes ago. She found the monitor listing arrivals and departures. Sure enough, his plane was on time, and he should be at the baggage claim, which was on the ground floor near the arrival gate. She headed that way, the short heel of her brown leather boots clicking the epoxy floor at an allegro tempo. Despite her disregard for the overpaid opinion generator, she did not want her punctuality to reflect poorly on the department or the institution, let alone her character.

A wall of people crowded the baggage carousel anxious to grab their bags and go, but Elizabeth could not locate Laroche. At the exit of the designated arrivals gate, adjacent to the carousel mob, there was a small wave of people, but alas, no Laroche. A second wave of people came through the gate minutes later, a little larger than the first group. Again, no Laroche. She waited, wondering if she'd fail to identify him in public. A half hour slowly passed.

Before she reached full-blown panic, a man of average height in an off-white Oxford emerged from the arrival gate. His sleeves were rolled to his mid forearm and the top few buttons were undone, exposing some chest hair. A black blazer hung from his left arm, and he towed a small black suitcase on wheels. His graying blonde hair was combed back, revealing a large forehead vis-à-vis a receding hairline. He looked like Gérard Depardieu circa 1998. That was her guy.

"Jacques Laroche, welcome," she said as she approached him.

"*Oui*. Hello. You must be Elizabeth."

Before she could say another word, Laroche was in her face, kissing both cheeks, his left hand touching her arm.

"It's a pleasure to finally meet you," she said, feigning sincerity.

"Likewise, Professor Buchanan has said many wonderful things about you, though he did not mention how beautiful you are."

"Is that so?" She smiled at the flattery.

"Yes. He holds you in high regard."

"That's very kind, but we should be going. The drive back to your hotel is about an hour."

They turned and walked toward the escalator, Elizabeth slowing her pace for the man.

"Did you have any delays?"

"No. Everything seemed to be on schedule."

"A long line at another baggage claim?"

"I wouldn't know. I always carry hand luggage. I hate the idea of having my personal items fondled by strangers."

"What was the hold up?"

"Hold up? I stopped for a drink at the airport bar. The wine on American flights is atrocious. Those little bottles of—what was it?— some cheap California wine."

Elizabeth stopped. "I waited forty minutes so you could have a glass of wine?"

"I would have asked you to join me if it were possible, but you know how security is these days."

She glared at him. *I knew it.*

"I suppose it may have been somewhat inconsiderate. I'm sorry for your wait."

"Athens has better wine bars than the airport."

Laroche trailed behind Elizabeth through the airport, back over the skywalk, and to the parking deck. When they arrived at her car, she opened the hatch to accommodate his suitcase.

"The Volvo 240 is a classic model," said Laroche.

"Sure."

They got in and before she could pull out of the garage and get onto the highway, he was talking. He began with the brief history of that Volvo model but soon moved onto the landscape they passed. Elizabeth found it odd how much he spoke, especially to her, a stranger, but it was not at all surprising. He was a critic. This was always the case for people in her field: they were either awkward and reticent or inveterate conversationalists. Laroche made small talk so effortless.

"You know, I don't think I've been to the Midwest. New York of course, many of the Ivy League universities, Los Angeles, and Chicago."

"Chicago's part of the Midwest."

"Is that so? I would have never guessed. An oasis in the land of suburban sprawl."

"That seems harsh and a little presumptuous, considering we just left the airport."

"So far, I've seen urban and commercial development, churches, signs for churches, and some farmland. We're not even thirty minutes into our trip. I enjoy the countryside. I truly do, but this seems rather depressing."

"It's hardly depressing."

"How is Athens? A town named after the cultural epicenter of Greek civilization."

"If we have time, I'll give you the tour."

"Describe it to me. I want to know what you think about it."

She wasn't sure if he was patronizing her or being sincere, but he seemed well-intentioned. Perhaps Harvey knew this would happen, knew the two of them would hit it off. She never took Harvey for being that perceptive. Maybe he was taking a chance with their interaction because who can really predict how two people will interact for the first time?

"It's a small college town with a rich history, and a quaint downtown, mostly architecture from the mid 1800s. There are pockets of beautiful, old homes in neighborhoods around the university. The town is full of trees, and this time of year almost anywhere you go, you'll have a patchwork canopy of color. The campus was one of the first settled in Ohio, so its design resembles other early American colleges like Yale or the University of Virginia. The town is easy to navigate, and most of us walk from place to place because everything is so integrated. Also, there are lovely little shops, and the people are mostly friendly. I moved here about fourteen years ago, and eventually bought an old house and settled in."

"I take it you really enjoy living there."

"I do. Midwest living doesn't bother me. I grew up in Indiana, went to Boston for my undergraduate, and then to Florida for grad school. I've had a taste of city life, and I prefer to live in a place similar to where I grew up."

When they reached the Athens University Hotel, just on the edge of campus, they noticed there was limited parking and many people wearing the school's hunter green and gold colors.

"This can't all be for the philosophy conference?" Laroche asked.

"It's not. These people are likely alumni here for homecoming weekend."

"It seems odd to have a conference on the weekend the university celebrates its inception."

"I think the idea was to have as many people on campus as possible to see the advertisements for the conference. You never know who might walk in. I know we have some philosophy alumni coming." She felt like she was reciting Harvey's marketing spiel.

"Now we're just advertising philosophy to the masses. How very capitalist. So American."

They got out of the car and walked to the lobby's front desk, Elizabeth leading. "The point isn't to exploit the discipline but to show what philosophy offers. That we aren't just wallowing in Cartesian dualism, Freudian symbolism, and goddamn Nietzsche." She looked at the worker behind the desk, clearly a hospitality management student. "I have a reservation for Jacques Laroche under the Department of Philosophy." The young worker typed on the computer's keypad and made small talk about how busy the weekend was going to be and how she'd likely have to miss the game.

"Room 157 on the first floor down that long hallway," the young worker said.

Again, Elizabeth led the way as if she were making sure nothing happened to him. "So why are you here if this goes against your principles? Why even bother coming to a place off your radar for a subject and group of people that mean nothing to you?"

"I admire your boldness. First and most importantly, your department chair paid me a lot of money, more than I would expect a small, public university to offer."

"I realize that."

"Secondly, I want to lay this whole subject to rest."

"How so?" Elizabeth asked. They stood outside his door.

"This area of study is a waste of intelligent minds. Time spent critiquing the position or predicting the future of our discipline is solipsistic. We don't need any more philosophy about philosophy. It's not even meta-philosophy. It's more like prophecy, and we are not prophets. I addressed the subject because it was brought to our attention with such force and welcomed with open arms. Now it is time to move on. If Thierry is to continue his work on that subject, that is his matter. But it is foolish and futile."

"That should make Saturday night interesting."

"Did you become a philosopher to make people feel good? I certainly did not."

She slid the key card into the lock and opened the door, taking a few steps inside to glance around the room. "When should I return? Harvey wants us to meet him at the department and then we will all go to dinner." She held the door, waiting for him to enter.

"You'll be joining, yes?"

"This is a dinner with the core faculty, so I'll be there."

He walked into the room and leaned his suitcase against the bed. His expression seemed to approve of the room's accommodations. For nearly three hundred dollars a night, this room ought to be up to his standards. "I won't take but a few minutes to freshen up. Why don't you just wait in here? Put the television on. We haven't finished our conversation. And you said you'd give me a tour."

She stood against the door, mid-decision, contemplating the necessity of staying or leaving, and then smiled as if to say—*sure, why not?* She stepped into the room, letting the door close behind her.

Ray Malone
In a booth at Moe's Place

NOVEMBER 2009

Sure, I know Harvey. Hell, I know a lot of professors from the university. They come in here all the time. We even unofficially call the place "Professor's Pub" because of it. From the moment we're open until last call, you'll see an academic in here with a drink. Usually, it's the look and behavior that gives it away. Otherwise, they'll tell you. They do it every time. And that's fine. I'm not trying to offend anyone by that observation. You should be proud of your profession. I'm happy to have their business.

But look around. Sure, it's an old bar in a college town, but it certainly isn't run like one. The place is clean, orderly, and, aside from the Athens U memorabilia and the vintage black-and-white photos on the walls, retains the old aesthetic: the cherry woodwork and bar tops, the original wide pine plank floors, and all this brickwork. You know this row of buildings was constructed right after the train depot in the 1840s. I know this kind of history because I've worked at Moe's Place for fifteen years, managed it for the last five. I'm here every day from noon until eight or nine o'clock at night. I see everyone who comes in, whether it's the families who want a decently priced meal (we're one of Athens top ten spots to eat), the guys who stop in for a drink each day after work, or the college students who made it their go-to.

But yeah, Harvey. He comes in a few times a week, usually alone, except on Fridays when he's with his wife. She's nice. A nutritionist and a yoga instructor. God bless her. Harvey is more of a red meat and bourbon kind of guy, which always made me wonder how those two got together. The whole opposites attract thing is bullshit. It didn't work for me and my ex-wife, but I guess in some cases it can.

What I like about Harvey is he talks to everyone. He doesn't think or act like he's better than anybody. That's why I get along with the guy. We know a lot of people, and we'll talk to pretty much anyone. Harvey would always say that bars and the streets are where philosophy was born, one of the few places where all kinds of people come together and talk about ideas and culture. When you hear someone like this guy, someone who seems to be pretty intelligent and important, say something like that, it makes you feel like you're exactly where you should be.

Now, I probably shouldn't be saying anything because I'm really not the guy to be spreading rumors or getting into other people's business. Then again, if you've ever worked at a bar, you know what to expect from people. When I heard about the girl being murdered like two weeks ago, I didn't think too much about it—other than it being horrible, of course—until I saw her picture in the paper and read about the weird love triangle. And then it clicked. She'd come in once when Harvey was having a burger. I don't have a photographic memory by any means, but that's his go-to when he's by himself. You have to try our burger. It was featured on that show *Diners, Drive-Ins and Dives*. You know, the one with Guy Fieri. That's why we have the life-size cutout of him over there on the wall. That was a proud moment. Anyways, like I was saying, it wasn't rare for Harvey to talk to people at the bar. Usually people he knew, but sometimes just random people. This particular evening in the summer, a young girl, probably late twenties with dark hair sat next to him and ordered a glass of wine. The two of them got to talking. It began casual, but you could tell they were flirting. Body language doesn't lie even when you've had a few drinks.

Honestly, I left to talk to someone at the other end of the bar. Maybe an hour had passed when they both got up to leave. They were clearly leaving together. I'm not saying anything happened, but seeing people leave together might put a few thoughts in your head about what they're going to do. And as I've said before, when you see this stuff happen enough, you pretty much know the signs. Harvey said goodbye, and she smiled. It's really no business of mine. I don't know, I would have probably left too. Can you blame the guy? I see people do it all the time. You know who is and who isn't going home together. The signs are always the same. Young, old, gay, straight, religious, nonreligious, married, whatever. It doesn't matter. Attraction is attraction. It's not something you can't easily fake, though I see that too. Trust me, you don't need a college degree to read people. They may come in different varieties, but the patterns are all the same. People are people. It doesn't matter what you believe or how you look at it—we're all pretty much the same.

The next time I saw Harvey, I asked about the girl. He said he walked her to her car and went home to his wife. I'm sure I gave him a look. I have a terrible poker face. He smiled and said, "Do you really think I would cheat on my wife?" I took his word and left it at that, even though it didn't set right with me. I wonder if it was worth it, going off with her. When that girl turned up dead in that apartment, Harvey was the one to find her. It's too early to tell, but I don't think he did it. Harvey's no killer. What about the other guy who was part of this "love triangle"? You see weird stuff like this on TV all the time. A guy tries to save his job and marriage by offing his mistress. Or the other guy gets mad and kills the girlfriend because he finds out he's not the only one she's banging. The whole thing just doesn't make sense. You think you know someone. I want to say he didn't do it. I really do. I can't wrap my head around something like that. I mean, if you want my honest opinion, he didn't do it.

Chapter 4

As the two men neared the College of Arts and Sciences, Dr. Thomas Dylan, with an éclair in one hand, the other gesturing wildly, his wiry, gray mop of hair flopping with each heated remark, recalled his last conversation with Dean Murphy. Harvey listened out of respect for the sixty-nine-year-old-soon-to-be-Emeritus, but he'd heard the story dozens of times, and they were already late to their meeting thanks to Tom's lack of time management.

"'Horseshit, Joe,' I said. 'Goddamn horseshit.'" He bit into the éclair. "He has the nerve," he said, mouth full, "to use that corporate jargon with me. 'Sorry, Tom. The university is restructuring by reallocating capital investments to more lucrative endeavors in order to reach near-term growth targets.' He couldn't just be straight with me."

"I know," Harvey said as he tried to pick up the pace. *If we walk any slower, we'd be traveling back in time.*

"The president wanted to renovate the place so he could leave this dump with the reputation that he changed the face of Athens. I told Joe we'd pay for it later. And all those assholes at the top got bonuses for the makeover, pats on the back from alumni and donors, and claimed it would attract more students. 'Show me the proof, Joe. Show me data that supports university betterment and improvement in overall student education.' I mean, Jesus. McDonalds just had a facelift, but they're still packaging the same insalubrious crap. Is that what they want?" He took another bite. "Athens University: Now servicing a million customers."

"I know, Tom. And here we are."

"I don't see what will be any different about this time," said Tom. "Joe will probably tell us Wal-Mart finally bought the place. Wal-Mart University, Athens Branch."

Harvey shook his head and sighed. "It's really not that bad."

"You're right. At least we'll have some geriatric to greet us at the entrance. 'Welcome to Wal-Mart U.' Hell, maybe they'll let me do that when I retire."

They entered the building and rode the elevator to the third floor. On this floor, clearly for university royalty, the walls were painted a dark red and accented with brushed nickel-framed prints of Getty stock photos with a single word under each like "Compassion" and "Tranquility." Some HGTV wannabe interior decorator really blew his load on this floor. They reached a door on the right labeled Office of the Dean. Harvey entered first, then Tom. A young woman, likely a student worker, sat texting on her phone at the desk next to the closed door of Dean Murphy's office.

"Can I help you two?" she asked.

"We're here to see—"

Before Harvey could finish, Tom blurted out, "No," and proceeded to barge into Dean Murphy's office.

"Sorry, he's . . ." Harvey shook his head. "Just being himself."

"Joe, has your office gotten bigger or am I losing weight?"

Dean Murphy looked up from his computer. "You're as rotund as always, Tom."

"Fuck you too, Joe." Tom laughed.

"It's always a pleasure, Tom."

Harvey trailed in and shut the door.

"Harvey. Why don't you both take a seat?"

The two men sat in the burgundy armchairs facing the dean's desk.

"This chair feels brand new," said Tom. "I bet you don't let the students sit in them, do you?"

Dean Murphy ignored the remark.

"So, these are the perks for selling your soul and sucking off the devil. How much are they paying you these days?"

"I see you've had your coffee today, Tom. How are you both?"

"Just fine and dandy," said Tom.

Dean Murphy looked at Harvey, his expression seeming to beg for some sign of congeniality.

"Fine but busy, Joe. Dr. Harlowe is picking up our keynote speaker from the airport. We set up for the conference early tomorrow morning. A lot ahead of us."

"That's good to hear. Well, there's no easy way to say this, so I'll just get right to the point. The decision to suspend or eliminate recommended programs and majors will take effect next academic year."

"Final nail in the fucking coffin." Tom threw both hands in the air.

"Joe, the vote doesn't happen until November 1," said Harvey. "With the upswing in enrollment, increased donor contributions, Harlowe's NEH grant, the attention to Thierry, and the conference—how are these not evidence of program viability?"

"Is it a promising and consistent event? Yes. But an annual conference with a few hundred attendees isn't really making a dent in anything. Sure, you bring in outside money, but we have STEM programs and professors bringing in millions of dollars in federal and private funding. There's almost no comparison."

"This is supposed to be our best conference. We'll get the publicity we need to advance to the next level. I just know it. More people, more exposure."

"It's homecoming, Harvey. Nobody's going to notice the conference. They'll be too busy with this weekend's events. Why on earth would you plan something on the same weekend as homecoming? It's like you wanted to see it fail."

Harvey didn't respond.

Dean Murphy continued, "You want to know what our other department chairs will be doing this weekend? They'll be attending the parade Saturday morning and then socializing with current students and past alumni at the Alumni Center where hopefully they can solicit donations or possibly recruit prospective students."

"You know that's just PR, Joe," said Harvey.

"Sure, but it works. Let me give you some statistics. When programs like Agriculture Studies, Business, Engineering, and Education Studies are bringing in the majority of students and funding, philosophy pales in comparison. Do you know how many students enrolled in philosophy or declared it their major this year? Twelve total, Harvey. Twelve. When Ag Studies enrolls roughly three hundred freshmen every year, it's purely economics."

"Compare apples to fucking apples, Joe."

"Fine, Harvey. You want apples? English had sixty. History had fifty-four. Even Anthropology had twenty-two."

"What about faculty and staff?" asked Tom. "The students? What's going to happen to them?"

"That has all been examined, and there are several paths the university's considering for implementing the budget reduction plan. It'll be executed campus wide, but let's focus on your situation. We would halt enrollment for philosophy and allow those currently enrolled the opportunity to complete their degree. We want to avoid any transfers. Granted, that would mean fewer courses offered, and the official closing of the department wouldn't occur until the last student graduated. Hence, Tom could retire with the buy-out, which would free up funds. We would keep the tenured faculty, Dr. Harlowe and Dr. Rausch, and terminate the remainder of Thierry's contract. You could move into an administrative role and possibly teach one course a semester. We would still offer a few philosophy courses once the department is shuttered and the program ended."

"What exactly do you mean by a few courses?" asked Harvey.

"We'll need to keep Logic and Ethics as those are required courses in several of our other majors. Dr. Harlowe could be absorbed by Women Studies while still teaching philosophy. Dr. Rausch could possibly teach a history course on German philosophers or something of that nature. I'm sure there would be an interest. Most likely, they, along with adjuncts, would teach the required introductory philosophy and critical thinking courses."

"That sounds awful, Joe," said Tom.

"And the rest of our faculty and staff?" asked Harvey.

"Unfortunately, their contracts would be terminated. They could re-apply for adjunct positions when they become available. We still need intro courses to be taught."

"Of course, you do, you low-balling son of a bitch."

"This is absurd," said Harvey.

Dean Murphy shrugged. "Another path, which is in the works, would be consolidation. The university would combine the lower funded, lower enrolled Humanities programs into a Humanities Studies degree. NYU and University of Pittsburgh are among many universities that have this program and are very successful with it. It's an economical solution to an expensive problem."

"This sounds like the university's Final Solution," said Tom. "Which makes sense, since you've already ghettoized most of us into Gordon Hall."

Dean Murphy didn't break.

"Joe, I saw the writing on the wall years ago." Tom stood. "I've fought the devaluation of education in this institution my entire career. I've worked to keep this place from becoming a glorified diploma mill. I've never fit in here, and that's fine. It's just sad to see that you're part of the machine that is killing this place. You've clearly 'Found Your Niche.'"

"If you would have taken a position like mine, then maybe you could have actually made a difference."

"Fuck you, Joe. You hollow man. No thank you." Tom stood and walked out of the office. He quickly poked his head back in. "Harvey, I'll see you tonight." He gave Dean Murphy the finger and left.

"For being such an eccentric guy, Tom has always been too serious," said Dean Murphy.

"He's not wrong, Joe." Harvey paused, sighed, and slouched in his seat. "Honestly, I don't blame you. But I also don't know what to do. I've tried to build this program into something that would attract more students, but it takes time. Now, we're looking at a university without a philosophy department?"

Dean Murphy leaned back in his chair and sighed, and then he leaned forward slightly and said in a lower voice, "Keep doing what you are. Try to make this conference big. Record and put it on the website or YouTube. Get some coverage in major publications. Draw attention to the department. Have students and faculty protest and write letters, which we're already seeing from other departments, and the vote hasn't even happened. Get other universities and people with some status to support you. More importantly, and I can't believe I'm saying this, make a lot of noise. You'd be surprised the effect that has. Whatever you decide to do, you have to inform your full-time faculty and staff before the final vote and press release. These things can get out of hand real fast and are usually not well-received. As far as we know, that's what stands. Again, Harvey, I'm sorry."

"It is what it is, Joe." He stood and left the way he came, taking the elevator to the first floor. His stomach ached, a mess of gurgling acid, most likely an alleged ulcer from the stress and drinking. As he began his trek back, he took out his cell phone and saw a missed call from her. He closed the phone and placed it back in his pocket, figuring he would call the woman back after the dinner. Perhaps his mood would be better.

The air seemed cooler now as he headed to Gordon Hall. Could they have been in Murphy's office very long? He glanced at his wristwatch. Three thirty-five. Forty-five minutes felt like an eternity. Harvey couldn't fix this situation, despite Murphy's insistence to *keep doing what you're doing and make some noise*. Is that not what he had been doing? There was more happening in the past two years than had happened in the last decade, yet they were being shit-canned nonetheless. The walk back felt so heavy and pointless. He was Sisyphus without the boulder.

In his office with the door shut, Harvey took a small glass and a bottle of Maker's Mark from the bottom desk drawer. He pulled the cork, poured two fingers, and downed it. He sat in his chair and turned around to face the window. His view: Gordon Hall's parking lot and the three-foot stone wall that bordered the side street. He leaned his head back and closed his eyes. A knock startled him out of his stupor. After blinking a few times and rubbing his face, Harvey quickly spun around in his swivel chair and grabbed the bottle of bourbon, setting both it and the empty glass in the opened drawer. "Co—" He cleared his throat. "Come in."

The door slowly opened, and Seymour's tall frame appeared. "I wasn't sure if you were still here, but Elizabeth and Laroche just arrived, and she's giving him a brief tour of the department."

"Oh god. Is it that time already?"

"It's quarter to five."

"Shit. How do I look?" He ran his fingers through his short, mostly salt than pepper hair.

"Truthfully? You look tired."

Sylvia Shepard
In a conference room of the Department of Philosophy, James A. Gordon Hall

NOVEMBER 2009

The administrative support in academia know everything. Don't take my word for it. Ask anyone in any department, and they'll tell you the same thing. And why do you think that is? Not only do we juggle multiple roles, communications, scheduling, finances, project management, resource planning, and logistics, but people cannot help themselves but to tell us every single thing that happens in their lives. It wouldn't be an issue if I only dealt with the clerical aspect of this department. Oh, no. I have to hear about the drama. And even though we're a small department, there is plenty of it to keep things interesting. Between students having near breakdowns regarding their romantic lives or their "mistreatment" by this or that professor to faculty conflicts, romances, and gossip, I sometimes feel like a therapist. It makes me laugh a little. All these years I've had a degree in philosophy I barely use when I should have had a degree in psychology. Then I could have at least charged by the hour. In all seriousness though, I know much more than I'd like to admit.

I knew Dr. Buchanan was having an affair. He didn't tell me this. I mean, who in their right mind would disclose something like that.

We're not that close. No, I ascertained this merely by observation and deduction. The signs were all there for the affair. Maybe not to the students or faculty. He probably just looked busy to them. I schedule his calendar, and I'm privy to a side of Harvey that even his wife doesn't know. The man is so protective of his time. Dr. Dylan might have been a more easy-going department chair, but Harvey has done a lot for this program in the last few years due to his diligence and hard work. All of this is attributed to his impeccable time management. He doesn't just have "things to do" for the day or the week. Each hour of each workday of every week, at least a month out, is carefully organized and detailed as to when and what he will do. Does he have free time? Sure, who doesn't? But that free or open time is typically reserved for "development," usually grading, planning, or the unexpected and rogue meeting that may arise as meetings tend to do.

But I know he was having an affair because he began having me schedule "conference planning meetings" in the beginning of August, usually in the afternoon during the week. When the academic year began, they would happen on whatever random day he wrote down the week of or even day of, which was unlike him. Dr. Buchanan said they were last minute talks with some of the academics or speakers and that I didn't need to confirm anything. I found that kind of odd because in years past, everything for speakers and submitted papers had been finalized by the start of the fall semester. The other odd thing was he didn't take the phone calls in his office. He said he'd prefer to take care of these outside of the office, never once indicating where he went. Strange, right? He always made a point to add location to the schedule if it was outside of the office.

I assumed he was creating an alibi if his wife asked. I figure, if you don't want anyone to suspect anything, don't bother making up stories you can't substantiate. Just don't say anything to anyone. Be evasive and don't bring attention to yourself: "I've been so busy, and I cannot recall." I would think someone who lives by logic and reason would understand this. It seemed to be more trouble than it was worth. Not that I know anything about the logistics of having an affair. I've been happily married for nearly thirty years to one of the professors in the Architecture Department.

Dr. Buchanan did, at one point, try to solicit an affair with me when I first started this job back in the early 90s. I never told anyone, not even my husband, because I didn't want to make it into a thing. Mind you, the only reason I took this job was because my husband's contract was contingent on the request that I also be employed at the university since we were uprooting our lives and moving to Athens. Although I had hoped for a teaching position, there were none available at the time, so they placed me here. I'm not complaining. It wasn't that we needed the money, but I wanted to work since our daughter was in grade school. The idea was if I got in with the faculty in this department, the chances of me getting a full-time instructor position would be better.

Dr. Buchanan's interest in me seemed Platonic at first. He was apologetic about the situation but glad to have someone who understood the coursework and not just another secretary. It really didn't matter how he felt because he wasn't the chair at that time. His power was limited, but I appreciated the sentiment, nonetheless. As the months went by, the more conversations we had, the more his behavior became flirtatious. I don't mind a little bit of flirting. I think it's unavoidable, necessary even. People are attracted to one another, and they blow off a little steam or flatter each other with some harmless flirting. It's a lot better than repressing that attraction until one day you both sneak off to a utility closet and ruin a perfectly good friendship or a twenty-year marriage.

As soon as Dr. Buchanan's flirting escalated to romantic advances, I politely made it clear that there was no way that would happen. And you know what? He stopped, and he never held that against me, personally or professionally. At least, not that I could tell. Looking back, however, maybe that kept me from advancing to a lectureship position. I know how easy it is to pull strings for an NTT appointment. The most I was offered was the chance to teach an intro class as an adjunct. It's an insult, really, one I'm still angry about. I try not to let it get to me.

Anyhow, when I saw Dr. Buchanan's photo next to the dead woman's photo on the news, I couldn't believe it. How did that even happen? But now I think about it and look back—it makes sense.

When I saw her picture, I distinctly remembered her visiting the department in the summer and meeting Dr. Buchanan. The timelines match up. Her visit was so ordinary that I thought nothing about it. She was with a group of prospective students doing a campus tour led by the Philosophy Club president. I usually remember the ones who show interest in this strange, old building. She had approached me, curious and enthusiastic about the building's history and had hoped to get a more in-depth tour of the place. I grabbed a small stack of stapled papers, history, really, and handed it to her. It was mainly some independent research I had done. It might seem strange to keep them on hand like that, but I had taken the time and gone through the trouble of obtaining this information. I wanted to make it available to whomever was interested since the university, oddly enough, provided very little record of it.

I took her down the hall of faculty offices before touring the rest of the building. I distinctly remember her touching the lettering on Will Thierry's office door, which I now realize was an odd thing to do. Then she turned toward me, her face expressionless except for her blue eyes. Those blue eyes that seemed to hold something back. She asked about Will. I probably went on a little too long about him, but then again who wouldn't? If anything, he added a little life to this department. We continued our tour through the rest of the building while I tried to keep her interested but also wanting to read the papers I had given her. I can provide you with a copy. You don't have to read it, but it is pretty interesting. Currently, the building may not seem as strange as it once was, given all its updates and remodeling, but it still has a disorienting effect.

I mentioned the plaque on the wall near the main entrance, the one that provides a glossy, inadequate history. Commissioned by James A. Gordon, a wealthy business owner in Athens and former Board of Trustee member to Athens University, in 1889, it was designed by the Italian architect Paolo Mezzanitti and executed by the late distinguished Professor of Architecture Ambrose Williams. Gordon Hall's structure was meant to embody the idea of the quest for knowledge, but it became *Il Labirinto di Pensiero Vuoto*: The Labyrinth of Empty Thought. It feels more like a crypt since the woman died. A place that harbors ghosts.

Chapter 5

At quarter after eight in the morning, Gordon Hall had an eerie sense of abandonment, a place long forgotten but still housing a presence. Will entered the Department of Philosophy and caught Sylvie looking down, concentrating on something. After a few seconds passed, she glanced up.

"Ope, sorry. I'm currently addicted to this word game my daughter downloaded on my phone. How are you on this lovely fall morning?" She brushed her bangs aside. Her beige blouse unbuttoned just enough to reveal some cleavage.

"I'm alright," Will said. "I take it everyone is at the Student Union?"

She smiled and leaned forward, elbows on her desk as she talked to him. In that position, her shirt hung slightly, and he could see the curve of her right breast and her bra's tan, sheer fabric. He tried his best not to look, keeping his eyes on hers, convinced she wasn't aware of the gap in her shirt.

"Except Tom. He brought the usual Friday box of éclairs," she said, pointing to the box on the table next to the office Keurig. "He took a few with a cup of coffee and is in his office, avoiding the conference for as long as he can." She rolled her eyes. "Harvey gave me the conference schedule and his 'revised' personal schedule, so I would know where he was while I 'held down the fort.' Truthfully, unless some random person with a new-found interest in Spinoza pops in, I'll be here by myself all day. Also, your student Jack Ballard was looking for you."

"Seriously?"

"Yep. He really has an affinity for you."

"I see the guy out in public one time, buy him a beer, and now we're best friends." He shook his head. "Anyway, I'm just dropping off some things at my office and then heading down to the Union to see what Harvey needs me to do. Would you mind copying his personal agenda for me?" He glanced once more through the space in her blouse. "I like your shirt, Sylvie."

She took the paper to the copier. "Thanks. I found it on sale at Macy's." She handed him the warm copy.

Will skimmed it on his way to his office. A lengthy spreadsheet dividing both Friday and Saturday into 30-minute increments from eight a.m. to eight p.m. He opened his office's door and flipped on the light. Every space on the page occupied by an activity. Was the guy just fully booked for the sake of looking busy or was he really this productive. Will set the paper on his desk and sat in his chair. It didn't matter. All Will could think about were his first words with Laroche. A number of different scenarios ran through his mind, imagined conversations he had rehearsed when he couldn't sleep or when he had a minute to himself. Each one ended with the Frenchman kindly accepting his new book and Will receiving an interview at the Sorbonne. It was an exercise in wishful thinking. After a few minutes, he left for the conference.

The Athens University Student Union bustled with energy, especially this early into the fall semester—the students eager, carefree, and within the window for dropping a class with a failing grade. Will entered the building near the student-run Starbucks, which prior to remodeling was the university-branded coffee shop Smart Beans, a name that begged for its corporate replacement. Attached was a lounge area equipped with several faux leather armchairs, half a dozen large flat screen televisions, and a black Steinway baby grand piano. The variation of sound and the level of noise from this end of the building could drive a person mad: the espresso machines' incessant grinding of beans and steaming of milk, the splintered conversations of students over-stimulated on sugar and caffeine, each television competing with the next to communicate a different version of entertainment, all of which were accompanied by a random person of dubious skill and style, stumbling through Lady Gaga's "Bad Romance" on the piano. The fact that there was a UNIVERSITY STUDY AREA sign posted was laughable.

Will passed through the dining hall that housed an enormous space with tables and chairs on the right and an attempt at multicultural eateries on the left, more or less the fast-food version of It's a Small World: Hardee's, Popeyes Louisiana Kitchen, Taco John's, Panda Express, Fazoli's, Einstein Bros. Bagels, and Subway. He took the stairwell to the second floor. The conference was confined to the modestly sized Burns Theatre and four large meeting rooms. Will entered a room with a sign labeled "Conference Registration" where a few students from Will's Death of Philosophy course set up tables equipped with all the accoutrements: glossy handouts, agendas, brochures for a variety of topics, blank name tags, pens branded with *5th Annual Athens Philosophy Conference*, speakers' books for sale, and finally a table with a jumbo size coffee maker and an assortment of donuts and muffins courtesy of the Athens U Catering Company, a.k.a. the hospitality management students. Jacques Laroche's books were splayed on a table, a bundle received earlier that week from his American publisher and included a twenty-four-inch cardboard cutout of the French philosopher, too big to set on the table, yet too short to place on the floor. One of the students brilliantly duct-taped the man's cardboard likeness to the wall behind the table.

"Morning, everyone," Will said.

"Good morning, Professor Thierry." Their responses staggered. Jack, of course, said, "Hey, Will."

"Looking good. Glad to see you've got this handled." Without a goodbye, Will left to find his colleagues.

Elizabeth and Seymour stood in the open hallway, talking. Just past them, Harvey held a cell phone, his free hand to his forehead and his face fraught with anxiety. Will greeted the two professors. Seymour's hands were slid into the back of his loose khakis, fingers on ass, no doubt, thumbs tapping his belt. It was somehow privileged information, a widely circulated rumor among faculty and students that the Seymour didn't wear underwear, and always stuck his hands into the back of his pants rather than into the pockets, which meant those long fingers grazed his bare buttocks. And then the guy had the audacity to offer handshakes to people. Thankfully, Will didn't have to break decorum with the refusal of a handshake since Seymour never offered. He had hoped it were just a rumor, but it was likely true. In academia, if a faculty member had a reputation for something, assume it was fact.

"Why weren't you at dinner yesterday?" asked Elizabeth.

Will hesitated. "I had a personal issue to take care of."

"I'm sure you did," said Seymour.

"The dinner couldn't have gone any worse, I suppose." She looked at Harvey still occupied on his phone. "Seymour caught him drinking in his office yesterday afternoon almost passed out."

"I didn't catch him drinking," Seymour interjected. "I said he smelled like he'd been drinking, and he looked tired, not passed out."

"Whatever. We all know he drinks in his office. Then he had a bottle and a half of wine at Il Treno and just kept thanking Jacques for his work and for making the trip to Athens. I cringed the entire time. It was another level of brown nosing."

"Probably the stress of the conference," Will said. *Again with the drinking.*

"He did seem preoccupied yesterday," Seymour said. "You wouldn't happen to know anything about that, Thierry?" He glared at Will.

"Not that I know of," Will said.

"Thankfully, Jacques can match Harvey's drinking," Elizabeth said. "Unfortunately, the only wine he would drink was this brand of Chianti that was a hundred dollars a bottle. Harvey paid, of course, but it was an awkward dinner. Jacques complained about the quality of the Italian food. He only responded to the staff in French. Then I drove him back to his hotel since I'm now his personal chauffeur." She rolled her eyes. "What a night."

Harvey interrupted, cutting the exchange short. "Will, I need to speak with you for a minute." Before Will could acknowledge, Harvey turned and walked away.

"I'll catch back up with you guys," said Will as he began to trail the man who was pure kinetic energy at the moment. "Hey, Harvey," he said, finally reaching him. "What can I do?"

"You should have been there. It was great. Jacques really warmed up to us. I even mentioned the study abroad idea, and he seemed receptive. I just talked to the caterers, and they should be arriving with food promptly at eleven. Could you make sure the students aren't screwing up anything?"

"Sure. Is everyone really on a first name basis with him?"

Harvey seemed to ignore the comment as he turned to walk one way while Will headed back in the other direction. Could there really be something else that begged Harvey's attention? Will stopped a few inches shy of the doorway where he had just greeted the students. He checked Harvey's agenda, hoping to answer his own question, and pulled out his pack of cigarettes. In earshot of the students' conversation:

"Why?" asked Stephanie. "We sit and listen to him talk for hours. How will this be any different? It's seriously an extension of his class and his book for that matter."

"Who cares about Thierry?" said a male student. "Laroche is the reason anyone actually wants to be here. I'm surprised he even agreed to come to this shitty place."

"Says the guy who flunked out of UCLA after one semester and came back home," said Stephanie. "Do you always have to compare everything to that place?"

"Fuck off," replied the male student. "Just don't be surprised when Laroche wipes his ass with everyone here."

"You included," said Stephanie.

"If you really think that, you clearly haven't been paying attention in class," said Jack.

Will finally entered, and someone made a hushing sound. "How's it coming?" He realized the other male student was the heavy-set guy with a beard and thick-rimmed glasses from his class who was known for being remarkably average and whose name Will could never remember.

"Fine," said Stephanie. "I just have to unpack this last box of Laroche's books. Then our in-house barista Jack will start the coffee."

Will looked at Jack.

"I work at a coffee shop, but like anybody can work one of these," said Jack.

"Sounds like you all have it under control. Do you mind if I leave my bag behind the table?" He pointed to a spot where the others had left purses and bookbags.

"Sure."

As Will set his bag behind the table, the student's name popped into his head. "Oh, and Patrick."

"Yeah?"

"With such brazen opinions and ideas, I'm surprised you don't have more to say in class."

Jack stifled a laugh. Will left and walked down the flight of stairs and out the side door.

It was a quarter till noon. Will sat on the far end in the second row of the Burns Theatre, counting down the minutes until lunch. Harvey stepped to the podium and addressed the crowd.

"We'll take an hour break for lunch. Because we are a little ahead of schedule, the caterers are still setting up the food. Please be patient, and within the next fifteen minutes, they should be ready to serve."

Harvey left the stage, passing Will without a word. Will quickly tailed Harvey. They passed several fold-out tables hugging a wall, outfitted with chafers and burners atop black tablecloths. Two young women in black slacks and white collared shirts arranged the equipment. Harvey continued into a conference room beyond the tables.

"How much longer until the food is ready?" Harvey asked. "We're ahead of schedule."

"We're doing what we can," said a man in black pants and a black collared shirt, "We'll have it ready by noon."

"You said the food would be ready before noon."

"It is ready, sir. We're just setting up in order to serve."

"Well, this needs to be perfect. Consider this a lesson in punctuality for your students."

Harvey turned around and left the man in mid-sentence. Will noticed the caterer shaking his head and cursing under his breath.

"I'm sorry," said Will. "He's stressed and clearly has never worked in food service."

"It's always the same at university events. Everyone complains about the timing or quality of food. And very few are satisfied. I really wish they would get outside caterers for these events. Academics are the fucking worst."

Without a response, Will left hoping to catch up with Harvey.

"Harvey," Will practically shouted.

Harvey turned around.

"I'll be back in a half hour. I have to stop home for something."

Harvey nodded and continued anxiously speed walking.

Will pulled his '98 black BMW into the driveway of his home. He killed the ignition and got out. Anne leaned against the back door of the house. He looked around, cautious of an unwanted eye, as he approached her. She wore her hair down, just about shoulder length. She smiled. He grabbed her waist and kissed her hard.

"Did you give him the book?" she asked.

"No. The French debutante hasn't arrived yet."

Will unlocked the door, and they both went inside. In the kitchen, Will opened the refrigerator.

"Do you want something to eat?"

"You're kidding, right."

He looked back, shutting the refrigerator door. Anne unzipped her sweatshirt, revealing her breasts. "I'll eat later," she said as she turned and walked out of the kitchen. She climbed the stairs and headed toward the bedroom like she had done it a thousand times before. Will was close behind.

When Will reached his room, Anne stood next to his bed, her sweatshirt discarded on the floor. Again, he kissed her. She pulled his head towards her neck.

Anne lay on her side in Will's bed, head propped on her hand, the blanket covering her legs. Will pulled on the pair of boxer briefs he'd been wearing. The digital clock showed 12:37. He'd rather lie in bed with Anne and fall asleep, his arms wrapped around her, her feet grazing his legs. He would caress her smooth skin all afternoon if he could, run his fingers through auburn hair. Even though he was present, the nagging feeling that Harvey would somehow find out crept into his mind. As soon as he dispelled the notion, the reality of Seymour's paranoid threats became very present. *What if he actually followed me home?* He tried to dress with urgency but fumbled at his belt. *Seymour is not following you.* He looked out the bedroom window but could only see the neighbor's house and the side yard.

"Are you worried someone saw us come in? No one is home at noon on Friday, and you know Harvey is the busiest he's been all year—"

"Seymour's threats have me paranoid as hell." Will left the room half-dressed and went to the front window of one of the extra bedrooms and peeked through the curtains. No cars, no people.

"Do you think we'll have a flat in the city or a small cottage just outside of town?" asked Anne.

"Let's not get ahead of ourselves," Will said, returning to the bedroom.

She mockingly pouted, pretending to be upset.

Will grinned. "We'll have a flat in the city. I hate the suburbs. I need people and noise. This place makes me stir-crazy. Going from Manhattan to Athens was like driving a car on the highway and suddenly throwing it into park. I just can't anymore."

"Those couple of days I spent in Paris during college when I backpacked through Europe." She paused. "I've never stopped thinking about it."

"If this next book does well and I get that position at the Sorbonne, this could mean a totally different life for us."

"I know, baby."

He walked to the closet and pulled a dark blue plaid tie off a rack. He wrapped it around his upturned collar, knotted it, and grabbed a charcoal blazer. "How's my hair?"

"Lose the tie and go look at the mirror. Should I lock up when I leave?"

"Do you plan on staying long?"

"I just feel so good in your bed that I don't want to move."

"That's fine." He walked to the bathroom to splash some water on his face. Then he ran his fingers through his hair.

"Come here."

Back in the bedroom, he leaned down to kiss her.

"I love you."

"I love you, too." He slipped his shoes on. "Not that you should be worried, but make sure no one sees you leave."

"Are you sure you don't want me to stop by the neighbors and tell them I fucked your brains out? I could leave them a note if they're not home."

"Funny. The Seymour thing just makes me nervous. I wouldn't be surprised if he were sitting in a car outside the house. Please be careful."

"He's jealous and old. You're young, handsome, and brilliant. And mine."

When Will returned to the conference about ten minutes till one, he noticed attendance had grown some, which eased his mind. More people, more distraction. The students had deserted the tables of merchandise, leaving good 'ol Patrick seated behind a table staring at his phone, no doubt texting or firing off a few Tweets about the gathering of minds, his excluded. *Maybe if you put down your phone,* Will thought, *you'd actually learn something about life.*

Harvey grabbed Will's arm, startling him.

"Jesus, where did you come from?"

"Laroche arrived fifteen minutes ago. You need to introduce yourself now since you blew off last night's dinner. The more comfortable you two are before the symposium, the better."

"Do I have a choice?"

"No."

Harvey practically drug Will to where a sizeable crowd gathered. He pushed his way through the cluster of bodies to the small opening where Elizabeth stood only inches away from the French theorist.

"Jacques, I'd like you to meet William Thierry."

The Frenchman eyed Will, sizing him up, and for a second or two said nothing. Will hoped their face-to-face relationship would not begin badly.

"It's good to put a face with the writing. *C'est avec plaisir*." He extended his hand.

Will shook it lightly.

"No, Monsieur Laroche, the pleasure is mine." *Why did I say monsieur?* Will hesitated, but then opened his messenger bag and pulled out an advanced copy of his book. It felt somewhat forward, but he offered it to Laroche. "I would appreciate your point of view on this when you have the time."

"*Merci*." He glanced at the cover. "Thierry is French is it not?" asked Laroche.

"Yes, it is."

"What part of France?"

"Actually, I'm Québécois," said Will with a degree of hesitance, "on my father's side, Italian on my mother's."

"And your French lineage?" Laroche paused waiting for an answer.

What? Will thought. "A conversation for another time."

"*Parlez-vous français?*"

Jesus Christ. Is this an interview about my Frenchness? Will thought. "*Un petit peu*," he said regretfully.

"Oh. Well, Thierry. We will need to continue our conversation later." He nodded and handed the book to Elizabeth who was now, apparently, the keeper of his things.

With nothing else really to say, Will thanked him and walked away. *What the hell just happened? You should have lied.*

Harvey gave a quick farewell on stage, concluding Friday's portion of the conference. Will considered approaching Laroche to redeem himself, but the Frenchman was swarmed by admirers. Every conference, no matter how big or small was always the same. Everyone wanted to be near the celebrity. Perhaps when they went out for drinks afterward, Will could atone. He relegated to waiting in the hall where he caught Seymour's magnetic glare. With the index and middle digits of his massive talons, Seymour pointed at his eyes and then in Will's direction. *Fuck this*, thought Will, and he beelined it out of the Union, avoiding, no doubt, more of Seymour's harassment.

Seymour considered it a small victory, the wunderkind retreating. He had to relay his elation in some way, looking to Tom still seated at the back of the auditorium.

"Tom. Do you have a minute to take a walk with me? I need to discuss a matter."

Tom, who was drowsy from too many trips to the donut table and the lack of an afternoon nap in his office, offered Seymour a blank stare. Finally, he responded, "What is it?"

"I'd rather discuss it more privately with you."

Tom begrudgingly heaved himself up and followed Seymour to one of the open conference rooms. Seymour shut the door behind him. "I have a strange feeling about Thierry and Laroche's interactions."

"What are you even talking about?"

"Earlier Thierry handed him his book and thanked him for reviewing it. I wonder why he would give the book to his nemesis. Is he wanting another bad review?"

"Nemesis? Seymour, again, what the hell are you talking about? It sounds like Will wants a blurb?"

"A man who is supposedly up for early tenure shouldn't be mixed up in compromising situations."

"I really don't know what the hell you're talking about. One, it's not like he blew the guy in the bathroom for a good review. And two, he's not up for tenure. Where are you getting your information?"

"I've heard things, and I know about the meeting you and Harvey had with Dean Murphy. I don't understand why we'd throw some inexperienced hack into a tenured position just because he wrote a pop-philosophy book. What about a proper search with a committee? I had to work my—"

"Let me stop you there. Will is not getting tenure. He's not even a professor here. In fact, his job is one of the few in jeopardy. And why? Because the university is shit-canning us. And resorting to behavior like this rather than doing your goddamn job isn't helping our case any. If Will wants to be in cahoots with Laroche, as you seem to be claiming, let him because he probably won't have a job here by the end of the year."

"We're protected, aren't we?"

"Is anyone ever safe? Murphy can say whatever he wants in a meeting to pacify us. If they want us gone, they'll find a way. For now, the tenured faculty still have their jobs."

Relieved, Seymour did his best to hide a smile.

"Wipe that shit-eating grin off your face. It's that kind of paranoid cannibalistic nonsense that keeps you from being a good educator. But keep your mouth shut until Harvey announces it, or I will choke you in your office."

It was quarter after eleven when Will settled inside his home after a few drinks with everyone. He mentally checked off the small accomplishments for today. *Perhaps this will actually work,* he thought. *Maybe Paris isn't too far off.* His post-conference interactions with Laroche were friendlier, more relaxed. He felt hopeful.

He scaled the stairs, having made up his mind to go to bed. As he approached his bedroom, he could smell a faint odor of perfume, a mix of flowers and something sweet like vanilla. Had Anne worn perfume earlier? These days, she only used essential oils. At the doorway of his bedroom, the odor was almost as strong as if someone had just sprayed whatever it was. Maybe Anne was trying to surprise him with some kind of aromatherapy. The scent was familiar, but he couldn't quite place it. He turned on the light and noticed the bedding was a mess. *I guess Anne didn't make the bed on the way out.* He discarded his clothes in the hamper next to the dresser, leaving his boxer briefs on, shut off the light, and got into bed. *The pillow reeked.* The attempt was nice but unnecessary. He tossed the pillow to the floor and grabbed another. The smell was not as strong. He closed his eyes and tried to remember why this scent was so familiar, his last thoughts before sleep overtook him.

Stephanie Green
At a table in the Student Union, Athens University

NOVEMBER 2009

What can I really tell you about campus visits that most people don't already know? It's a very simple process. When I'm involved with the general campus tour, which is most of the time since the philosophy major is less popular, I take students to the same sites around the university. We begin at the admissions building and hit all the spots that would likely draw the students to this place. We start here in the food court because everyone needs to know where to eat, then to a newer building to show them the updated digital classrooms, then to the rec center where we emphasize all of the activities that help relieve stress like yoga, smoothies, and hot tubs, then to the stadium where I give them a scenario about home football games and school spirit, then we walk past the greens near some of the older, more aesthetic architecture and the scenic spots, and then through the quad past Cox library, all the while providing them anecdotes about college life, some funny and some heartfelt, in order to feel a sense of belonging—there really is an art to this. Sometimes I will take them to a staged dorm room to plant that seed about living on campus. I try to show prospective students how they will "find their niche." The saying is actually "Find Your Niche," which is a stupid motto because how many of these kids even know what their niche is let alone the definition of the word. College gives them a map to help them find what they are interested in, but they won't really discover who they are or what they value in life until they are practically finished with school. That's just bad marketing. If I know there is a group of students who are legitimately interested in Philosophy or Classics Studies, I'll take that group of students to Gordon Hall. I think the main reason we have anyone on this smaller tour is because they want to see the building. It's pretty unique. I've heard that it combines many styles, which is why the university kind of hates the building. It doesn't really go with the rest of the campus design. At least that's what Sylvie said. She knows the whole history behind it. Typically, I leave the group with Sylvie so she can discuss that, and then like Ariadne guiding Theseus through the labyrinth, I show them some of the weirder parts of the building, such as the strange spiral hall design and the Italian stonework, and parts that have been remodeled so it's less confusing than its original design.

Do I remember any particular students? Not usually. Sure, we don't get many that come into the philosophy department, but I do so many of these tours that I might see fifty to a hundred faces in one day. Sylvie is the one with the great memory. It's why she knows so much about so many obscure things. But you can't put "good memory" under specialized skills on a résumé, and I'm really just trying to get as many meaningful lines on mine, like leading these campus visits, so I can get into a decent graduate program. I'm not trying to be a lawyer. I want the PhD. I want to do what Dr. Harlowe does. She's an amazing woman and a role model for women in academia and the field of Philosophy. We need more women to breathe life into this discipline and transform it, rather than talk about its death like Professor Thierry and Dr. Buchanan do. Also, Dr. Harlowe wouldn't get caught up in some scandal like those two. She wouldn't try to take advantage of students, and she certainly wouldn't murder anyone. That's the problem, really. It's always the men trying to exert their will onto women, inappropriately talking to or touching their students, gaslighting them and making them think they are so special when really, the creeps only want to get into the next pretty girl's pants. Derrida did it. Sartre and Heidegger did it. And I'm sure there are many more. You don't see Martha Nussbaum or Judith Butler or say, Avitoll Ronell trying to coerce their students into affairs. Sure, Simone de Bouvier did, but that was part of her feminist philosophy, and it was all consensual. She was truly trying to chip away at the patriarchy. It's almost always men who are violent perpetrators, acting as if women owe them everything, like women are the reason why they do the things they do. Maybe we don't want that kind of attention, their toxic masculinity.

All that aside, I was hopeful and kind of naïve when Professor Thierry arrived because he was a young up-and-coming philosopher, and it made Athens University seem like a cool place to be. When he ditched his classes the week after the conference, I felt responsible to be the one to lead the way and make a complaint. And once I made my case to other students, they followed. Some people probably thought I was being petty or a bitch, but it's our responsibility to do what we have to do to get the most out of our education. And professors should not be able to do whatever they want because they are tenured, prestigious, or some hip guy with a popular book. That not's fair to us, and it makes a mockery of higher education. But who really knows now what it'll be like because of this whole scandal? I just need to continue to work hard and not let everything happening ruin my chances of getting into a good grad school.

I guess what I'm trying to say is that I don't remember the dead woman. Sylvie says the woman was part of one of the summer groups last year. She's probably right, but I really couldn't tell you either way. I do however know someone who knows something about her. I promised him I wouldn't tell anyone, but given the circumstances, it would be wrong if I didn't say something. At the time the information didn't matter to me, and he seemed like he needed to tell someone. Since we were talking or dating or whatever, he trusted me. But isn't that how gossip gets started? If you don't want anyone to know then don't tell anyone. That seems pretty simple, but people have these like internal struggles where they need a release (*i.e.,* tell someone) or they will go crazy. His story was kind of weird, and I was shocked to hear about everyone involved. The incident was sort of funny but really strange, gross even, but I really don't know what to make of it.

I wasn't there, so I can only speculate. It seems pointless for me to try to relay the story to you when I'll likely get something wrong, so you might as well get it from the source. I mean, what professor would ask his student to do something like that? Thierry had to have known what he was getting them into. So, your best bet is to just get a hold of Jack Ballard. He could tell you all about it. And, damn, does he have a story. It all makes me wonder what kind of person Professor Thierry was before he came to Athens.

Chapter 6

Saturday morning.

Harvey staggered into the kitchen, rubbing his temples, the first step of shaking off his expected hangover. He put the coffee on and took a long, loose shit while skimming the headlines of *The Washington Post*. Upstairs in the Buchanan household, Anne slept with the comforter pulled over her head. She dreamt of a room full of geriatrics dressed as sports mascots, and though her body felt heavy and dense, she attempted to instruct them in Bikram yoga. She moved as if encased in a Jell-O mold while the giant Muppet-like figures mirrored her, sweat pouring off their synthetic fur. She awoke from this dream every Saturday morning, a dream worthy of Freudian interpretation or maybe just a sign she might be thinking too much about work.

A few streets over, Seymour sat in his solarium near a cast iron wood burner, drinking coffee and reading a book about the German Labor Front during the rise of the Third Reich. He pictured his young German father on a scaffolding, plastering the walls of a building, spreading the brown undercoat over wooden lathe. As his father observes two young SS soldiers standing on the corner of a street smoking cigarettes and laughing, he feverishly spreads the mixture with a sense of pride from his part in constructing the building, a structure destroyed from a bombing years later. Seymour's wife sat at the kitchen table eating wheat toast in front of a small television that displayed the week's events.

Elizabeth woke up in a bed that wasn't hers, quickly realizing she was in Laroche's room. She could hear the sound of water running from the shower as she gathered her things and told him through the door she would return at ten. He asked if there was a decent bakery in town where they could have pastries. She told him she knew the perfect place before she left to drive back to a house that was far too large for one person, though it has been her home for nearly fifteen years.

Tom sipped a cup of hot black tea and ate a chocolate éclair leftover from the previous day's purchase. He sat in his recliner wearing yesterday's clothes, reading a worn copy of *Swann's Way*, a book he had not read since his French literature course in college nearly fifty years ago. Given his impending retirement, he found a sudden interest in revisiting the past.

Finally, there was Will who awoke from a dream, or rather a nightmare, his heart racing and his chest covered in sweat. The scent in his room was Sweet Lavender, a specific fragrance Lily had worn, one she bought on occasion from a small boutique a few blocks from where they had lived in Washington Square. The owner of the shop claimed to have made all the skincare products inhouse from ingredients she gathered from remote regions of the world. The aroma of the perfume so faint in this moment he felt as if it were merely a memory, some involuntary notion triggered in his brain by the dream. He sat up, feeling the usual morning discomfort from a full bladder, his biological alarm clock indicating six a.m. Will shuffled to the bathroom to relieve himself. As he stood in front of the toilet, he recounted the dream though some of the details were blurry, confusing.

In the dream, Will walks on a brick road in downtown Athens. Everything feels closer together and tight, giving him the impression he is larger than normal. The atmosphere is dark—the black and white shades of film noir—and Athens is a maze of sorts. He turns a corner, then another, and observes a woman in a long black coat walking on the opposite side of the street, her dark hair hiding her face. They proceed in unison, practically a mirror image, mimetic. He turns the corner, yet again, to walk down an alley and sees the back of what looks like the same woman. With each step he takes, she moves in perfect tempo, as if she's an extension of him. He follows her until she turns the corner. He hurries to catch up, feeling as though he will lose her, but when he rounds the same corner, there she is. He continues following her on this path until he reaches a main intersection, the exact center of town. On each corner stands a woman, four total. They are identical to the one he was chasing or running from (could he be doing both at the same time?), and their backs are to him. How he ended up in the middle of the intersection is unclear. He shouts, "What do you want?" The words trickle slowly and slurred and taste metallic. He attempts to open his mouth wider to yell, but it won't budge as if wired shut, and he strains to force another "What do you want?" The words are barely intelligible, garbled. No reply. He takes the main street toward the university. He looks back, and the women walk in opposite directions, though one seems to be following him. He crosses another intersection. The streets are barren. He quickens his pace to a sprint, a task that feels dense and slippery like running in water. He's not sure where to go.

Now, he stands at the front entrance of Gordon Hall, and the building seems massive. The inscription above the door reads *LASCIATE OGNE SPERANZA / VOI CH'INTRATE.* He walks inside to what looks more like a funhouse maze than an old building. He thinks he'll find solace in his office if he can just get there, but the halls twist and turn. He sees himself running in several directions at once like an M.C. Escher lithograph. Random sets of staircases. He takes one, but they all look the same. The feeling of falling is ever present. He runs upstairs, but the orientation is relative, first right-side up, then sideways, and then upside down. It's all the same. He passes painting after painting of different philosophers like a hall of bizarre family lineage. Each looks like versions of Harvey, as if he had dressed in costume for the portrait. The first has a moustache and blank stare like Nietzsche. Another has glasses, a pipe, and exotropia like Sartre. Still another with two huge tufts of white hair and mutton chops, Schopenhauer. Descartes. Foucault. Angela Davis. Confucius. Socrates. Hypatia. All Harvey. The eyes of the paintings literally follow Will. There is the crackle of chamber music playing throughout the place, like something from a phonograph.

Finally, Will reaches his office. The door is glass, and the light is on. A woman sits at his desk reading his book in a way that conceals her face. He tries to open the door, but it's locked. He kicks it once. Nothing. He kicks it again. Nothing. He has the strongest urge to be inside that room. Some outside force moves, pushes him. He looks for something to throw through the glass, but the hall is empty. He kicks a third time, but the door opens right before his shoe connects. He loses his footing and falls several feet, floors, miles down, down until his body hits the ground. Long blades of grass, rye, and wildflowers surround him. He stands and realizes he's in a field of Queen Anne's Lace. Daybreak. The scene is a melding of several places and times. A large group of women in the distance, the ones from before, close in on him. They seem so far away but approach with haste. They swell in number, becoming hundreds maybe even thousands. They're like ants swarming on a granule of sugar or a ripened strawberry. But something is off. As they near, he realizes they have no features, each face nothing but pale smooth skin.

And like before, he wakes up just as they reach him.

Will returned to his bedroom, picked up the pillow from the floor, and brought it close to his face. Its smell made him wince. He placed it on the bed, put on a pair of jeans and a sweatshirt, and headed downstairs to the kitchen. He grabbed a pack of Turkish Golds from his messenger bag and headed out the front door. He lit a cigarette and sat in an Adirondack chair his parents had given him years ago. He had had the dream twice before, both times within the first couple months of moving to Athens. *Why now?* he asked himself. He exhaled smoke. Perhaps it was the stress of everything. It's always the stress.

He glanced at the ashtray on the small wooden table next to him as he flicked the ash from his cigarette. Wait. He looked again at its contents. Among his snubbed butts was a single black filter. He picked it up and smelled it. A clove. More accurately, a Djarum Black. *Where the hell did this…* Instantly, he could taste her mouth—the sweet residue of smoke on her tongue. He tossed the spent filter on the porch floor. *There's no way. This could be anyone's.*

He took a hit: deep breath, long exhale. He couldn't block the thought of her sitting in his chair and smoking on his front porch. A series of images of her flashed in his mind.

"No," he said. "Just a weird coincidence. Could be anyone's."

After a final hit, he snuffed the cigarette and went inside to shower.

The day went much like the previous one. Reluctant to arrive at the conference too early and run the risk of having another awkward exchange with Laroche, Will went to his office and looked over his symposium notes. He'd been preparing for months, but no matter how comfortable he felt about his part, he knew he couldn't prepare for the unpredictable. Ideally, if they each act with a level of civility and ethics, while minding their time, sure, things should go well. Will had no issue with professional courtesy, but Laroche was a wild card—the seasoned contrarian whose snarky pragmatism left little room for niceties. The only way to ready oneself for Laroche was to anticipate the flaws, however miniscule, in one's own response and correct them. One could not just expect the Frenchman to be satisfied with any answer because a pause was an invitation for an attack. Also, being familiar with abject humility helped. After spending roughly an hour running through notes, he lost interest and felt like it was more important for him to have a presence at the conference. Technically, he helped organize this thing, so networking was expected. Given that his name was on the schedule twice today, one for the symposium and the other for reading an excerpt from the new book, Will needed to mingle with others. As Harvey had drilled into his brain, they must bring as much attention to this place as possible.

Will arrived at the Student Union around ten a.m. In the open green space known as the Quad, shared by the library, the Honors College dorms, the Student Union, and the president's hall, there was a small stage with a DJ and a row of tables under tents offering everything from Argonaut merchandise to program information to alumni perks. About a dozen banners and signs of different shapes and sizes marked the celebration: Athens Homecoming '09: Defend the Fleece. For a stupid slogan that had so little to do with the actual Greek myth, the phrase brandished everything, and people wore it with pride as intended. There were even little golden fleece towels with "DEFEND THE FLEECE" embroidered on them. People of all ages and income brackets swung the towels over their heads. If only someone in the philosophy department had thought to brand something, even if it seemed cliché and commercial. A T-shirt with a silhouette of The Thinker along with the caption "The unexamined life is not worth living. —Socrates" and on the back "2009 ATHENS PHILOSOPHY CONFERENCE: V." Why hadn't anyone proposed that? Why hadn't he thought of that until now? They could have been the school colors, even sold alongside the school merchandise. And in the same vein, why didn't Harvey set up a booth at the Alumni Center for after the parade? They could've dumped a couple of adjuncts and student workers in it. They could have even been talking to alums about cutbacks. It was as if they were inviting the university to shitcan them.

Given the shouting from and swaying of the hunter green and gold bodies, the students were starting their celebration early. The DJ played an EDM version of Miley Cyrus's "Party in the U.S.A." Inside the Union, Will could still clearly hear the music and shouting from outside, which could be problematic, distracting even, for conference goers. When he reached the designated conference area, a relatively large group of people mingled, a dull roar of splintered conversations. Will searched the crowd for Laroche. Maybe the two could discuss hiring a language tutor and a genealogist to help bolster his Francophilia. So far, no sign of the Frenchman.

Inside the room with refreshments, Will found Elizabeth picking through the pastries, examining them with the precision of a food inspector.

"Something wrong?" Will asked.

"All of it looks perfectly edible, but Jacques complained about finding a decent bakery for a pastry." She rolled her eyes as she continued to peruse the sweets. "God, he's so annoying."

"Why am I not surprised. Is he here?"

"No. You can relax. He's getting ready in his hotel room. I'm supposed to head back to pick him up."

"Head back?"

"Don't ask."

"Grab two of the croissants and ask one of the caterers to put them in the oven or toaster oven for a few minutes. I don't think he'll notice. How did you become his personal assistant?"

She stuck two croissants into a small brown paper bag. "Because I hate myself just enough, and I'm trying to get through this weekend."

Unsure of how to respond, Will changed the subject. "I'm going to sit in on a few readings. I'm still surprised you didn't prepare a paper for the conference."

"Honestly, Will, I haven't had the time." She folded the bag. "And I'm annoyed and disappointed that most of the speakers are white men. That's not going to happen next year."

"I had input into a lot of this, but Harvey had the last say on the list of speakers. I'm headed to a reading on the state of black consciousness from a Morehouse professor."

"I bet he's white."

"No," he said with uncertainty. "You can't teach at an HBCU if you aren't black."

"Of course, you can." She dropped the brown bag of pastries into a canvas tote. "We have a number of white professors here who teach the Black Experience. Have you seen our Pan-African Studies Department? Worse contradictions have existed. I guess part of the black experience has been having white people tell black people what they've experienced and how they've experienced it. I'm sure that's a hoot for the African American students who take the course. Alright, I'm off to get these things toasted. Don't forget we're going out afterwards, so plan for a late night."

"Will do. Good luck."

Sure enough, Elizabeth was right. The Morehouse professor was indeed white, in his mid-forties, and regularly adjusted his large, black, thick-rimmed Wayfarers. His paper titled "Philosophy's Death Shudder and the State of Black Consciousness" was an overly enthusiastic argument about the lack of representation in the field of philosophy due to the fact that most [white] philosophers considered Africana philosophy and race theory to be branches of Pan-African Studies. People of color who attempted to assimilate into the former discipline were not considered philosophers but rather culturalists and thus relegated to the latter. He wasn't pushing for some brand of the death of philosophy but argued that Western philosophy's racism was limiting its ideological expansion. Africana philosophy was expanding and challenging the discipline, allowing it to move in new directions. The solution, from the Morehouse professor's perspective, was to add the study of Africana philosophy to every philosophy department thus ensuring black philosophers the opportunity for a real permanent place in the field. But until that happened, philosophy would repeatedly feel that death shudder as it has in recent years. It wasn't quite clear how he addressed Black Consciousness or if he even did, but it made for a provocative title.

When the man finished, he was met with modest applause. As Will looked around, he saw the attendees were nearly all white aside from two young black men in the back, one of whom was in Will's course, a student by the name of, um, Jeremy? Yeah, Jeremy. He was sharp but said little in class, usually meeting Will in office hours to discuss the material from time to time. Jeremy raised his hand.

"Yes, in the back."

The student stood. "So, like, I'm a double major in Philosophy and Pan-African Studies here at Athens University, and I know that even though it's in the course catalog, the Department of Philosophy doesn't offer Africana philosophy. But there are many courses in the Pan-African department that cover this topic extensively, and even one of the professors who teaches these courses has a PhD in philosophy. So, I guess my question is how exactly is it feasible to add the study of Africana philosophy to 'every' philosophy department?"

"Well, there is no clear path for developing a concentration in Africana philosophy for each university's unique situation. It's a case-by-case basis. Some may offer courses at the graduate level, while others will only offer courses at the undergraduate level. But the idea is to plan, implement, and develop these programs nationwide, which would provide more philosophers of color opportunities in philosophy departments."

The Morehouse professor appeared satisfied with his response.

The student continued unphased. "This whole conference is addressing the fact that philosophy as a career, as a field of study, and as a set of ideas is dying. Based on Professor Thierry's book and other sources, many philosophy departments are struggling financially and unable to put more bodies in seats. So how exactly is a department that can barely pay its bills going to find the funds to hire more faculty, let alone a black philosopher who specializes in Africana philosophy, one who teaches courses that may actually compete or conflict with Pan-African Studies? And furthermore, from what I gathered, the whole point is to gain the interest of more black students thus creating more diversity and normalize careers for people of color. It's like, rather than just trying to encourage black students to study philosophy for like the same reasons that Dubois, Angela Davis, or Cornell West studied, you're basically baiting us by using our identity. Why not just offer barbeque and hip-hop at the student orientation if you want more black students? It'd be cheaper."

The student's friend laughed.

"I. I. I'm sorry if I offended you," said the professor, beginning to walk back his ideas, "or made this seem like some kind of academic affirmative action. I assure you it's not. My observation at Morehouse and other institutions that offer Africana philosophy as a concentration, whether on the undergraduate or graduate level, has matriculated more students of color, overall. More students equal more funds, which in turn creates more positions for faculty. Diversity is always a precursor to progress."

"With all due respect, the one flaw I see in all of this, for whatever reason you keep ignoring, is the inherent racial bias of the system. Bro, you're teaching Africana philosophy at an HBCU, and you aren't even black. I mean, according to your theory, your position should be filled by a black professor. And that fact alone should make it clear that despite my scholarship and dedication to philosophy, my white counterpart who applies to the same faculty position that I'm just as qualified for is more likely to be offered the position."

"Well, I don't think that—"

"So, the only death shudder I foresee is the one from the black philosopher when he realizes that he's not getting the job because some hip white dude has an interest in black culture."

One of the moderators for the conference, an adjunct, silenced the microphone of the Morehouse professor, and shouted, "Thank you for your input, but we must set up for the next speaker to stay on schedule," then awkwardly clapped, hoping to encourage the rest of the room to join. Jeremy left before Will had a chance to talk to him. He wanted to suggest the student write an article about this or, at the very least, thank him for the name drop. An article of that nature could easily make it in the *Chronicle of Higher Education*. He'd talk about it next time they had office hours.

Harvey moderated the dialogue, interspersing small apologies and comments about the noise outside from the homecoming festival, which had not decreased in volume since it began this morning. Three men sat at the table on stage, each with his own microphone: Will on the left, Laroche on the right, and a professor from Yale in the center, a nice buffer between the two. The stage lights were turned up all the way, a mistake made by the lighting personnel no one bothered to address. Although none of the men complained, Will's anxiety exacerbated his awareness of the light's heat and the perspiration on his forehead. Will had said something to spark Laroche's annoyance.

"Well, that's where I think you're wrong, Mr. Thierry. The humanities will never be a lucrative part of the university. This was not their intent, and it is certainly not their place in today's society. They thrive because of donors, endowments, people of the profession with a vested interest, and above all, prospective students. The Arts and Humanities suffer without these forms of support, without the necessary attention to garner funds or the proper encouragement to study these subjects. The oldest and most reputable schools will likely continue to have thriving humanities programs, more specifically philosophy. Many mid-level and public universities struggle to keep these programs viable because they do not fit into the adapted corporate model that plagues most American universities. In Marxist tradition, intellectual thought is the antithesis to this model, which is the brutal irony of the entire situation. The professionalization of philosophy rather than philosophy itself is becoming an endangered species."

Will focused on the physical: the perspiration under his armpits, his dry mouth, the lights' heat and glare. This compounded his anxiety, or maybe his anxiety was the real culprit. What the hell was his problem, really? The discussion had only just begun. He took a drink from the glass of water near his microphone. He looked to the front row where Anne sat. She was gorgeous in her black dress with her hair done, and she even wore heels for the occasion, an oddity. She caught eyes with him, and they shared a look, which should have been encouraging but Will interpreted as pity.

"I think you're right in that respect, Jacques," Will responded. "But consider Latin. It's a dead language, but most universities teach Latin in their language department to an extent. Why? Because it serves a functional purpose, albeit mostly for history's sake. It's the basis of many languages, and it's still pertinent to logical argument and practicing law. Latin has its own set of rules, like logic, that must be taught. But as other spoken languages developed and dialects became the preferred vernacular, Latin's usage and necessity declined until it was pronounced dead, unless you're a lawyer or a Roman Catholic. Then *pax vobiscum*."

A few scattered laughs, nothing too enthusiastic.

He continued, "And I find it highly unlikely that anyone is encouraging younger generations to study Latin, let alone make a career of it. Yet, it is still taught, and new permanent positions are being posted every year. Just look at the employment data from the Society for Classical Studies. Philosophy attempts to use logic but because it has splintered off into so many different specialized areas, what we know as philosophy mimics other areas of study: literature, history, science, linguistics, and mathematics. And it's being taught much like those subjects. So, I see it dying, in a sense, like Latin and being taught like language and mathematics, similar to Derrida's thoughts on metaphor, so to speak."

There was a short pause. Harvey cleared his throat and read from his script.

"One of the most well-respected public institutions in England recently ended its philosophy program and closed the department. Another college in Philadelphia did the same. These are just two of the many examples where universities have made the decision to do such. There has been a twenty percent drop in philosophy majors since 1979. If this trend continues, we could see a chain reaction occur where universities suspend or discontinue majors and close departments, creating a surplus of philosophy professors but a very limited number of jobs, essentially making these individuals obsolete in academia. Students observe this phenomenon, and regardless of their desire to pursue a philosophy degree, they don't because the job market appears non-existent. Student enrollment decreases. Lack of enrollment leads to department closure. So, hypothetically speaking, this continues until there are only a few institutions in the world that offer philosophy. How likely is this scenario? Are there theoretical safeguards to prevent what seems inevitable or is this the fate of the discipline? Dr. Fowles from Yale, you may answer first, then Thierry, and finally, Laroche."

"If we look at Weston College," said Dr. Fowles, "we'll see that although their philosophy department was shuttered and the major discontinued, a semester later everything was reinstated. People immediately realized the travesty of that decision. Philosophy is at the foundation of Liberal Arts education, and although the general public may not completely appreciate or understand what that means, they realize the effect it would have on the scholarship. They understood our field's uniqueness: it feeds the mind like science and mathematics and nourishes the soul like literature and the fine arts. Even the required intro courses nearly every student takes contributes to the development of deep, critical thinking. What they did, the students and faculty of the college, was ban together and write letters to the college and protest the travesty. They publicized this event so much so that the college was met with a tidal wave of criticism they could not ignore. Realizing its enormous mistake, the college immediately responded to the uproar by reinstating the major, the department, the faculty and staff, and the students who were a part of the program. Much like other European countries and parts of Latin America, when people collect for a purpose, it is powerful and produces change. It also didn't hurt that Noam Chomsky and Martha Nussbaum among other prominent figures in philosophy wrote complaints to the president of the college criticizing the college's actions and thus causing donors to threaten to stop funding."

More laughter, clapping. A few cheers.

"Professor Thierry."

"With regard to Dr. Yale's sentimentality toward social uprise or unrest, it's a nice anecdote, and I think it works for politics and social change. But if you look at the history of philosophy on a timeline, you'll see that there were lulls in free thought, proceeded by eras where people created amazing philosophy: the Socratic era, the age of Reason and Enlightenment, the Germans of the Weimar Republic, and the postmodern and post-structuralist movements of the 60s, 70s, and into the 80s. Societies were divided and a greater amount of the public accepted such ideas, especially academics and intellectuals. Universities are where some of the best writing, thought, and research is produced. When the focus of education shifts from acquisition of knowledge to acquisition of money, there is a clear problem.

"When young people are placed in a position to choose a career, the main priorities are money. What is the cost of this kind of education in relation to the salary of the corresponding career? Granted, that is a reasonable approach to choosing a career if personal wealth is the sole factor, but that is not typically the mindset of someone choosing to study the humanities. They are interested in self-discovery, human contribution, and authenticity.

"What it comes down to in our current society is demonstrating that philosophy can be lucrative and that a department is viable and will benefit the university, perhaps not in the ways in which the STEM departments do, but in ways that are equally extrinsic as they are intrinsic. No one is going to 'find their niche' if there isn't a variety of dynamic programs that meet the needs of the current and incoming student population. The humanities have always aimed at advancing and benefitting humanity in numerous ways. Formulating new ideas and ways in which we view the world and attempt to interact with it and each other is the foundation of liberal arts education."

"You really believe," Laroche cut in, "that your death of philosophy rhetoric will benefit all of humanity? That by studying the death of philosophy people will view the world in new ways? What about the people of Papua New Guinea who know nothing about this subject and will never know anything about it or starving children in developing countries who don't need ideas but need food and medical care or the appalling number of women who are sexually assaulted worldwide? How indeed does this enrich their lives in any way?"

Will wanted to call bullshit on Laroche. The Frenchman was baiting him, being a provocateur. This was merely tennis, and Will just needed to keep hitting the ball back to Laroche.

Outside, he took out a cigarette and lit it. "Fuck," he said aloud to no one. "It doesn't matter what I say," he trailed off and took a drag from his cigarette, finishing the words in his head, *that asshole makes me look like a fool.* He exhaled smoke. The Q and A portion of the symposium had to be better than this. With his back to the Union, he looked out at the Quad.

The events were winding down, and students were likely heading to off-campus parties as custodial workers slowly cleaned the grounds. He looked to the half-demolished building formerly known as Rear Hall, which was demarcated by a chain-linked fence, caution tape, and several signs that warned unauthorized individuals from crossing. The building's architecture, unlike the Georgian and Federalist style of the early Athens University halls or the Gothic style of Gordon Hall, was plain and bland, a long, three-story rectangle of yellow brick from the late forties. It could have been any building constructed at that time in the city of Athens. When it was built, Rear Hall first housed the Cox Library, but as the college grew, the Manasseh Cox Memorial Library was erected, a towering structure of fifteen floors on the adjacent side of the Quad. All that the old building held at this point, before demolition, was the Center for Distance Learning and Tutoring services, which conveniently moved to the Student Union's lower level as part of the Campus Enhancement Program. What Will loved so much about this old building was the view he had enjoyed from this very spot for the last two years. On this side of Rear Hall, there had been nine large stained-glass windows depicting great minds from history: Socrates, Plato, Aristotle, Cicero, Homer, Virgil, Dante, Shakespeare, and Chaucer. Like saints on display in a Catholic church, these colorful mosaics represented human thought.

Standing here admiring these figures was one of the few times Will ever felt reverent toward anything. He knew his work paled in comparison, but it had given him hope for what was possible, what could endure time. But the glass was gone, mere vacancies, the openings covered in plastic. The building would be down in the next few weeks given the workers' progress. The day they shattered the glass Will had stood in the same spot and watched, sicken by the whole scene. The donor of the stained-glass figures had long since been deceased, and despite some minor protest, the university deemed the cost of salvaging the windows too great. Will had petitioned to take the stained class to Gordon Hall and put it on display in different parts of the building, but it seemed the university wanted nothing to do with that. As Will finished his cigarette, no more than a few yards away, a student stood next to a bench, hunched over and vomiting. He wore a T-shirt with the phrase "Athens University Proud." Will shook his head and walked back inside the Union hoping the second half of the symposium would be less uncomfortable than the first.

[PROOF COPY]

DOWN THE GARDEN PATH (*MEZZANITTI IN ATHENS*)

From researching Paolo Mezzanitti's time in Athens, Ohio, I have concluded that some of the historical records were likely destroyed, revised, or abbreviated. The intentional loss or possible destruction, as I suspect, may involve something more sinister at work by removing this archival information. It is still somewhat of a mystery as to why the Italian ventured to Ohio, let alone Athens, a town that at the turn of the 19th century had little connection to the nation—a frontier hub of education and a small farming community with a gristmill producing corn, wheat, and rye flour. Despite the introduction of the canal in 1836 and then the railroad in 1860, the town was merely a sojourn between Philadelphia and St. Louis. Few sources have supported any real insight or motivation as to why the Italian traveled through Ohio, a trip less direct and ideal given the Appalachian Mountains and the connecting trains. Most assume he was on his way from Manhattan to Chicago, a city densely populated with Italian immigrants from his hometown of Genoa. At this time, landscape architecture was booming, and Mezzanitti had spent nearly a decade working in the parks system in New England.

Because little is known as to why exactly he came to this rugged Ohio town or how he was commissioned to design the building known as James A. Gordon Hall, I have had to piece together what limited sources were available from the Athens County Public Records, Athens University Historical Archives, Athens Historical Society, and the most important and treasured source, the recently acquired private journal of Mezzanitti[1].

There is not a detailed account of this period of time in his life (about one year), and piecing together the narrative has relied partially on the theoretical. Due to the obscurity of the architect, there are few[2] who have researched and written about him, most of which is in Italian. The architectural historian Fabio Calvi, in his book *L'Influenza Italiana nel Disegno Americano,* has suggested that Mezzanitti simply took the wrong train due to his lack of proficiency with the English language. Rather than traveling the train route from New York City to Chicago, a route located along the Great Lakes, he mistakenly took the route through southern Pennsylvania. When changing connecting trains in Athens, as well as being met with delays, the Italian wandered the beautiful campus and happened to meet the right people at the right time. Unfortunately, there has been no evidence of travel or passenger logs to confirm this theory. Another source, *The Architecture of Athens County,* a locally published book by the Athens County Historical Society, briefly states that Mezzanitti was a visiting lecturer whose designs were chosen for the commissioned building project of James A. Gordon Hall. But after exhaustive research through public records, the Athens University Archives, and Mezzanitti's journal, I found no information to validate this account. Therefore, I offer the following theory, which is substantially more rooted in recorded factual evidence, albeit seemingly mundane at first, that the Italian was on his way from North Carolina to Ohio to interview for a teaching position.

After working in New England, he traveled to Asheville, North Carolina in 1889 to visit the Biltmore Estate, without invitation, to view the extravagance of the landscape and home designed for George Washington Vanderbilt II with the intention again of working with

---

1   See Appendix C for full journal translated by Mario Boiardi, my friend and connection to the Italian architects.

2   Fuller, Martin. *Obscured View: Architecture of the Avant-Garde.* University of Massachusetts Press, 1999. An encyclopedic work and labor of love I extensively researched and wrote to shine light on the lesser known, but no less talented, architects who deserve recognition for their daring and innovative work in architectural design.

renowned landscape architect Frederick Law Olmsted whom the Italian was a laborer and an assistant[3] in the restoration and redesign of the Niagara Falls Park via the Niagara Reservation in 1887. While eager to provide service to the great landscape architect, the Italian had hoped for the opportunity to meet Richard Morris Hunt, a leading figure of American architecture, and study his design of the Vanderbilt mansion. None of these opportunities came without obstacles.

According to the Italian's journal, neither Olmsted nor Hunt cared to associate with him during this project for reasons such as his age and ethnicity:

> *In 1889, I was only thirty-one, Olmsted was sixty-seven, and Hunt was sixty-one—both in the twilight of their careers. Each man insulated himself from the laborers, only communicating with the few designers. Despite my work on Olmsted's former projects, it was clear the architects would not associate with cheap and unskilled immigrant laborers. They believed we [Italians] had a reputation for deceit and violence. They called us stupid and worthless dagoes.*

Mezzanitti, however, found a way of breaking into the elite circle by lying about his age and involvement in the construction of the Villa Durazzo-Pallavicini's garden, a famous and beloved park in Genoa. He embellished his formal education and apprenticeship with the esteemed architect, set designer, and professor Michele Canzio as well as his father's reputation as a garden designer in Italy. Although the latter information was true, he had told them his family was appointed as the garden's caretakers and added fifteen years to his age by adjusting dates to certain professional documents and growing a very thick and convincing mustache. All of this drew the attention of the architects, and the Italian labored part of the day and spent the other part assisting Olmsted.

Although Mezzanitti associated with the architects, he was never fully able to penetrate the group's close circle. Nearing the end of his year there, he made the transition from the Biltmore Estate to

---

3   Uncredited

Athens University based on Olmsted's insistence that he apply for a lecturer position in the Department of Architecture at the Ohio State University in their landscape architecture program. Before departing, the Italian obtained letters of recommendation from both Hunt and Olmsted, praising him for his intellect and abilities in both areas of design. What is curious about the letters is that Mezzanitti forged both. His reason was simple: the architects refused to give him their recommendation. It is important to note that during this point in America's history, anti-Italian sentiment was growing[4], and to be affiliated so closely in any way would have soiled one's reputation. In addition, most men of this profession were either Anglo-American or French, so Mezzanitti truly had no real place in the lineage of American Architecture at this time. Be that as it may, the Italian carefully observed and practiced the writing styles of both men, thus creating two letters to use for future professional endeavors. Having letters from two of America's most distinguished architects proved valuable in the latter part of his career. Prior to this occasion, Mezzanitti had created dozens of counterfeit letters from other accomplished individuals in his field, some as early as his days attending university in Genoa.

The forgeries, his apprenticeship with Sr. Canzio, and his study of Humanities likely influenced his sense of design. He discusses briefly in his journal how he valued the images in the arts that were viewed as odd and unconventional, like the scenes from painter Hieronymus Bosch and poets Dante and Ovid:

> *I had very little interest designing gardens or structures that people deemed fashionable or great. I wanted to design structures that confused and displaced, the kind of design that would leave a lasting impression on people, something pointing to the ethereal or metaphysical. Surprise and curiosity over praise and recognition. Sr. Canzio's Villa Durazzo-Pallavicini garden is an achievement in style and greatly admired. It is at once a theatrical design that incorporates the English*

---

4   So much so that on March 14, 1891 a mob hanged eleven Italians in New Orleans for their alleged involvement in the murder of police chief David Hennessy after some of them had been acquitted at trial. It was one of the largest single mass lynchings in U.S. history.

Romantic style of a garden, Dante's Divine Comedy, and
Chinese aesthetic. But it lacks the grotesque that was present
in the Renaissance, the kind of images that evoke the feelings
that we are told not to feel.

Mezzanitti began his technique making slight adjustments to others' designs, incorporating faces and symbols in ways that were puzzle-like or akin to a mosaic, which may be seen as an early use of collage in architecture. Some have even described his work as early pastiche. He often ridiculed the people who commissioned the work by adjusting the designs, and if he were caught, the result was often an early dismissal from the project. At the Biltmore Estate, unbeknownst to the sculptor, Mezzanitti fashioned mustaches and erect penises onto a dozen of the "more flaccid" statues and decorative stone carvings. Due to this approach in his designs, and his sense of humor, many of his early works[5] were unfinished or completed and credited by other architects.

Although the Biltmore project still had an anticipated five more years until completion, the Italian welcomed Olmsted's new opportunity. The academic position was merely a stepping-stone to acquiring more money in order to travel to San Francisco, a land of gold that he had heard about since his youth in Genoa[6]. In his present state, Mezzanitti was merely a vagabond moving from place to place with no real residence and very little money.

Mezzanitti took a train to Ohio in early 1890. To the Italian, Ohio could have been any state in America west of Pennsylvania, east of the Rocky Mountains. When the train stopped at a small depot in Athens, there was a delay[7], forcing him to find a place to wash and eat before boarding the next train. While wandering and observing the city, the Italian lamented the fact that "this town in no way resembled the illustrious city of the Greeks, but the town and the university it housed were curiously intertwined." Because recorded facts are few and

---

5   see Appendix D for complete list of works, both credited and uncredited

6   Mark Twain had circulated this information about San Francisco when he visited Genoa in 1867 as recorded in *Innocents Abroad.*

7   No records were found to verify the incident.

he did not write about where he had stayed in Athens, it is uncertain whether Mezzanitti had planned to take the next train or if he had stayed in one of three known lodgings: the Athens Inn[8], which was the leading hotel at the time and a more expensive option; the Burns Bed and Breakfast on the more scenic north side of town; or the lodging attached to the train station, catering mainly to transients and travelers. One would ascertain that out of frugality and sheer necessity, he chose the depot's lodging. From another excerpt of his journal, he observed the campus greens and gardens: "[Because of] the geographical isolation, the landscape had the effect of stumbling upon a secret Eden. The designs were unmistakably Olmsted's work." However, despite the institution's establishment in 1810, the campus design could not be credited to Olmsted who was born well after its construction. One could likely speculate that a very young Olmsted had in fact been part of a later design collaborative as the university expanded, or perhaps an architect whom Olmsted had known or studied under or whose designs he had observed was responsible for the landscape. This is only speculation and thus digresses from the Mezzanitti narrative, yet it is odd that an institution would not want to attach such a figure to the university's legacy.

Mezzanitti's interest only increased as he explored the campus, observing both the landscape and the buildings. He had thought the place was an "oasis in the middle of the forest, much like the Biltmore Estate." This kind of American design intrigued the Italian because it was as if "Americans valued community alongside nature, manmade beauty in congruence with the natural world." He recognized the Americans' need to create a kind of utopia within the wilderness, "Cain establishing civilization outside the Garden." The university borrowed designs from Georgian architecture[9] and Chateauesque qualities. The

---

8   Later acquired by Athens University in 1982 and remodeled and renamed aptly Athens University Hotel. I've stayed there on two occasions when researching Mezzanitti's time in Athens. The accommodations are generous, the beds are comfortable, and the in-house dining is delicious and reasonably priced.

9   Rufus Pendleton and Brigham Supper, early Federalists granted by

gardens had even reminded him of the gardens his father had worked on for Sr. Canzio in Genoa.

The Italian found his way to the Department of Architecture and met the faculty. They were averse to meeting him, due again to the prevailing attitude toward Italians, especially in this area with its majority white Protestant population, and in a town this small and only recently settled, Mezzanitti was an outsider in every sense of the word. However, he discussed with them his surprise and admiration for the campus and its architecture, explaining how he had been working with Hunt and Olmsted and was in transit to Ohio State University to apply for the teaching position in Landscape Architecture. The irony was that there was no department or program by that name, let alone a position available in the nonexistent department. The Italian learned from the faculty that both Athens University and Ohio State University were developing rival programs in landscape architecture, essentially forecasting which university would become the preeminent school in that area of study.

In addition to institutional competition, Mezzanitti discovered Athens was seeking designs for a new building on campus, not necessarily a centerpiece for the campus but a structure that incorporated the university's educational philosophy—the building would be a physical depiction of these ideas and values. The Italian was confident that with the many forged letters of recommendation, as well as the projects he had[10] been a part of, he might be considered for the building project. At this point in time, he was "desperate for money and would take any opportunity afforded him." However, there was a suspicion raised in his mind about the motives of both Hunt and Olmsted, since they provided him with the information about the phony faculty position. According to his journal, Mezzanitti felt a deep contempt for the two men, not only for the false lead but also

---

George Washington through the Ordinance of 1787 to charter the first college in the Northwest Territory, had wanted to replicate the architecture from both Virginia and Massachusetts, keeping with early-American designs.

10   Or had not

because his assistance at the Biltmore Estate, although modest, was never credited nor listed anywhere in historical records, another act of erasure to the Italian's work[11].

Mezzanitti gathered his letters and qualifications and met with the university president to inquire about the design submission. At this time, before the establishment of a campus layout and building commission, the president's office was directly involved in university-wide matters. The president agreed to meet with him after receiving his materials. During their meeting, as outlined in the Italian's journal, Mezzanitti discussed his former projects, the previous meeting he had had with the professors of the architecture department, and university's vision for the new structure. The Italian could perceive that the president was reluctant to share the information about the building, despite the evidence of qualification. This treatment was familiar, the way Americans reacted or responded to him with skepticism, assuming he was thieving, deceitful, violent, or would take advantage of their women, never once acknowledging that he was from Europe's most culturally and historically significant region. Nevertheless, the president shared the vision for the new building: the design should embody the heart of education or the quest for knowledge. A structure like this would be a functional monument, displaying the university's commitment to humanities education. The president wanted Athens University to be the first to do such a thing and had secured private funding to do so. The donor was a member of the university's board of trustees: James Alexander Gordon. Gordon, a financier, wealthy landowner, and very large man who commissioned the design and construction, said he would pay whatever amount necessary to ensure that the project was completed, and the building would carry the prestige of his family's name as one of the founders of not only Athens University but also the town of Athens and even America.[12]

---

11   Again, see Appendix D for complete list of works because no one should have to toil and produce work just for it to be disregarded or appropriated. Acknowledgement is the truest form of flattery.

12   Gordon had argued his ancestors were among the early families in Virginia alongside Washington and others. As part of the early Northwest

Although the president had expressed interest in two other architects who had submitted designs, he was eager to see what Mezzanitti would propose given his work with Hunt and Olmsted, two men who had been involved with designing some of the country's leading university campuses. The Italian left the meeting and immediately began drafting a layout for the building. Unfortunately, it is difficult to understand the steps he undertook for the design he drafted, or rather envisioned, because he did not record designs in his journal.[13] There are some musings about the design, and given some of his earlier design work in gardens and landscape and even his later architectural layouts, it can be assumed that Mezzanitti obtained pleasure from making structures, whether buildings or landscape, with unusual components and compositions.

The Italian chose his labyrinthian design as his interpretation of the pursuit of knowledge. He noted that as he was pondering the layout, his mind often wandered to Dante's *Divine Comedy* and Daedalus's Labyrinth. So, Mezzanitti made two designs. The first resides in the Athens University Archives, and the second is likely in his collection of architectural drafts and drawings. Nevertheless, the design that was presented and accepted by the president and board of trustees had the slight appearance of a maze. When viewing the three-floor schematic, one will note that the ground floor is actually a winding hallway, leading to a lecture hall in the center that accommodates roughly 150 people. The second floor had space for offices and classrooms with two sets

---

Ordinance land treaty, Gordon's family had left to settle and charter an institution of higher education. Some historians have traced Gordon's lineage not to Samuel Gordon of Virginia, who indeed stayed in the town of Fredericksburg, but to Nathaniel Gordon of Maine, the convicted and executed slave trader. This is laughable and could be why there are no Gordons recorded or mentioned in the establishment of Athens or the university.

13   It should be noted that Mezzanitti did not record any of his designs or notes pertaining to his designs in *this* journal. I speculate that this was his personal journal, and he had a dossier containing drawings, notes, sketches, prints, etc., a collection I am close to obtaining from a private collector. One more piece in the Mezzanitti puzzle.

of stairs directly in the center of the building leading from the north and south sides to a single hallway in the center of the third floor thus dividing the second and third floors in half, like an isosceles trapezoid. The third floor would likely house various Humanities departments on either side. The second design, however, was the same basic shell, and the one Mezzanitti had favored. Although we do not have the second design, as previously mentioned, one can see the sketch imbedded within the schematic of the original design, as if a code from the Italian. It would make sense that the design be transposed over the first given the unique layout and dimensions. In the alternate design, the first floor was one long, winding hallway without classrooms, and the same lecture hall at the center. Unlike most academic buildings, or most buildings for that matter, where the stairwell to the next floor is located in or near the entrance, Mezzanitti had placed the stairs in a bend in the hallway, an unusual placement. The staircase was also intended to be a twisting wrought iron structure that went all the way to the roof of the building. There may not have been an obvious logic to the Italian's design, but there was an internal logic. The actual stairs ascended to a seemingly random location on the second floor, an intentional dislocation. His goal for the second floor was complete negative space, but the kind of support beams that would have to be used to allow that kind of void on an entire floor would have been costly and challenging. In addition, Mezzanitti knew his design would not be accepted if the floor were not being utilized, so he put seven rooms in a kind of step stone layout, disconnected from one another. The third floor remained exactly the same, office space. The exterior was akin to the Chateau style, a design no doubt influenced by his time at the Biltmore, but bordered more on the Gothic style, making it the most recognizable building on campus, departing from the Georgian and Federalist style.

In his journal, he wrote of the inspiration for the design:

> *The building would resemble nothing seen at this institution and would be a place of intrigue. Following the American's desire for beauty in the midst of wilderness, the exterior would mimic old, French castles. Upon entering, though, there would be an overwhelming sense of confusion and*

displacement. Unlike Daedalus who built the labyrinth to imprison the Minotaur, I will build this first floor as a maze that leads to a large amphitheater with a lectern. The students will wander the hall in search of knowledge but will indeed become frustrated in doing so. When accessing the second floor, there will be nothing but empty space. One should feel the void when walking through this level. It contrasts so drastically from the first floor but should give a similar feeling of displacement or uncertainty. Finally, when they journey up the staircase on either side of the single hallway, they will finally arrive at their intended destination. As in Dante's Divine Comedy, purgatory was an upward journey and limbo was a place for those who may have accomplished much, great writers and philosophers, but they received no punishment, nor reward—they merely existed, like Sisyphus.

The concept is explained with brevity and pulls from so many different sources[14], and even his inspiration isn't quite true to form, even contradictory in theme. He submitted his design, the more acceptable layout, and the committee approved[15] with some minor modification to the exterior (the two turrets had been removed), citing the expense was too great for the ornate features.[16] The Italian was paid half the money allocated for the architectural design, fifty-five hundred dollars, and would be paid the other half upon the project's completion. The building was estimated to take exactly two years to complete. Mezzanitti requested that he be sole actor with his design and construction team,

---

14 I have spent many hours studying the building and attempting to decipher the indecipherable. Although an academic and an intellectual, I have labored over text upon text, artwork upon artwork, architectural design upon architectural design to supply an exhaustive interpretation of the structure. Perhaps with the continuous help of colleagues, I will one day provide the origins of each aspect of Mezzanitti's labyrinth.

15 It is no surprise his design was chosen given the recommendations of both Hunt and Olmsted and the uniqueness of his composition.

16 Had the turrets been kept in the design, this may have been one of the earliest examples of Collegiate Gothic, predating the halls of Bryn Mawr College and Princeton University, though one could argue that the building does fall within the Gothic style.

meaning he did not want any input or interference from the building committee, Gordon, or the president, which is often an issue regarding this kind of project.

To say that Mezzanitti was ignorant of the process would be an exaggeration, having worked on dozens of large-scale constructions, but he had never been sole architect thus far in his career. The execution of this project was new territory. This commission was the largest sum of money he had received for his work to date, and that should have been enough for him. Yet the Italian could not ignore the original vision he had for the building, a vision he wanted to see through to the end[17]. So, he began to subtly incorporate parts of his original design. Each night after a full day's work, Mezzanitti would redraw the schematic, adding another minor detail, which gradually restored the integrity of the original design. However, during the construction of the exterior, the Italian petitioned for the use of the original design, which included the turrets, not to the committee or even the board of trustees, but to Gordon himself, once more citing the Biltmore Estate as an example of what could be. Unfortunately, Gordon could not oblige the Italian's desire. In a moment of spite, Mezzanitti paid a mason, an Italian *scalpellino*, two hundred dollars to carve an inscription above the entryway, a characteristic of most buildings from that era. Rather than James A. Gordon Hall or even Gordon Hall, the lettering read *Il Labirinto di Pensiero Vuoto*, which translates to The Labyrinth of Empty Thought[18].

17　Much like Mezzanitti's labyrinth, I too attempt to create a work, unhindered by editorial discretion, that fully encapsulates the life and essence of the Italian, detail by excruciating detail. To write a biography of such depth and exactitude would take decades and thousands of pages. A book of that magnitude would cause such an uproar in the field of Architectural History that it may even change the way architecture is taught in America. Alas, I am bound by contract to a book of no more than 500 pages if I hope for it to see the light of day.

18　Years later the university attempted to remove the lettering, but due to the incorporation in the stone, the lettering could not successfully be removed unless a complete restructuring was to occur. The inscription was then covered for a time, but the Athens Historical Society, through a

The construction of the building seems rather commonplace. The university had a vision, a donor, and an architect. Aside from the duplicitous professional documents and the calculated incorporation of the original design, everything was going according to the university's wishes. The one issue that arose was a resentful faculty member in the Athens University Department of Architecture by the name of Ambrose Williams[19]. Williams had met Mezzanitti when the Italian first arrived in Athens and was immediately skeptical of the nature of his journey, especially regarding the position at the other college. He had his theories, and given the public view of Italians at that time, Williams had speculated that Mezzanitti was either a swindler or a spy for the other college here to sabotage the development of their program. In addition to his doubt, Williams also had another item at stake: his design for the new building.[20] His was one of the other two designs that were under consideration, and it was not until his design was declined that he decided to investigate Mezzanitti's background. Having apprenticed with Olmsted early in his career, he wrote a letter[21] inquiring into the identity and recommendation of Mezzanitti. It was months before Williams received an answer from Olmsted, but the response confirmed part of what he had anticipated. Neither Olmsted nor Hunt had written the Italian a letter of recommendation, and the man had only worked as a laborer and was a general nuisance at Biltmore, defacing the statues with his aesthetic adjustments. Also,

---

lengthy legal process, was able to have the veil removed, so to speak.

19   I am aware that it is my duty as a biographer to refrain from inserting my opinion of the individuals and narrative, but I cannot emphasize enough how much of a scoundrel, a coward, and an insecure sack of shit Williams was. If it were not for his cutthroat measures, we would likely regard Mezzanitti in a different light in American architecture.

20   Williams' design was not chosen due to its lack of imagination and how it closely resembled Pendleton Hall, the first building constructed at the university's conception and subsequently named after the co-founder Rufus Pendleton.

21   The brief correspondence between Williams and Olmsted can be found in *Frederick Law Olmsted Papers* published by the Library of Congress.

Olmsted never once mentioned the work or assistance on the New York Central Park project. Williams immediately took the letter to the university president to discuss the Italian's fraudulence. It had been ten months since breaking ground for what would be Gordon Hall—the exterior was complete, and the framing for the interior was in place.

In a meeting with Williams and Mezzanitti, the president presented the allegations. The Italian denied Williams's accusations, questioning his credibility and the authenticity of the letter: "Mr. Williams claims I never received recommendation, never assisted Olmsted, but somehow I defaced statues. What power I possess that I can be somewhere and nowhere at once, powers that cause stone statues to grow facial hair and become aroused." The Italian claimed his admiration for the university and his dedication to the building project, reminding the president that this building was a monument that would gain the attention and respect of other architectural and educational institutions. They might even be a model for other campuses. The president said he would consider both sides, present this issue to the board of trustees, and decide whether any further actions needed to be taken.

Given the reality of his situation, Mezzanitti feared the worst. He packed his bag that evening, bought a ticket for the first train out of town, and by dawn boarded for Chicago, leaving the altered blueprints and taking the fifty-five hundred dollars they had paid him. With a half-finished building and the possibility of public embarrassment, the university assigned Williams as co-architect[22] to finish the final stages of the project. Rather than causing a scandal and involving the authorities, the university fabricated a story about the project where Mezzanitti and Williams intended to work together, combining the Italian's imagination and the American's craftsmanship, to create a building so unique to represent the kind of world-class education Athens University offered. Williams was paid a small price of twelve hundred dollars for finishing the project. An *ex post facto* building permit was created naming Williams as the architect of record, thereby relieving the university of any further discrepancies or liability if future

---

22 Talentless hack

legal issues were to arise.[23]

Over the years, Gordon Hall has had modifications made to conform to evolving building and safety codes, such as a rear entrance, an elevator, clearer signage, and updated electrical and lighting. The university had attempted to demolish the building sometime during the late eighties for reasons that are not completely clear[24], but again, the Athens Historical Society intervened, deeming the building an important piece of architectural history for the town. This is by far one of Mezzanitti's greatest works of architectural design, despite the lack of full acknowledgment and the honor due to an individual with such uncanny abilities, sense of imagination, and originality. The only

---

23   One discrepancy, and I place this piece of information as a footnote because it came from a professor in the Athens History department who wishes to remain anonymous, was James A. Gordon's relentless pursuit of Mezzanitti once he had vacated Athens. Gordon had hired a private investigator and a hitman with the intention of finding the Italian and murdering him. The rumor was that because of the building debacle, Gordon, not the university president, was the laughingstock of the elite inner circle in Athens. He was foolish for pouring so much money into the vanity project led by a filthy, deceptive Italian. The inner circle even brandished the nickname "Minotaur" since the labyrinthian building was in part for him. Gordon spent thousands of dollars trying to find and kill the Italian but to no avail. He was likely the reason why Mezzanitti was erased from the university archives.

24   Minutes from a Board of Trustees meeting dated 29 February 1984 provides some insight into this matter. Glenn Wagner*, the assistant director for the Office of Institutional Advancement at Athens University, provided a proposal for the demolition of the current Gordon Hall due to the "inconvenient location" and "conflicts with the vision for project 'Learning Landscape'" and "could potentially halt future construction." Again, the meeting notes had few details and that proposal was later denied in a future meeting citing "historical preservation." The Athens Historical society provided me their "cease and desist" letter that was dated 19 March 1984.

*It should be noted that a conflict of interest could be assumed due to the fact that Wagner is Gordon's great-grandson and has on several occasions attempted to take legal action to propose the construction of a new "more honorable" building.

way one would know even a fraction of this history is from a largely inaccurate plaque on the wall of the lobby of Gordon Hall, and even some of the educated that roam this labyrinthian structure, students and faculty alike, do not know this man's name, let alone his genius.

Part II

Out of the Past

Like a gentle breeze blowing in the summer's stillness, rustling the leaves as the Queen Anne's Lace swayed, Lily Zephyr drifted into town one day near the end of July. She pulled a borrowed Honda Civic into the parking lot where a large white sign with navy blue lettering announced "Graybeard Suites." The two-story building looked like an ordinary motel. She had called ahead earlier that month to reserve a room, one of the few places listed on the town's website that rented month-to-month and in walking distance of the university. The landlord had said she was lucky. The place was usually all booked up by this time of year due to the influx of students. She had snagged one of his last rooms.

Inside the leasing office, she browsed the stacks of brochures on a table next to the front desk. Lily wasn't interested in the local wineries, downtown festivals, or weekend farmer's markets, but it did create a backdrop for Will, walking from booth to booth, table to table, lingering to study something that caught his eye, a small basket of ripe strawberries, a watercolor from a local artist. A man, possibly in his late fifties or early sixties with long sandy hair pulled back in a meager ponytail and a beard of mostly gray, asked if he could help her. She was here to sign the lease and move in. Larry, as the man introduced himself, wore Birkenstocks, faded blue jeans, and a button-up flowered shirt. Lily put the brochures in her purse when he told her there were some really great things to do here, especially if she liked the outdoors. Also, the student tenants threw great parties, and hell, he even partied with them a few times. And did she know, originally, the Athens Motor Inn, the previous identity of the not so historic building, was supposedly a landmark spot for truckers in the 70s? Jefferson Airplane and Buffalo Springfield even stayed here when they played at one of the local bars. This place is famous, man. The guy was a random fact generator of town history, and he obviously didn't know what famous meant.

He quickly wrote up the lease and photocopied her driver's license. The rent was five hundred bucks a month, utilities included, a pretty reasonable price if you asked him, and she had enough to cover roughly six months, if necessary. But it shouldn't be. Once she signed the document, he would show her to her room. If everything played out as she had hoped, she would be back in New York within a month or so, back to her normal life, perhaps a new life. She had left a boyfriend who wasn't happy about her departure. She left him with an excuse simple and frequently given in relationships, the semantics of which were often dubious at best: time and self-discovery.

* * *

Her apartment was modest. Larry said he had recently remodeled everything, even though it still looked like a motel room and faintly smelled of stale cigarette smoke and mold; the flaking gray paint on the exterior walls exposing yellow brick indicated how recent. The room had a full-size bed, a small round Formica table in the corner with two chairs, a loveseat, and a kitchenette, which consisted merely of a mini-fridge and a slender two-burner stove next to the sink. When she settled in, Lily set her sights on Athens University. She dialed the number for admissions on her iPhone. Once connected, it was only a matter of touch-tone options before an admissions assistant, most likely an eighteen- or nineteen-year-old student, spoke about scheduling a campus visit. Lily described her interest in majoring in philosophy and wanted to meet with someone from the department during her visit.

"Absolutely," the girl answered. "I'll check with their administrative assistant to, like, find out when they have an informational meeting with a current student or professor. Please hold for just a moment."

When the girl returned, she listed several dates the department had set for prospective student tours. The next available was Friday, two days from now. Lily confirmed the date, not as if she had anything scheduled for that day. She was to arrive at the Student Union at eight o'clock in the morning. Lily thanked the girl and ended the call. She grabbed her purse on the urge to take a walk and see the town. Although she'd been driving for the last nine hours and would soon crash thanks to the coffee and Adderall, she wanted to explore and stretch her legs. What did his new home look like? What were his favorite spots? Who had he spoken to, had made laugh or cry, had kissed? Maybe she would spot a little café or a bench under the perfect tree, places he would have gone to in New York. Maybe she would know and understand what had drawn him to this place. *Where are you?* she wondered.

* * *

Walking to the downtown took maybe ten, fifteen minutes at most, but it was uphill and the previous several-hour car ride didn't help. As she crossed the bridge over the Athens River, the asphalt pavement underfoot ended where smooth red bricks began. The town felt old, but like working class old: the buildings lacked the frills and ornate façades of the Gilded Age. It reminded her of some of the small towns along the Hudson River as one headed north to Albany, a trip she would often take with her family when vacationing in Lake George. The buildings had a glossed look to them—recently renovated, like senior citizens with plastic surgery who dressed in the latest fashion. And like so many places in America, the original bones of the town had been preserved, but the guts or spirit of the place was young. No wonder Will had been drawn here. He probably felt like he was home.

Lily walked along Main Street, noting the shops and small restaurants that occupied storefronts, an independent bookstore and coffee shop. She chose what looked like a random boutique and walked inside. A young girl with a nose ring and tattoos in a lacey sundress stood behind the counter. She talked a little about the store, focusing mostly on what she could help Lily find. All the shop's items came from local crafters and artisans, the girl claimed. The small section of Doc Martins on display didn't appear locally made, then again cobbling was a dying art and more of an investment than the owners were probably willing to make. Lily grabbed a wide-brimmed hat the shade of espresso and tried it on. That looks perfect on you, the girl gushed. Lily paid and left. The car ride had caught up to her, and she felt tired. So she grabbed something small to eat from the next spot she saw and took it back to the apartment.

* * *

Lily felt foolish and out of place sitting through the presentations about how great and exciting college life would be at Athens, how they'd learn so much about themselves. She laughed to herself as weepy mothers and beaming fathers repeatedly embraced their children who were just at the threshold of losing their remaining innocence, ready to send them off to their future, which would no doubt be full of alcohol, bad choices, and half-assed coursework, the proverbial life-changing experience. It didn't matter the location; all colleges were pretty much the same. The times she had spent with friends at the universities around the city, the parties, the CUNY courses she took but never completed. It all felt the same.

She collected a dozen or more orientation handouts and placed them in a folder featuring a photo of the university's main entrance, a large stone archway with the Athens U seal stamped on the concrete below. In bold, white Helvetica typeface on the bottom right corner were the words ATHENS UNIVERSITY. FIND YOUR NICHE. What a stupid tagline. Could have easily been *When You're Here, You're Family* or *Take a Look, It's in a Book, Athens University.* Any slogan would do as long as it felt like your slogan. The presenters always made a point to enunciate, faces contorted like children scrunching their noses and smiling with all teeth then immediately shooshing, when pronouncing *nee-shh*, correcting parents and prospective students who pronounced it *nitch*, one even remarking on how "nitch was such an ugly word and you know what it rhymes with."

Despite her boredom as the presenters pandered to the masses with the usual emotional nonsense about higher education, empty nest syndrome, and future leaders, Lily was grateful to learn the campus layout with the help of a tour guide. She carefully observed and noted where each building was and which departments they housed, scribbling on the map she was given earlier that day.

As the tour ended back in the Union, prospective students were ushered to current student leaders who could better inform them about their intended major or program of interest. A girl with medium length red hair and jean capris introduced herself as the president of the Philosophy Club. *Stephanie* in purple Sharpie on her name tag. She led a group of seven or eight, including Lily, from the Union down a long stretch of red brick walkway to James A. Gordon Hall, home to several of the Humanities departments. Stephanie told them the building's layout was a little weird and confusing at first but manageable.

"Expect to get lost a of couple times your first year here," she said. "I know faculty who still wander the halls or walk into the wrong classroom."

They entered Gordon Hall and twisted around a long hallway and up a flight of stairs and then around a corner and another and another, then up a single set of stairs until they reached a very narrow landing on the third floor and faced a door labeled PHILOSOPHY DEPT. / CLASSICS DEPT. Someone commented that the building was like a maze and how weird it was to have to climb all of these steps (where's the elevator?), and Stephanie replied that Sylvie in the department could tell them all about it if they were interested. She led them to a conference room to discuss their potential future as Athens U philosophy majors.

When the conference room cleared, Lily wanted to find him, wanted to know where his office was and where he lived in this middle-of-nowhere town. All she had to do was ask, but it had to seem natural. *Be cool, not obvious. You need to show genuine interest.* She slowly approached Sylvie's workspace as the woman smiled and gave her best to the other prospective students who departed.

"I heard you're the person to talk to if I want to learn more about this unusual building," said Lily.

"Guilty," said Sylvie. "Have you had a chance to tour the building?"

"Maybe?"

"I tell Stephanie she needs to take the students through the whole place. Why don't we walk around, and I can tell you a little more about it? The history is very interesting."

"Would you mind first showing me around the department?" Lily asked. "I'm just curious as to where the professors' offices are."

"Sounds good. My name is Sylvie, by the way, if Stephanie didn't already tell you."

"Elli."

They shook hands, and Sylvie led her around the department, first stopping at the office directly behind her. The door was open.

"Dr. Buchanan? This is Elli, one of our hopefuls. I'm going to show her around the department."

A man in a light moss collared shirt looked up from his desk. He stood and walked toward them. "It's a pleasure to meet you, Elli."

"Likewise."

"I'll be away from my desk for a few minutes." She looked at Lily. "You will be seeing a lot of Dr. Buchanan if you decide to enroll in our program."

"I hope you choose to matriculate to our institution." He stared intently at her. "So many people act as if philosophy is a dead subject. That it has no place in our current society. But philosophy is more relevant now than ever. At Athens U, we strive to provide students with many opportunities and resources, such as our yearly conference, Philosophy Club, graduate school placement, our student-run publication, and world-class faculty. I hope you choose our institution. Just let us know how we can help with that."

"Thank you," said Lily.

He gently shook her hand before they left his office.

"Dr. Buchanan really believes in this program, and his dedication to the students shows that."

Lily smiled. Sylvie continued down the short hall and pointed to offices, providing the corresponding professor's name and some brief biographical information. They stopped outside of Will's office. Lily peered into the window alongside the door. She would see him soon. She felt it, almost like he had never left.

"Are most of the professors out of office during the summer? Like William Thierry for example." She pointed to the black nametag on his office door, running her finger over the lettering.

"Will is our visiting lecturer and philosopher-in-residence, so he stays away from the university most of the summer. Dr. Buchanan and I are usually the only ones here. Sometimes the other professors will teach a summer course or come in occasionally."

"Where is he visiting from?" asked Lily.

"He came from New York University, just a wonderful, young, smart person. He's a bit of a rock star around here. The students love him." Sylvie's thinly veiled affection was obvious.

"He sounds like someone worth meeting."

"Absolutely. And you will during fall orientation."

Pausing, she searched for anything to stay on the subject of Will. "This is such a quaint town. I take it the professors live nearby?"

"Almost everyone in the department lives in the neighboring streets," Sylvie said, as they turned around and walked back toward the entrance of the department.

"You don't say. That's so convenient. From what I've seen, it seems like a nice place to live."

"Athens is a really special place. Ask anyone. You'd be surprised at the number of alumni who eventually move back. There is something magnetic about this place. I really can't say enough good things about it."

"Are the faculty and students a pretty close-knit group?" asked Lily.

"Given our relatively small size, we try to foster a nurturing environment where the students really feel like they are a part of something. We don't want them to be just another number. Sometimes the faculty and the senior students will go out for drinks after events and such, or we'll do department get-togethers. I think you'd feel at home here."

"That sounds fun. Where's a good place for drinks?"

"Moe's has great food and is an Athens institution. It's never too crowded with the two floors and patio. Then again, we usually go pretty early in the evening. Dr. Buchanan is there a few times a week."

"That sounds great."

"It is. So where are you from if you don't mind me asking?"

They walked into the hall and descended the stairs to the second floor.

Shit. "I'm from, um, White Plains, New York. But I have family nearby. They knew I wanted to go back to school and recommended Athens. They even offered me a place to stay. From what I've seen so far, I really like it here."

"I'm so glad. Now, about the history of the building. I think you'll find this very interesting."

* * *

Lily wore a black dress and lipstick the shade of cranberries when she went to Moe's for the second time. She ordered the same drink, a glass of the house cabernet, and sat in the same seat, third from the end of the bar. However, the bartender was different: a stocky guy, possibly in his late forties, maybe fifty, with a head razored bald. Some of the customers, likely regulars, called him Ray. He seemed friendly enough.

There was no mistaking that Lily looked striking, given Ray's what's-a-beautiful-woman-like-you-doing-in-a-place-like-this-kind-of-greeting. Her dress fit her form but not too tight, cut just above the knee, and she wore flats rather than heels so as not to draw too much attention. Her dark hair lay in loose waves over her shoulders, shining in the dim light of the bar. She was Ava Gardener in *The Killers*—well, her shabby chic look-alike. She waited, knowing perfectly well what was in store for the night, what she must do to set this plan in motion. Was she ready? She had to be. What other way was there to get close to Will?

The first time she had stepped into Moe's, however, was the evening of the campus visit. She had worn a black tunic T-shirt and dark jeans, her plain clothes from that day. She was merely scoping out the place, getting a feel. A trial run. There were few, if any, expectations that night. She had ordered a glass of wine and, roughly twenty minutes later, had ordered something small off the menu: fried artichokes in a lemon butter sauce. The food wasn't terrible for a bar. After finishing another glass of wine and carrying on a harmless conversation with a young male bartender, she had left. On the walk back to the apartment, she had wondered if Will had experienced what she experienced now, to feel out of sorts in a place that lacked energy and noise, to be in a town devoid of personality. Had he thought about her his first night here?

This visit was different. Take one, action. The defining moment. Perhaps Will would walk through the door, or some other actor would take the stage as her supporting role. Would she wait until he noticed her, or would she get up from the bar and leave, and as she passed him, he'd catch her perfume's scent, a smell he would remember, like in some old detective movie? She worked out scenarios in her mind to pass the time, possibly even preparing herself for the real thing, even though she was never one for much preparation.

And then the man walked in. His eyes seemed tired. He ambled to the bar; the heels of his brown wingtips clicked with each step on the worn hardwood floor.

"Hey, Harvey. How's it going?"

"Long day, Ray," he said as he sat a seat away from Lily. "Just glad to be having a drink right here."

"Maker's Mark?"

"A double on the rocks."

Lily sipped from her glass and casually turned away from Harvey, enough so she wouldn't draw his attention and make it seem like she had nothing better to do than to listen to his conversation. There were two other people at the bar, a counter that comfortably seated eight. Although it was six o'clock on a Wednesday, the booths along the walls were full of people eating food, both families with children and couples in conversation. Lily wondered if any of these people were professors from the university; maybe someone other than Harvey knew Will. A half dozen black round tables with chairs were empty in the center of the place. They would probably fill as the night went on. Two young female servers, college age, busily bounced from booth to booth, intermittently replacing drinks and taking orders. They both wore cut-off jean shorts and green T-shirts with white lettering on the back that read "Moe's Place / Try Our Damn Near Famous Burgers." Pop music played in the background. She took another sip of wine.

"You mean to tell me the university is gonna shut you down just like that?"

"That's what I've been told, Ray," said Harvey. "But we're on the verge of doing something big. From hiring Thierry to securing more private donors to fund this year's conference to our faculty awards, I figured we were doing a hell of a job. It's always about enrollment numbers though. Always. If only I could figure a way to partner with Agricultural Studies, then we'd be in business. Pastoral Philosophy." He laughed.

Lily listened, wanting to know what Harvey knew, to plumb his mind of all the experiences he had had with Will. What kind of guy was he? She couldn't wait any longer.

"Sounds like you need a vacation," she said.

Harvey and Ray both turned to her.

She flashed her deep blue eyes at them. "And maybe another drink."

"You're telling me," said Harvey. "People think being a professor is so prestigious. It's not, not at all."

"Oh yeah?"

"Maybe it was thirty years ago. Not now. But I doubt you'd care to hear about it."

"I've got time to kill."

"Once you spend nearly a decade in school and nearly a hundred thousand dollars in tuition, you start your career underpaid, overworked, and usually part-time. You barely make enough to cover a mortgage, let alone any debt you've accumulated from student loans. If you're lucky enough to secure a full-time spot, you still aren't making more than 50k, and you're teaching around a hundred students a semester, but at least you have healthcare. If by chance, you snag the coveted tenured position like I was fortunate enough to do, you're expected to have your hand in so many other things aside from teaching. Research. Publication. Committees and boards at every level. Jesus, the general bureaucracy of it all. You're so goddamned burnt out by the whole thing that you can't really enjoy it, not even in the summer because the vultures are circling to grab any summer course they can teach, hoping to pay for the vacation they all want to take. And the best part is that once you have it, there's no way in hell you're giving it up either because what other job has this dynamic?"

"Is that so?" Lily quickly got in.

"Yeah. I mean, yes, the faculty are vultures when it comes to summer teaching, but I suppose it's not all that bad. There's about one year right in the middle of your career where you really are happy and fulfilled. It's called sabbatical." Harvey laughed and took a sip. "Plus, higher education is really the only place where weirdos—excuse me, *eccentrics*—who lack social and professional skills can have a career. And don't get me started on rank and discipline specification. Everyone, and I mean, even the freaking adjuncts, are comically territorial about their specialties. And their great stories about meeting a celebrity writer, educator, theorist, or philosopher are never great stories, ever. They're unbelievably embellished, worst than some of my students' most asinine excuses. And don't even think about retirement because you didn't make enough to actually retire comfortably. Luckily, you can teach until you die. The students don't care either way. Be the old fart in the tweed blazer, the faded cardigan, the bowtie and suspenders. Give the students something to talk about. It keeps things interesting. Okay, I'm done ranting."

She smiled at Ray and looked back at Harvey. "Sounds lovely."

"Just a dream. Oh, and did I forgot to mention that we're all paranoid backstabbers?"

"At least you're honest and help people," she said.

"I can't confirm either of those."

She continued. "I just travel around the country and, basically, wreck people's lives." She was sure he didn't recognize her. He made no gesture in the affirmative.

"So, what's your line of work?" asked Harvey.

"I'm the person who makes it harder for you to claim something on your insurance. And if by chance your claim is covered under your policy, a policy you probably haven't read, you aren't getting nearly what you should. Because I'll be damned if I don't have someone at our organization price out the cheapest equivalent and then put that number in an equation that depreciates it accordingly no matter how pristine the condition was."

"That sounds rough. You're a professional dream crusher."

"I'm an independent actuary. I travel most of the time to different insurance organizations and agencies and assess their risk and loss. Very boring. Lots of numbers."

"Then you're not from around here."

"I'm here working at the local Farmers Insurance office." She sipped her glass of wine, realizing she only said that because she barely remembered passing the sign on the way in. Hopefully, he didn't know anyone who worked there. "And no, I'm originally from New York. I mean, I still have a shoebox of an apartment on the Lower Eastside that I pay for regardless of how little I'm there. I sublet to a friend."

Harvey emptied his glass. He glanced at Ray who was helping a couple at the end of the bar. His gaze returned to Lily. "How long?"

"Long enough." She smiled. "Projects can go anywhere from a few weeks to a month or more. Back in early 2007, I was in southern California for about three months when they had that terrible drought and like the worst wildfires to date there. They even called it a 'firestorm.'" *It actually paid off listening to your brother-in-law talk about work*, she thought.

"You are brutal."

"Just doing my job. You can't predict life."

"I suppose not. Did your company put you up somewhere in town?"

"I'm staying at the Graybeard Suites."

Harvey laughed. "Why the hell did they choose that place? The least they could have done was the University Inn."

"Who really knows? I'm sure someone Googled month-to-month, and that looked most appealing. You know how websites can be. You get someone to touch up a few nicely shot photos and the place has a retro boutique appeal. Then you get there, and it's another dump you hope doesn't have bedbugs or cockroaches. It was central and decently furnished, so I was told. As far as the clientele involved, our company doesn't bother with researching location demographics. They pick the hotel or apartment, and I go. Sometimes I have a say, but no one knew where the hell Athens, Ohio was. It's fine, really. I've been in worse."

Harvey looked again in Ray's direction. Lily hesitated, wondering how she could steer the conversation, take it a little further. She couldn't miss a beat. *Be consistent. Play it cool. Get him hooked and interested.* Then a thought grabbed her, one she had the day she checked in. Harvey put his finger up to grab Ray's attention.

"Since we're on the subject, what's the deal with Graybeard Suites?" she asked. "The name, the guy. I don't know if I quite get it."

Harvey turned to Lily and grinned. "This area, believe it or not, was a pretty popular spot in the 60s and 70s, around the time I was a teenager just graduating high school. There were even a few musicians who went on to make it big. Some things actually do come out of Ohio."

"Oh. A hometown boy."

"Yes and no. That's a story for another time. That place—"

"The Athens Motel?"

"Athens Motor Inn. It was the only inexpensive motel in town at the time since the hotel at the train depot had been turned into a restaurant. The place was bought by an Athens' townie, a burned out quasi-hippie guy named Larry Welch who's about ten years older than me and used to sit outside the bars, usually shirtless, and just play his guitar and smoke pot. He was one of those guys who somehow, by luck, managed to find people stupid enough to invest in his projects despite his inability to successfully manage a business. Basically, a bunch of other burnout townies with some money. This city is full of them. He poorly ran a coffee shop for about a decade, which was bought out by Starbucks to his fortune, before acquiring the motel."

As he talked so effortlessly and with such confidence, Lily wondered what he thought about Will, what he knew about Will's life in this small town.

"When Larry bought the place, sometime in the mid-90s, he intended to name it Graybird Suites, but evidently, he had smoked too much the day he registered the business with the state and the city, and when writing the name, he had been distracted by someone in the office with a gray beard. No lie. He didn't realize his mistake until after he had remodeled and opened the place. This was just what I had heard from a few people around town, but they are pretty reliable sources. A few weeks after the placed opened, a city official told the guy the sign didn't match the name on the registry. So instead of paying the fee to change it in the registry, the guy just changed the lettering on the sign."

"That's crazy." Lily laughed and touched his arm. "And I thought the guy wearing the Hawaiian shirt at the rental office was good ol' Graybeard himself."

Harvey laughed. "Oh no. Larry grew it after the sign was changed. I guess to fit the persona."

"You ready for another one?" Ray asked Harvey, finally returning from the other patrons.

"Let me get this one, Harvey," said Lily. "That way I won't be drinking alone in a strange town."

"Nonsense. There is nothing strange about this town other than Larry and his entourage. I should buy you a drink."

"You get the next one." Her smile was playful.

"Fair enough. I don't believe I caught your name."

"Elli," she said, hoping that didn't spark a memory in his overworked, alcohol saturated mind. "Graham."

Their conversation carried on for about an hour. Harvey had moved to the seat that separated them. They laughed. They flirted. Their commonalities were few, but Lily had chosen the pretext: arouse his interest but don't flatter him too much. Connect but don't make it seem like they were star-crossed lovers. She carefully constructed her stories—her lies built out of omissions, half-truths, and wine. There was little, if anything, at stake on a personal level for Lily, but in the scheme of things, this was everything. It meant being a step closer.

Finally, when there was a lull in the conversation, enough, but not too much, alcohol in their systems, and tabs were paid, she considered her next sentence very carefully. She had to say it, though it filled her with anxiety. The knot in her throat accompanied by the ache in the pit of her stomach caused her to vacillate. What kind of contract was this, or more precisely, what would she offer this man in his mid-fifties that he wasn't already aware of when he moved a seat closer to her? *Fuck it. Why not? What's the harm?*

"Wanna come back to my place for a drink or something?"

Harvey's expression reflected a combination of shock and consideration, likely entertaining the idea. He glanced in Ray's direction. The man's back was turned, and he was engaged in a conversation with another guy, clearly out of earshot. He looked back at Lily.

"I don't know about that. It's been a long day, and I should probably head home."

"I'm just asking you to keep a girl company, no pressure." And Lily figured by home, the man meant wife, given the ring on his finger, the one he did little to hide. There wasn't a point to make a case for why he should go home with her. Why look desperate? Then again, maybe just dangle the carrot.

"It's nice to finally know someone in town."

"I'll tell Ray I'm walking you out to your car."

Lily stood and walked toward the door, closely followed by Harvey. She smiled and winked at Ray as she walked by. He raised his hand, a motionless goodbye. Harvey whispered something to Ray, turning his expression to a mixture of suspicion and doubt. And then they were gone.

* * *

That night, Lily and Harvey slept together for the first time. The experience was fast and intense, the only proper fuck with a stranger. She had reservations concerning the whole matter, although they were few, which kept her from fully committing to the act. Sure, she propositioned him, a married man, to the apartment, and, once inside, had been the first to set the carnal act into motion, but it was a means to an end, transactional. Give him just short of what she knew he wanted, and he would want more. He'd offer more for it. And it wasn't difficult to know what a man like him desired. Get close, but not too close. She imagined herself next to Harvey and next to him, Will. Harvey was the gatekeeper who could provide her what she wanted. But in this moment, she was ready to let Harvey do to her what he would.

Despite taking the lead, she was responsive. The ritualistic ebb and flow of sexual reciprocity. The pace quick, the passion strong. It was no time before they were naked, and she was on top, digging her hips into his. After a few minutes, she told him to "fuck me hard." He rolled her over and thrusted, his arms quivering at his own weight as he held himself up. He breathed heavy and softly bit her neck, his stubble scratching her clavicle. She moaned, careful not to overdramatize. *The illusion of pleasure.*

The only light in the room came from a streetlamp's glare through a small space in the curtains. She opened her eyes and looked at his face. It appeared distinguished in the dark, the good features accentuated, almost exaggerated like a wooden carving, the flaws practically nonexistent. No lines or redness, the products of age and excessive drinking, the wear and tear from living was gone. The waft of bourbon from his panting might have been nauseating if she herself had not been a little drunk. She could tell he lost himself in her. She looked down and noticed Harvey's small, hairy belly, and for some reason found it endearing.

When Harvey finished, he lay on his back and Lily on hers. She told him it was "so good." She didn't really want to flatter him, but silence can leave a person wondering the strangest things. Harvey's chest rose and fell at a more moderate pace. She turned to him. Even in the faint light, she could see he wasn't looking at her or in her direction but rather at the ceiling, typical. She wondered what he was thinking, if all philosophers thought the same thing after sex. Did they attempt to make some larger meaning out of it? Or did they find the whole act too human to even put into words? Maybe he was thinking about his betrayal to his wife? Or was sex, well, just sex?

Will would put on a pair of his boxer briefs, grab a cigarette and a lighter, and go sit on the sill. He'd light a cigarette and then open the window just enough to let smoke out. He'd stare out the window overlooking Bleecker Street and would tell her something about love. He'd blow smoke and would say something like, "The concept of the soulmate is a fabrication, which is why we should treat every romantic relationship as if it were simultaneously the most important and of no consequence." His version of pillow talk, apparently. She didn't always agree with what he said, but he seemed sage-like in those moments, nearly nude, often bathed in streetlight, looking at the city. He could have said anything, and she still would have been in love.

Harvey stood and turned on the light. He looked at Lily, his eyes gliding over her body. She half smiled.

He gathered his clothes and dressed. "I want to see you again."

"Maybe some time next week."

"It's a date."

She told him the number to her prepaid cell phone. He grabbed his phone from his jacket pocket and had her repeat it as he entered the number and titled the entry "Insurance." Then he left.

* * *

"Hello."

"Miss me?"

"Lily? I almost didn't pick up. Why did you block your number?"

"I lost my phone and picked up one of those prepaid phones."

"Where are you?"

"Do you miss me?"

"Of course, I do. I haven't seen you in almost a month. Really, where are you?"

"Traveling."

"Where, Lily? Where are you traveling to?"

"I'm not traveling to anywhere. I'm already there. In Paris."

"Seriously, Paris?!"

"Yes, Paris. You know. The Eiffel Tower. The Louvre. Baguettes. I've always wanted to go there."

"What the fuck? We could have gone together. I have vacation time."

"You told me to get shit figured out, and that's what I'm doing."

"I know I said that, but you couldn't have done it, oh I don't know, closer to home?"

"I told you I need to do this by myself and for myself."

"I…I can't believe this. I really can't."

"Don't worry. I'm fine."

"I'm not fine. How are you affording this?"

"Don't worry. It's not expensive. I'm just staying in a hostel and seeing the sights. I'm coming back, you know."

"When?"

"Soon. I love you. You know that, right?"

"I don't know."

"I do. I told you, I just need to do this."

"For how long?"

"As long as it takes. I'll be back sometime soon. I'll call you again."

"How soon?"

"I love you."

* * *

Harvey took her to the City the next time they went out. He told Lily the restaurants were better than the ones in Athens, and they were. She likened it to parts of the Village where she'd go, a mixture of modern bistros and ethnic fusion food. However, the City was also forty-five minutes northwest of Athens, and they would be less likely to see someone he knew, which he made crystal clear. Harvey would pick her up in his burgundy Volvo SUV and take her to a reasonably priced restaurant, always paying cash. They called this a date, and on these dates, they would drink wine, and Harvey would talk about his days as an undergraduate in Athens, stumbling upon the philosophy of Sartre and other existentialists that would lead him to grad school and then become his life's work, his time spent in France, and his desire to leave Athens and the department to spend the rest of his days in Paris. They would sometimes walk the streets to the small stores and enjoy watching people and just absorbing the general atmosphere of this place. The whole experience felt so much like something she had done with Will so many times before.

Lily enjoyed dates with Harvey and quickly realized she couldn't just rely on the man to talk only about himself. He asked her about work and if she knew this person or that person at the insurance office. At first, she had shrugged off the inquiries, but then made it a point to emphasize the nature of her business was confidential, and she did not attempt to get to know those with whom she worked, largely because she didn't spend much time with them. A little bit of research one day and she had the ins and outs of what she did and which department it was with, always making a point to redirect the conversation, if at all possible, especially when the topic of her departure would arise. There was more work with the agency than was anticipated, and they left it at that. She knew an expiration date would change the dynamic somehow, and she liked what this was.

Lily was the woman men daydreamed about when they were driving in cars with their wives, the woman that made them forget about their children and distract them from their routine lives, the woman who could not be kept. They did things for her, not the other way around. Yet it was usually held together by a false pretense, except with Will—at least in the beginning when it was new and somewhat pure. Now, she just wanted Will or some form of him, maybe some kind of closure or some indication that he still loved her. Then she could go back to her real life rather than this simulation. This wasn't even an affair, at least not by her definition. Maybe on Harvey's end it was an affair, the end where he snuck around with a mixture of anxiety and excitement, lying on several accounts, and having sex with an attractive woman half his age who wasn't his wife. Although the wait for her was agonizing at times, and she would often wonder what she was doing, feeling like she was doing nothing, Lily didn't want to prematurely force anything and somehow ruin whatever progress she had made, albeit progress wasn't easy to measure.

And then one night in early September, Harvey moved the subject of conversation to Will. Lily had been smoking a cigarette by an opened window in her apartment. Harvey had, at this point, made it a habit of talking mostly about work.

"I could see real potential in Will," he said, "despite his adjunct position and the recent release of his book. When I hired him, I became his professional mentor because Will didn't know a damn thing about the politics of academia and how to position yourself and strategize. I taught him that, the pecking order that exists, how to approach senior faculty and administration, how to get money from within the university, and how to make an impact so that the president of the university and the deans of each college know who you are. I took him to all the important events, even the stupid things like the monthly faculty social club, and practically introduced him as a son. I showed him how to hustle in this industry. Publish or perish doesn't mean shit to the administration. They don't give a fuck about your recent article touting Husserlian Phenomenology as a Kind of Introspection in a journal they've never heard of. Network or no work: you have to connect yourself to important people or you'll never go anywhere."

"How'd you know he'd come here? I mean the jump from New York City to middle-of-nowhere Ohio seems a little—oh, what's the word?—underwhelming. How did you sell that?"

"Very funny. It's not like this is North Dakota or Idaho. There's plenty to do in Ohio. Will made it perfectly clear he couldn't move up in the NYU system, even with the book, and wanted something different, wanted to move on. It helped that he grew up in or around Buffalo, which is technically part of the Rust Belt. So, by transitive properties this place would feel more like home. I made him an offer that I knew he couldn't get anywhere else, at least not at that time."

"You made him an offer he couldn't refuse, Godfather?"

"Funny. The teaching load was small, the pay was high, and it gave him a quiet place to work on his next book. We put him in faculty housing, rent free."

"You have faculty housing? Like a dorm for professors?"

"Of course not. We have a number of houses and apartments located close to the university. He's in a house near mine. This way I could keep an eye on him and give him better access to me, again, as his mentor."

"I see. That seems smart on your investment."

"And because of that relationship, Will and I planned and curated the entire conference. I gave him a lot of authority in choosing panelists and speakers. Hell, the theme of the conference is based on his book *Death of Philosophy,* though the focus is Laroche."

The conversation continued, focusing on the specifics of what would happen in a few weeks. This is what Lily wanted: more Will. She encouraged Harvey to keep talking about Will and their relationship. He seemed to be such an important person in Harvey's life. He was the best thing to happen to the department in years, and Harvey sounded optimistic about the future. They would be part of some Midwest Renaissance instead of just flyover country. The information produced an aching feeling inside of her, more so than before. Will had accomplished so much since his departure, and she wasn't a part of any of it. Will had left her behind.

* * *

One Friday near the middle of September, Lily walked into Moe's. She had seen Harvey's SUV parked out front when she drove past the place for no real reason but to get out of the apartment, grab a bite to eat, do anything but sit by herself and play on her phone or obsess about Will. A strange curiosity tugged at her when she saw his vehicle: who was Harvey with? Maybe he was meeting Will or having a beer with colleagues.

Inside, she sat at the bar, ordered a glass of her usual, and took a menu. No sign of Ray. Maybe he was off or in the back. She opened it and read over the specials: Tuscan woodfired pizza, braised short rib, half a chicken, or chef salad. She discreetly glanced behind her and scanned the booths and tables. Sure enough, she saw him in the corner of the room in a booth with a woman. It had to be his wife. Harvey never exactly described the woman but only mentioned her in passing. She was much younger and more beautiful than he had made her sound, though she was rather plain: short, straight auburn hair cut just above the shoulders, thin with soft features, small breasts hidden by a white cardigan, and a subtle smile that made her seem pleasant. Come to think of it, Harvey hadn't said a thing about her.

Lily watched them as they talked and ate dinner. Their body language suggested neither one was fully acknowledging the other, Harvey talking, not skipping a beat, as he cut and forked pieces of steak into his mouth and his wife half acknowledging, picking away at what looked like a salad of some sort. Lily couldn't hear their conversation, but she knew the signs. The wife continuously looked around the room from face to face as if she'd rather be a member of any other party than the one she was with. Once even, the two women met eyes, but Lily played it cool. She didn't look away immediately but allowed their gaze to last for a second or so longer than what might be considered socially acceptable. Then turning away, Lily sipped her wine. They didn't look happy, though they didn't look unhappy, either. Perhaps, just bored. *I bet she's cheating on him, too,* she thought. *I would be.*

Lily finished half her meal of grilled salmon on a bed of jasmine rice, the dryness of both masked by some kind of miso glaze, and downed the last gulp of wine. She ordered another glass to hold and sip, though she had no intention of finishing it. About the time Harvey and his wife finished their drinks and were paying the check, Lily got an idea. It came so quickly that it filled her with a kind of manic shiver. Why hadn't she done this before or at least thought of it? Perhaps the timing wasn't right, but then again, she had just learned of where Will lived. This whole endeavor was about timing. It couldn't be reckless like last time. It needed to be perfect. She quickly paid the check and walked to her car. She waited. No more than five minutes later, the couple walked to their vehicle. They pulled out and passed Lily. She gave it a few seconds and then followed. She didn't actually know where they were going, but since they headed in the direction of the university, it had to be home, hopefully. Sylvie said they all live near the campus. He turned down the street that bordered the campus to the west. He made a left onto the next street. Lily did her best to follow as far back as possible in the old, borrowed Civic. They were the only two cars on the street. As Lily rounded the corner onto Walnut Street, able to finally read the sign, she caught a glimpse of the back end of Harvey's vehicle in a driveway, about five houses in. Lily passed slowly, making sure she could identify the house the next day. Her concern wasn't with Harvey's home as much as it was with Will's, whose residence should also be on this street, whichever house that was. Nothing struck her as characteristic or defining of Will's home, a certain car—did he still have his old BMW?—or the curtains opened with a light on. She would make the trip as many times as she needed to find him.

The next day, she parked her car on the street that bordered the university, far enough away from Walnut Street so not to raise any suspicion, not that Harvey even paid that kind of attention to anything other than himself and his work. Will wouldn't recognize her car, a model that probably one in ten college students had. She got out and went to their street and then walked on the opposite side. She studied each house as she passed, trying not to be too obvious. Just make it look like a leisurely walk on a Saturday afternoon. She passed Harvey's house, which appeared vacant. Again, each proceeding house did not provide any indication of Will's residence. Who knew what professors did on the weekend in this place? She reached the end of the street and turned right, figuring she could loop around, get to know the area a little better. Lily spent nearly two hours walking around the neighborhood, having passed the mystery house five or six times, each lap spent looking for some noticeable or defining characteristic. Nothing.

The following day, she drove down Walnut Street, going the same direction as before, passing Harvey's house and then slowing to a crawl so she could peer into windows or open garages. The day was sunny and warm, but she didn't see people in their yards. Perhaps on Sundays, families were eating lunch after church or visiting their grandparents. Another bad idea and a wasted trip. Maybe a visit to the philosophy department would have been a better choice. What the hell was she thinking? As she crept past each home, on the front porch of house number three past Harvey's, she noticed a man sitting in a chair, reading. The closer she got, the more distinguishable his features became: younger with short, dark hair and wearing jeans and a black T-shirt. He smoked a cigarette. And as she passed the place, she realized it was Will, looking exactly as he had the last time she saw him. He was lost in a book as he blew smoke from his mouth. Realizing how slowly she was driving, Lily sped up until she reached the end of the street. Then she turned left and raced down the side street heading back toward downtown.

Why didn't I just pull into his fucking driveway? she thought, scolding herself. *We could have said hello like normal fucking people do.* The ache inside her was more apparent now than ever. She rushed the moment and convinced herself she couldn't turn around and go back. "What the fuck," she shouted as she hit the steering wheel with her fist. It wasn't fair to have to wait all this time only to see him for a moment. In her head, she would have pulled into his driveway, Will looking puzzled and then visibly surprised, even happy. He would have met her in the front yard with a tight hug, one that struggled to close the space time created. He would have invited her in, each catching the other up on the last two years of their lives: Will apologizing for leaving, Lily apologizing for how things had spiraled in New York. They would have kissed, undressed, made love on the couch because the bedroom was just too far away. She would have stayed with him while he finished out the year, no, the semester, and then they would have returned to New York. But that was only in her head. She pulled into the Graybeard Suites and parked her car. All she wanted to do was sleep away this moment and these feelings, dream about what could have been. With her face next to his, she would say, "I'm sorry." But she wasn't sorry. In fact, he should apologize.

Instead, she laid her head on the steering wheel and cried, but no one was in the parking lot to notice.

* * *

"Why are you doing this to me?"

"You told me I needed to deal with my issues, and that's what I'm doing."

"This isn't what I meant. Are you still in Europe?"

"No, I'm back in the states."

"Where?"

"Maine."

"Why are you in Maine?"

"Family. I wanted to be with them."

"I didn't know you had family there."

"Do you miss me?"

"Of course, I do. I missed you the moment you told me you were leaving. Are you even coming back?"

"I told you I am. I just want to spend time with family I haven't seen in years."

"I don't know why you had to do this. It's like I don't matter to you. I don't know why I'm putting up with this."

"Because you love me, and you know I'm coming back."

"I'm not sure you are. I assume I'll never see you again."

"You will."

"When?"

"Next month. I'll be back next month."

"Really?"

"Yes."

"Can you at least give me your number so I can call you?"

"I don't know."

"You don't know what?"

"I'll see you soon."

"Come on."

"You can just call me on my regular number."

"I have been and texting. It goes straight to voicemail. I thought you said you lost your phone?"

"Sorry. I did and then I got another one, but it was being weird in Europe. It should be fine. Don't be upset."

* * *

"How is everything with Will and the conference?" Lily asked. They were en route to the City to have a late afternoon lunch.

"He seems a little more together. Laroche's hotel is booked. I have one of our faculty scheduled to pick him up at the airport. And I'm just busy putting out fires."

"When is the conference?"

"The weekend after next, which means I probably won't be able to see you."

"It's fine. I figured that might happen." Lily's mind wandered for a moment as she saw a road that passed under the highway and continued into a wooded area off in the distance. "I was wondering, Harvey," she said, still staring out the passenger window. "What would you say if I told you I wanted to go to the conference? Not the whole thing. Maybe just one of your talks."

"I would suggest you don't." He shifted in his seat, straightening his posture.

She turned to him. "You've talked so much about it this last month. I want to see what you've done." She hooked her arm around his and squeezed it tightly.

"I don't think that's a good idea. There will be a lot of people there."

"All the more reason I should go," she said. "I'll blend in. Nobody knows me anyway." She slid her right hand on his thigh, her fingers inching up the inseam of his khaki pants until her hand was on his crotch. "I'd really love to see you in action." She rubbed the bulge in his pants, feeling his dick swell.

"I'd love to say yes, but I don't think it'll work. What do I tell someone when they ask who you are? Say my wife?" He looked at her and then back at the road ahead.

"Why would anyone ask that question? It's not as if I plan to latch onto you or try to have a conversation with your wife."

"I like the part of my life you exist in. Plus, it's too risky and distracting."

Lily let go of Harvey, pulled her black cardigan around herself, and crossed her arms as if she were cold. She returned her gaze to the passenger window. "I really don't know why it's such a big deal. It'll be like I'm not even there."

"It's just too stressful, too many moving parts. I'll make it up to you after the conference."

"If I'm still here." She sensed Harvey move, probably shooting her a look, but she didn't care. "I just mean I don't know how much longer I'll be working here. It's been two months, and that's close to the longest assignment I've ever had. I'll probably be leaving any day now."

"Shouldn't you know how much time you have left?" asked Harvey. "I would think a person in your position would be privy to that knowledge."

"Of course, I know how much work I have, roughly. I only said that because I'm irritated. I just want to make the most of this before it ends."

Although she spoke the words, she didn't mean them. What she needed to do was act, make a scene, draw some attention.

* * *

Lily knew she would go to the conference, and both Will and Harvey would be painfully aware of her presence. Unlike in New York, where she had acted recklessly out of spite, here she had shown restraint and patience. What seemed to be a little over two lonely months in a place she neither liked nor enjoyed felt like an eternity. Cooped up in this shitty shoe box of an apartment in this stupid town in the middle of nowhere, stuck fucking a guy twice her age and still no chance at Will. She wanted to cry, but that was a waste of time, much like these last few months.

She sat at the head of her bed, legs crossed in lotus position. Flipping through television channels could have been a distraction if she had a TV. She sipped a cup of licorice tea, imagining she is in his house, begging him to take her back and telling him it would work out this time. They would work out this time, and she'd break it off with her boyfriend because it was Will she wanted. Maybe she took him for granted the first time, and maybe he was more concerned with his work. They were both in different places in their lives, and they could make this work. They could have what they left behind because you don't just stop loving someone, right?

When he had left New York, she had been much more forceful. She had done things she wasn't proud of and created a false narrative, though it felt real, but she had done it out of love. After that day in Central Park when they had fought, and those men had attacked him, she knew she should have said something, but she was so angry. It wasn't her fault someone wanted to stand up for her. At least someone was actually willing to come to her defense this time. He shouldn't have made such a scene and brought it to that point. At least she had Nick.

Now, she was just a stranger. She wasn't Will's girlfriend. She wasn't a guest. None of this felt real. Sure, she knew Harvey, and with a little more time, she could probably make him do anything. Would he really betray Will like Nick had? Maybe if he had enough motivation or reason. From what Harvey had said, people here clearly loved Will. She played with the ideas in her head, what she should have done. She should have enrolled as a student in the classes he taught: fifteen weeks of staring into her eyes and having to pretend that everything was normal. Why hadn't she done that if she was truly willing to do whatever it took to get him back. She should have cut and dyed her hair, pretended to be another person and have him fall in love with that version of her. She had made it nearly impossible for him to stay in New York, or at least at NYU. He didn't even tell her to her face that he didn't want her. He just left. She knew he still loved her.

She pulled a photo from her purse. It was a Polaroid of the two of them that she had taken when they were lying in bed in Will's apartment one afternoon. He had been reading, and she had grabbed her camera, had pushed his book down, and had told him to smile. In the photo, Lily smooshed her face into Will's cheek. She stared at the photo, reliving that moment, and then placed it back into her purse.

She had to haunt him, make him feel her existence in the subtlest ways and in the most unexpected place. Will had no idea she was here, which made her feel like she had accomplished nothing. She sat on her bed, head resting back on the wall, her eyes closed, thinking. His home, his office, the conference—that order. She knew where she needed to be.

* * *

It was mid-October, and the air was brisk. A breeze blew Lily's long dark hair, and she pulled her maroon cardigan around herself, crossing her arms. She considered the Student Union, but it didn't feel right. Maybe it was too early in the day, and what if she ran into both of them together. The whole thing would be ruined. She took a walkway that eventually led to Gordon Hall. Once there, Lily went to the back of the building. Sure enough, in the designated lot was Harvey's Volvo right next to what she believed to be Will's dirty BMW, the one he had stupidly owned in New York, if he still had the thing, a car that was already old when he had bought it and was more of a nuisance than anything.

She entered through the back door and moved quickly through the halls, then up the stairs to the second floor where she made a few questionable turns, but when she finally reached the stairs leading to the third floor, she stopped. Her nerves kept her from making the final ascent, but she needed to do this. She climbed the stairs to the third floor and entered through the Department of Philosophy's door. Instead of the woman who had talked to her about the building, there was a young guy sitting at the desk.

"Can I help you?" he asked.

"Where's the woman who—"

"Sylvie? She's at the conference but should be back within the hour. What do you need?"

"Nothing, really." She came all this way, and she didn't have a plan. "Can I take one of these?" she asked, looking at the stack of conference schedules next to a candy dish on the bureau's surface.

"Uh, yeah. It's supposed to be good. Jacques Laroche will be there."

"Thanks."

Once outside, she knew where she needed to go. She left campus, heading for Walnut Street—her pace steady, neither quick nor leisurely. She glanced at Harvey's house as she passed, clearly vacant. Lily didn't dwell too much on Harvey. There was little about him that concerned her, mostly, but the closer she came to Will's, the more anxious she became. Her heart beat faster; her skin tingled. It felt difficult to swallow. Why did he do this to her?

As she neared Will's house, a woman walked down his driveway. When she turned onto the sidewalk, she caught a glimpse of Lily, which brought a look of surprise to her face. It was Harvey's wife. The two women locked eyes as they neared each other. Lily smiled. Harvey's wife sheepishly smiled back and then looked away. Lily stopped at the foot of the walkway to Will's front porch. She glanced back, watching Harvey's wife until she disappeared into their house. *You weren't supposed to be here,* Lily thought. *Is Will the other guy?* Lily stepped on each of the sandstone squares that led to his porch. She saw an Adirondack chair next to a small table, made of the same sun-bleached wood, with an ashtray on it. She walked onto the porch and sat in the chair. It was hard and at an awkward angle.

She pulled a pack of Djarum Blacks from her bag, took out a cigarette, and lit it. It crackled as she inhaled. Looking out at the neighborhood, she exhaled the scent of cloves from the side of her mouth and tapped the cigarette on the brim of the ashtray. This is what he saw every day and what it felt like to live this kind of life in the suburbs. It was quiet. Cardinals sang. The idea of someone seeing her wasn't a concern. When she finished, she left the last bit burning in the ashtray and, without lingering any longer, walked to the back of the house.

Like she thought, there was a back door, which looked like the original. She tried the doorknob. Locked. She glanced around. From her vantage point, she was out of sight from wandering eyes. Taking out a credit card from her bag, hoping the door wasn't bolted, she slid the card between the edge of the door and the jamb. Stiffly, she jabbed the card in the direction of the latch and turned the knob until it clicked. The door popped open, and she stepped inside.

In front of her were two sets of steps: a long set to the basement, and a short set to a closed door, likely the kitchen. Her heart pounded and her palms sweat as she ascended the few steps. She wiped her hands on her jeans and turned the knob. It creaked open into the kitchen. She peaked her head around the door, looking in all directions.

The kitchen was simple, plain. The place was clean, nothing but a coffee pot on the counter. The kitchen led to the dining room, which had a wooden table and chairs larger than the one in the kitchen, half covered by papers. Lily ran her fingers over the vacant part of its surface as she passed, collecting dust that she just wiped on her pants. She crept softly through each room. To her right was the living room with more cream-colored walls and light oak floors, but this might have been the room where he would entertain guests. There was a boxy, brown leather sofa and armchair positioned around an oval shaped coffee table. On the wall nearest the driveway was a fireplace with bookshelves on each side full of books. A single lamp stood in the far corner. Even for a single guy, these were rather stringent surroundings. She passed the front door and turned to walk upstairs.

The second level had three bedrooms and a bathroom. The one bedroom had a handful of brown boxes, some open and some taped close. *Packing or unpacking?* The other room had a small desk and more boxes, a study of sorts. Will's bedroom door was open like the other room. Again, it was clean and plain like most of the house. The only furniture was the basics: a chest of drawers, a queen size bed, and a nightstand with a digital alarm clock on it. The bed was meticulously made. Harvey's wife, no doubt.

Lily set her bag on the nightstand and yanked the covers down, got into bed, and pulled the blanket up to her chin. She caressed the mattress, knowing it was his from the apartment in New York, the bed she had slept in, had fucked him in. Turning onto her stomach, she put her face in his pillow, breathing in deeply through her nose. The pillow smelled faintly of him, as if he had just left the bed. In a way, it turned her on. Memories of his body close to hers flooded her brain. She unbuttoned her pants and slid her hand beneath her underwear, touching herself as she dug her face into his pillow. She wanted him to be here with her the way he had been before, to touch her, to be inside of her.

When she finished, she lay there on her stomach and looked towards the only window in the room. In her mind, their relationship had never officially ended. If they had been married, they'd merely be separated, estranged. Why couldn't she live in this house with him? She noticed a few branches of a red maple tree through the window; some of its leaves were bright crimson and mixtures of orange and yellow, giving them the collective appearance of flames. If the wind blew too hard, the flames would scatter and scorch nearby houses, setting fire to the other trees until all of Athens was burning. Then they could leave the town ablaze. She grabbed the other pillow on the bed and pulled it close to her. She closed her eyes and fell asleep.

Lily sprang up, startled, looking around frantically until she saw the red numbers of the clock. She had slept only a few minutes. She got up, leaving the covers disheveled, reached inside her bag, pulled out a bottle of her perfume, and sprayed it on the bedding. Vigorously, she pumped the little bottle until losing patience and snapped off its nozzle. She dumped the remaining contents on the bed like a priestess anointing with oil. The room filled with the aroma of sweet lavender.

Lily left the way she came, shutting the back door behind her.

* * *

The next day was a very different process. First, Lily showered and got ready around noon, then walked downtown and smoked a few cloves. It felt strange having been in Will's house and his bed. The experience left her with none of the feelings she once had in his apartment. In this town, she was alone, out of place, and not feeling like herself. She was a *flâneur*. The lack of motion and noise in her life made her anxious, stir crazy. Over the past two months, friends had been calling and texting her, asking about her trip and why she hadn't sent them pictures, wondering when she would return. Her lies were the same to them as they were to Nick. The friends understood because they knew her. This kind of thing wasn't unusual for her. Eventually, she wandered into a small café to order a turkey croissant and a bowl of tomato bisque and wait. It seemed like that was all she was doing these days. Waiting.

* * *

Lily arrived late to the symposium, not so late as to be noticed but enough so that the speakers were already on stage, and there was no plausible way she would accidentally run into Will beforehand. The Burns Theatre inside the Student Union was small, and the back rows suited her best. She sipped a latte from the resident Starbucks. The lights had been slightly dimmed to highlight the stage. Lily quickly found an open seat in the second to the last row. Harvey was just now introducing Will to begin the discussion. Honestly, Lily didn't pay much attention to what they were saying because the genuine sight of Will for the first time in over two years produced mixed feelings. She wanted to run onto the stage and kiss him on the mouth and tell him how much she ached to be with him. Then she wanted to throw her coffee in his face and tell him what a son of a bitch he was for leaving her, for never saying goodbye. *The look of surprise and sadness on his beautiful, scalded face.* Her head filled with scenarios of violent embrace.

The men on the stage talked for nearly forty-five minutes. Lily watched both Harvey and Will, but she didn't hear a thing. Harvey's combed back graying hair and the broken capillaries in his cheeks; the shapely dark eyebrows and soft young skin of Will's face, the way her hand felt in his short, gelled hair. She could have them both if she wanted, but not here or with these kinds of circumstances. Well, she had had them both. But everything was too close, too connected. Maybe transplant them back to New York, Harvey in Long Island or on the Upper Westside and Will could return to the Village or better yet to Williamsburg. Then she could still have Nick. Then she could—a swell of applause sounded, cutting her daydream short. Lily glanced at the stage. Will seemed distraught.

"There will be a ten-minute break," said Harvey, "and then we will resume with the question-and-answer portion of our evening."

The men walked off stage as the front-of-house lights were turned up. People's chatter filled the room, some stood, while others remained seated. Lily wondered how she could get their attention, even if only just a look, without having be the one to do it. She eyed the young man sitting next to her

"Excuse me."

He turned his head toward her. "Yeah?"

"I'm not sure exactly how the Q and A works?"

He made a strange face that implied, *it's literally in the title of the thing.*

"I know, stupid question," said Lily, "I came in late and missed the introduction."

"The way they've been doing it for most of the conference is you raise your hand, and someone brings you a microphone. Then you ask a relevant question. It's that simple."

"This probably sounds strange, but I have a question that I would like them to answer, but I have an issue with speaking in big crowds. I forget what I'm going to say and become a stuttering mess. It's like so embarrassing. I'm hoping you might be able to ask it for me." Lily smiled and shrugged her shoulders.

The young man she proposed this to couldn't have been older than twenty-three or twenty-four. She thought he seemed nice enough. "You seem sweet enough."

He smiled. "Sure. I don't mind as long as I don't have to try to explain anything."

"No. You shouldn't have to do anything other than ask my question."

"Okay."

Lily had read Will's book, even though she hadn't been listening to the men talk, so she had something in mind. She took the schedule out of her purse, turned it over, and began writing. *Once philosophy has reached its theoretical end, then what will happen? What kind of transformation will occur and who will determine that?*

"Direct it to William Thierry."

"That's it?"

"Yes. That's it."

* * *

"We're going to begin the question-and-answer portion of this evening." With the auditorium lights turned up, every face in the audience was visible. Harvey took a sip of water from the glass on his podium. "This will be roughly a half hour to forty-five minutes depending on the number of questions and the length of their responses. I apologize if we cannot get to them all."

Lily looked at the guy next to her and whispered, "You're so sweet." She touched his shoulder. He grinned and raised his hand. Lily, satisfied with having to do very little on her part to be seen, would just sit back and wait to make eye contact with Will. He was all that mattered at this point.

"You, sir, in the..." Harvey trailed off as he pointed to the man next to Lily. "Bleh." Harvey was no longer looking at the man who had stood to ask a question but locked eyes with Lily. She smiled, and he cleared his throat into a clenched fist. "Excuse me. In the blue plaid."

"This question is for Professor Thierry," said the young man. He glanced at Lily and then continued with the question.

Lily's eyes moved from Harvey to Will, and, sure enough, he was staring at her. All expression and color had left Will's face as the young man finished the question, but Will kept his eyes on Lily as if in a trance. She was as stoic as ever, not once wavering in expression. With Harvey, the smirk was necessary—it signified playfulness, not malice. It let him know she could not be controlled, but she wasn't there to punish him either. However, with Will, it was something of a different nature. She felt a heaviness as they stared at one another. Rather than heavy, the exchange was dense, as if the matter in the room was compressing together due to the pull they had on one another, so dense that it would take all her energy just to turn her head, look away. She felt as though they were becoming the same person, bound by forces unseen. Moving to this town, the affair with Harvey, being inside Will's house like she was his lover, and always only at arm's length from seeing him. These were the pieces of some irregular jigsaw puzzle. And finally, in his presence, their surroundings faded like an old tube in a black and white television. The look. That's all it was, and it put Will in a nearly catatonic state. *I'll always find you.*

"Will, don't take *too* long to formulate a response," said Harvey. "We only have forty-five minutes."

Laughter.

Will seemed to come to and glanced at Harvey, whose wide eyes looked cartoonish, and then back at the young man in blue. "I, I'm sorry. Do you, uh, mind repeating that?"

The man repeated the question, and Will and the French philosopher discussed the matter for a brief couple of minutes. For the rest of the session, Will kept looking at Lily as if he were seeing a ghost for the first time and trying to reason it away. Maybe upon the next glance, she'd be gone and someone else would be in the seat, and he could have some sense of relief. She knew she had him. She had made her mark. This was what she had been working towards.

When the Q and A came to an end, Lily exited the auditorium as quickly as possible. If this were going to work, they couldn't meet just yet. She left the Student Union through the closest door. The air outside was cool. She brought her cardigan close to her body and walked in the direction of her apartment. After a few steps, panic seized her. *What if he actually tries to follow me?* She began running and reached a pace she didn't think she was capable of. She ran, bag bouncing off her back, and as she neared the edge of campus and turned onto Main Street, it was only a few more blocks until she'd be away from it all.

* * *

The next day around ten in the morning, Lily's phone rang. It was Harvey.

"Hello," she said, sweetly.

"What the hell kind of stunt was that, Elli?"

"You said you wouldn't be surprised if I showed up. You could have fooled me."

"Well, I was. Believe me. Thankfully, I kept my composure. If someone had recognized you—"

"But no one did because no one knows me. You should calm down. I left as soon as the Q and A was over. No harm done."

"It didn't make my night any easier."

"I tried to be more formal about it, but I finally got to see what you do. I was turned on just sitting there."

"Stop. Not now."

"What happened to your protégé? He clammed up."

"Will? I don't know. He was fine during the discussion, even though Laroche treated him like a rag doll. One minute Will's engaging, the next he's speaking like he's on a delay."

"Maybe he saw a ghost?"

"What?"

"Did it ruin your night?"

"No. I think, all in all, it was a success. Though he did act strange the rest of the night."

"What do you mean?"

"He seemed out of it when we got to Moe's. He wasn't himself, kind of on edge, staring off, looking around a lot."

"I wonder what spooked him."

"Maybe stress. Anyway, when do I get to see you again? I think you owe me for that stunt."

"I take it you've forgiven me already."

"It was crazy for you to show up. Anne would never have done that. I suppose it's one of your best qualities. The way you just do what you want."

"How about you come over right now so I can do whatever I want? I'm still in bed, and I'm wearing nothing."

"I wish I could, but I have to go to the homecoming game today."

"The offer stands all day."

"Maybe."

"I'll be waiting."

* * *

Lily walked into the philosophy department. At the front desk was the same student she had met the first day of the conference.

"Hi. I need to meet with Professor Thierry."

"Usually, he's in class until eleven on Wednesdays, but he's not here today."

"I just need to give him a paper."

"You can put it in his mailbox."

"Actually, I'd just prefer to slide it under his door."

"That's fine. His office is—"

She was already walking in the direction of his office, turning down the hallway and passing a couple of open doors, briefly glancing in each doorway to see if it were occupied but avoiding eye contact with anyone. She knew he would be in class but didn't realize he wasn't at the university today. That made this task a little easier, hopefully. She stopped in front of his office. The door was shut. She tried the old knob, but it was locked. Taking out a credit card, the one she used at his house, she quickly jammed it in the space where the latch was and wiggled the card. The door opened almost instantly thanks to the old hardware and university neglect. The room was dark, but its contents still mostly visible. She found an empty shelf and placed the book flat in its center. She didn't linger, closing the door as quietly as possible. Her body tingled, and her heart raced; the whole act made her want to sprint out of the building, but she kept her cool. As she neared the front desk, she had the urge to ask the guy where Will was. He told her, candidly, that no one had seen or heard from him since the symposium, which was, like, not normal for him. A few students had complained to the chair about it just today. The chair's door to his office has been closed since. She considered what he said, thanked him, and left.

* * *

Harvey closed the door behind him. Lily sat on her bed, knees bent and pulled to her chest. She was on her phone, texting a friend, passing the time. She glanced at Harvey and then back at the screen.

"Well, hello to you too," he said in a mock-hurt tone.

"I figured you weren't going to show up like the last couple of times."

"You know I couldn't come over then with all the homecoming and after-conference bullshit I had to do. The administrative follow-through is always a headache. And I still don't know the state of our program, even with the positive turnout." He slipped off his tan jacket and set it on the chair next to the small table.

She looked up from her phone. It had only been a little over a week since the night of the symposium, since Will saw her. The curtains were closed on the large picture window as they always were, largely out of necessity, a characteristic that made this place feel even more like a motel. The only light came from a combination of the window on the back wall and a lamp on an end table next to her bed.

"I'm finally able to see you and forget everything else." He came closer to her and touched her shoulder, gently moving his hand up her neck until his fingers were in her hair. She looked up, and he kissed her.

"I need a drink of water." She got up and walked to the small refrigerator, opened it, and grabbed a bottle of water. She took a sip and set the bottle on the counter. Harvey was already taking his shirt off. Lily walked over to him and let him kiss her as she unbuckled his pants, an act she had done so many times before, but there was something about this time that felt off, artificial. It was as if she were watching herself from another room. Harvey began undressing and kissing her body, which felt good despite the previous fact. She laid back on the bed and Harvey went to get on top of her when there was a loud thud.

He jumped, startled. "What the hell was that?"

"It sounded like a bird hit the window."

Harvey walked to the door and looked out the eye hole. He shook his head and came back to her. Lily put her foot up to keep him from getting back in bed. She slid to the edge and grabbed his penis, which began swell. She glanced at the window, thinking about what bird may have broken its neck as it flew into the glass, when she noticed a forehead and a pair of eyes looking at her. The unexpectedness of that sent a shiver through her, but rather than shouting, she stared at the set of eyes and put Harvey's penis in her mouth. She stared at the person in the window. Within a minute, whoever that was disappeared.

* * *

"Hello."

"Lily, what's going on?" Nick asked, voice raised.

"Nothing. Are you alright?"

"Where are you? You said you'd be home by now."

"Calm down." Lily got up from her bed and began pacing around the apartment. "I'll be home soon." She chewed the nail of her index finger. "I'm still in Maine."

"Bullshit. What's going on?"

"Don't yell at me. Nothing's going on. I'll be home in a few days."

"I was just on the phone with Will, and he said he saw you. Several people saw you." He paused. "Well?"

Lily hesitated. "I don't know what you're talking about."

"Will thinks you're in Ohio. In Athens."

"That's crazy."

"He doesn't happen to think so. He's acting all nervous and weird."

"I haven't seen Will since he left. You know that. And I don't even know where fucking Athens, Ohio is."

"Well, he happens to think you're stalking him and messing with his head."

"I'm not. I'm nowhere near Ohio or him."

"I don't like this. It's really fucking weird. We haven't spoken since he left, and he calls me out of nowhere claiming you're stalking him. That you've been inside his home."

"I'm not fucking stalking him, and I've never been in his home." She took the phone and hit the bed several times before bringing it back to her face. "He always does this. He makes me out to be the psycho." She started to cry but held back.

"He's questioning me like I should know, asking me where you are and what you've been doing. I can't even answer those questions, and I shouldn't have to."

"You don't believe him, do you?"

"I really don't know what to believe at this point. You up and leave because you need to get away and travel. I get that, but I don't hear from you for months. I really have no clue what you're doing. I don't know if you're actually with your family because I've never met any of them."

"What are you saying?"

"People who love each other don't do this. And maybe you should just stay where you are. Maine. France. Ohio. Wherever the fuck it is. This is not what I meant by dealing with your issues or your past. This is way beyond that."

"But." He had hung up.

This was the last conversation she had with Nick, draining any hope she had of returning to a life with him. She figured there was little chance to repair that relationship. What did he even know? It was just speculation at this point. Nick had told her she needed closure with Will if she would ever move on with her life. He practically pushed her to do this. And nothing felt closed. It was wide open. She was not grounded. There was nothing connecting her to anything, just a vague idea floating in the moment. Even though she had been living apart from Will for the last few years, he never left her mind. In her thoughts, memories, dreams, nightmares, and everywhere she went, she wished he were there with her. He haunted her as she now haunted him. And that's how she came to be with Nick. Will's closest friend, he was the person who knew him best. He anchored her to the past. It was the way she could always be close to him. Now, she was close to Will and far from Nick, but it all felt lost, and she felt alone and estranged.

What was the point? She had felt good, as if everything were coming together. Why hadn't she thought that Will would call Nick? She assumed the wedge that had driven them apart also had severed all communication. Clearly, she was wrong. But it had to be getting to Will or else he wouldn't have interrogated Nick with so many questions as Nick claimed. This was the progression of things that would bring it all to the end. An end where Will listened to Lily and realized that they were meant for each other. This was the point. Or was it eroding away and turning into shit and decay? She needed to do something drastic, something that would send everything on a collision course. There had to be a tipping point.

She called his phone, a number she had found in Harvey's phone one evening when he was at her apartment in the bathroom during his post-coital piss. It was simple but necessary.

The phone rang and went to voicemail. She did her best to settle herself, so her message would sound somewhat intelligible. After the tone, she didn't say anything for a few seconds. Finally, she spoke.

"Will. Hi. It's uh . . . well, it's Lily. This is so weird, but I'm in Athens and wanted to see you. I'd leave you my number to call me back, but I'm sure that would give you all the more reason not to. I'm at the Graybeard Suites in Athens. My room is 203 if you want to catch up. If not, that's fine, but I think it would be really good to see you. Bye."

She felt nauseated. She didn't want to be so direct, but what choice did she have? The phone call assured her this was now an imminent possibility, and she wasn't a stalker.

Harvey was supposed to come over later in the day, so Lily thought a shower would take her mind off the call she had just made. There was so much going on in such a small space. She couldn't believe after all this time of moving slowly and somewhat methodically that she would let it all explode or implode. Something was coming apart.

She undressed and took a shower, letting the water run over her pale body, the heat of the water flushed her skin. She stood there for several minutes just feeling the hot stream of water hit her flesh. Then she washed herself and shampooed and conditioned her hair. When she was finished, she wrapped herself in a white towel and blow dried her hair. She dressed in tight blue jeans and a light gray sweatshirt, not bothering to put on socks or shoes because she hadn't planned to go anywhere. She went to the kitchenette and took a box of licorice tea out of the cupboard. She poured a mug of water from the tap and placed it in the microwave for two minutes. When the timer went off, she dropped in a tea bag and let it steep. Maybe after she saw Harvey tonight, she would up and leave, perhaps never confronting Will. Her elusiveness would leave a lasting mark, and he might follow her. Love is always about the chase.

And then there was a knock at the door. She waited, unsure, thinking that Harvey wasn't supposed to be at her place until later. She walked to the door, unlocked and opened it. In the doorway stood Will.

"I'm glad you're here," she said.

"Me too. . ."

Part III

Philosophical Investigations

Nick Lynch
At his home in Greenwich Village, telephone interview

APRIL 2010

I was in total shock when I heard the news he had murdered her. I mean, I still am. Jesus, it just happened like six months ago. I never would have imagined Will doing something like this, and I've known him a long time. He was a good guy, intelligent, kind of quiet. Never violent, rarely upset about things. We grew apart these last couple of years since he moved away, but he was at one time my best friend.

I don't recall exactly how Will and Lily were introduced. It was the summer of '05, and Will and I had gone to a party at my friend's loft in Greenwich Village. This guy was a childhood friend who came from money and lived excessively. His place was huge, and he had shit all over the walls: artwork, instruments, photographs, whatever. Everything was a conversation piece. While I was chatting with a few people, I noticed this girl looking at a painting. She was thin with long, dark brown hair, just standing there by herself. Don't get me wrong. I wasn't really looking to pick up anyone, but sometimes you see what might be the perfect moment, and you know you'll regret not taking it. So, I stood next to her and asked her what she saw. She turned to me, I smiled, and we both turned back to the painting. A sad kitten in a white ruffled collar, she said. I tried to be funny and said I saw an eighteenth-century advertisement for cat food. Then I introduced myself. Her name was Lily, and she had wandered in with a group of people she didn't know. I told her she was in good company because I didn't know most of the people here. I offered to grab her a drink. A dry red, she said.

I went to the kitchen to pour her a drink and get another beer for myself. I couldn't have been gone for more than five minutes. When I returned, she was gone. I scanned the room but didn't see her. I asked a couple of people if they saw where the girl was, the one who had been in front of the cat painting. No one knew.

I walked upstairs and made my way toward the balcony, thinking she might have gone out to catch a view of the neighborhood. As I passed the little study, I happened to glance over and who do I see? Will and Lily. Will leafed through some old book while Lily sat on a desk. She actually seemed interested. My moral dilemma: do I hand her the wine and stick around, trying to pick up where I left off, or do I let Will continue to entertain her? These situations can test friendships. I entered the room with an exaggerated smile and introduced them with all the irony I could manage. "Will, I see you've met Lily. Lily, this is William Thierry, the smartest guy I know."

They both looked at me a little confused. I handed Lily her wine and Will the beer, and I told Will not to get too attached. "Discuss boring things while the rest of us drink and be merry and talk about paintings of kittens in ruffled collars with women of dubious intent." Then I left the room. Who the hell sits in the library at a party? Later that night, I got a text from him saying he had left and was walking back to the apartment. She must have already broken his heart. He was kind of a delicate flower. I finished out the night there and left around three in the morning.

I woke up around nine and made a pot of coffee. I remember leaning against the counter, looking out the window over the sink, nursing a minor hangover, when I heard Will's door open. I turned to ask Will how his night had gone but instead met eyes with Lily. She wore only a tight black tank top and underwear. She made a shy, almost embarrassed expression that quickly turned into, I don't know, maybe that look you get when you realize you know someone—sort of surprised but also kind of familiar. She said she didn't expect to see me again as she turned and walked toward the bathroom. Will had to have told her we lived together. Maybe not.

When she returned from the bathroom, I asked her if she wanted some coffee. She stopped short of Will's door, hesitated, and then accepted my offer. That was the moment I knew what kind of person she was. One-night stands sometimes have the potential of turning into something more but not with someone like her. I had a feeling she was going to break his heart. I didn't know anything about her at the time, but I had a feeling. She didn't care about decorum. She didn't care she was standing in her underwear after snubbing me and spending the night with my best friend. I didn't just want to know more about her, I wanted her to stay here in the kitchen with me for as long as she possibly could. It probably sounds crazy, but I wanted to pretend I was the one who had taken her home, that she was actually walking into my room and getting back into bed with me. So, I poured us each a cup of coffee while she took a seat on one of the bar stools at our old tile counter. We talked until Will woke up, and then she collected her things, dressed, and left. And that was the beginning of their yearlong relationship.

When Will met Lily, he had a book contract with some university press. He'd wake up early, like four in the morning, and work on edits. Then he'd teach a few classes, and in the evening, they'd see each other. It wasn't long after that, maybe a month or so, he was waking up later, and she was spending the night more. I'd come home after work, and they'd be smoking cigarettes on the fire escape. I could always tell she was there because she smoked cloves, and the smell settled in the apartment. I still live in that apartment, because you'd have to be crazy to give up a place as nice as ours in this part of the Village, especially for what I pay.

. . . I'm not going to say I don't know what it was about her. I think there was this sense of mystery, like she had a secret. Yes, she was beautiful, but not what's typically beautiful today. She had sort of a gypsy-like, bohemian look, something you might recognize in an old black and white movie or silent film. Young Heddy Lamar,

Elizabeth Taylor, or even maybe more appropriately, Audrey Hepburn. References my grandfather might make, no doubt. It's not what you see in magazines or social media, unless you happened upon Italian Vogue or some French magazine, which you'd never find in the convenient store. It was a classic look—long dark hair and smooth, milky white skin. She didn't care about bronzer or too much make up. You don't see women with that kind of beauty unless you're watching an indie or foreign film. When Lily walked into a room, something all of a sudden felt vacuous. No, it's like a high. Lily could walk into a room, and you almost immediately felt like you were missing something and simultaneously euphoric. There was some urgent sense of longing, and it radiated from her. Something so simple as talking about an odd painting or how she could walk out in a tank top and underwear and give you this kind of look as you offer her coffee that just breaks every bone in your body.

Will totally ate her up. He had never experienced a girl like her before. She would take him to all these different clubs and bars. She introduced him to a whole new group of people, who didn't necessarily become his friends but made for an okay time. He hung around them mainly to appease her. He'd say they were more ego than substance. She described them as "eclectic," which usually translates to pretentious, elitist, adult children who either are supported by their parents whom they loathe or work some shitty retail or food service job that they love/hate. They just hang around and try their hand at a bunch of things, whatever grabs their attention at the time, but never really know much or become good at anything. But of course, that makes them an expert on everything. I can't stand these types, but the Village is full of them. They discuss pathetic hackneyed versions of ideas about literature and culture like they are changing the world with their conversation, each one agreeing or awing at the other. Will was on another level, writing about cultural theories or ideas, and when it came to those people, he was considerably patient given the way they would act. Lily introduced him as the guy getting his PhD at NYU who was publishing a book about philosophy. Like she or any of them even had the first idea about what that meant. Of course, they all acted like it was no big deal and *who couldn't talk about philosophy because we philosophize every day we are alive?* I'm sure after every time they hung out with her friends, he wanted to fucking kill himself. They are seriously the dead end of Western civilization.

Regardless of her friends, Will would stay out with Lily until three or four in the morning and then end up back at our place. He'd be up by nine or so, work on edits for the book, go teach a class, and by the time he was back, she'd be up and have coffee made. They'd smoke cigarettes and drink coffee on the fire escape, talking for hours. She'd take him on these little excursions around the city to places like the Chinatown markets and play with the kids in the street, constructing fantasy lives for themselves with what they saw or who they interacted with. They'd crash people's parties, much like the first time I had met her, to see what those people were like. They'd take the subway to Harlem and go to a blues club she had heard about, not really knowing anything about the place. They'd order drinks and listen to some live music. He loved telling me about all of it, and I didn't mind listening because he was happy and obviously falling in love with her. And in this regard, Lily was good for him. She took him out of his head and comfort zone. But I was jealous. I knew it then, and I know it now. Seeing the two of them just reminded me of what could have been if she hadn't walked away and met Will at that party. But I knew their relationship had an expiration date. They were on different paths.

When Will's book was finally published, things with Lily changed. Will's book sold specifically to philosophy departments throughout the country, or at least that's what he said. In the realm of academia, he was getting a lot of attention. The book was Will's main priority, which I think was clear to Lily. And why shouldn't it? That was a huge accomplishment, and not to mention how well it was doing. He was invited to read at some of the local universities around the city over the next few months, maybe November through January. I remember Will going out less and coming home earlier. Although Will's behavior or routine changed some, Lily kept the same lifestyle. She'd stay out long after Will came home and stumble in around four in the morning, drunk off her ass, if she didn't stay with whomever she was with. Sometimes she was just a little intoxicated, but there were occasions where she would return blackout drunk and spend the night on the bathroom floor. Will would wake up early the next morning, get her cleaned up, and into bed so the bathroom was available. Maybe she was retaliating for the lack of attention he now provided her. People cope differently, sure, but this felt self-destructive and selfish. And he acted like it wasn't a big deal or that it didn't happen as often as it did. Her behavior took a toll on him, but it didn't change the way he felt about her, so he said. It was definitely the beginning of the end.

It's been my experience that when couples start spending less time together or behave with indifference, it means they feel less of a sense of obligation to one another. There's a disconnect. What I find interesting was Will's motivation for fulfillment. Will changed his previous lifestyle to accommodate her because she did something to him. Now that his book was finished, and he was getting involved in matters related to the book, his obligation shifted to that. The connection they had seemed to be gone.

. . . Will's first book reading, which was at Columbia University, went well. Their philosophy department scheduled Will to be part of a Colloquium Series, an event that announced him as an important new voice in contemporary philosophy, at least that's what he had said. He had invited his parents, whom he hadn't seen since graduation, which meant this would be their first time meeting Lily. With some of the NYU philosophy faculty attending, along with quite a few others from Columbia and the surrounding area, there were nearly two hundred people in attendance. Despite his anxiety, Will did an excellent job. His age and experience weren't even an issue because he clearly knew his subject. He read well and answered questions from the audience, and even towards the end, he had a minor debate with a man who called Will's book anti-philosophy. I don't know why I remember that. What was most memorable about the night, the real reason I'm even bringing this up, is the way Lily behaved around Will's parents. She was a totally different person, like she was trying to win them over. She said all the right things and was so polite and personable. Will's mother whispered into my ear a few times about Will possibly finding *the one*. His father said she was a keeper. I find it funny how people can think after one meeting that people are destined for one another. Given the façade she had constructed, she could really manipulate a situation. Even with the introduction to his parents, a moment that solidified Lily as a real part of his life, that reading was far less important. The event at The New School was the real turning point in their relationship.

Will had called me and said she had shown up pretty drunk and was acting belligerent. I hadn't planned on being there because I had been to like three of his events already. But I told him I would stop by and do my best to make sure she was alright. When I arrived, Will was standing next to Lily with his hand on her lower back kind of guiding her, clearly frustrated. The moment she saw me, she yelled my name and stumbled over to me. It was really bad. I told her I was on my way to grab a drink and maybe a late dinner at Dempsey's and had just stopped by to wish Will good luck. I asked if Will wouldn't mind me stealing her. She said he didn't care whether she was there or anywhere else in the world and agreed to leave with me. I remember Will and I made eye contact. He was obviously relieved. She and I left and got some food, a lot of water, and a few more drinks. What the hell, right? She seemed to be in a better mood and wasn't on the verge of blacking out, typical Lily, but she needed sleep. Nothing good was going to happen in this state. We walked back to the apartment. She talked most of the time about Will changing and not wanting to have fun anymore. The amusing part was that Will hadn't changed. That was Will. He was not a fun person. He was a good person but not a fun person. His work was his main priority.

Once we were inside the apartment, she thanked me for a better night than she would have had. Then she grabbed my head and kissed me. I knew this was not how I wanted it to go, so I walked her to Will's room and put her to bed. We did our best, I would say, to pretend that that didn't happen, aside from the looks that people give one another when they have secrets they choose not to share with others. It's that secret that no matter how small or insignificant it may seem, it's still your unspoken connection.

I think a week or so later, I had taken a personal day and stayed home from work. Will was teaching at the university. Lily and I were alone. It seemed coincidental, but I'm sure subconsciously we had created that scenario. I don't really remember the circumstances of it that well. I had just taken a shower and was either walking to or from the bathroom, probably just in a pair of jeans, and Lily had come out of Will's bedroom, which was right next to the bathroom in the apartment. The near collision was so sudden we startled one another, and my first reaction was to grab her waist to keep her from running into me. She kissed me, which probably seemed like the next logical step in her mind for that encounter. It tasted sour, likely morning breath or the byproduct of vomiting from a night of drinking. Whatever the case was, I couldn't stop kissing her. I remember thinking how I didn't want to betray my best friend, but the feelings I had for her and the way she dug her pelvis into mine at that moment as we stood there—the only option was to go to my room.

Like the drunken kiss, we never talked about that morning. Things between the three of us stayed relatively the same. Will had planned a trip to his parents for the holidays that would have included Lily, but she told him her mother would disown her if she didn't spend it with her. Will left for Buffalo a week or so before Christmas, and Lily went to her mother's townhouse. I was certain I wouldn't see either of them for weeks, but right after Christmas, maybe a day or so, Lily came over. We fucked for days. It was incredible, a nice break from reality.

When Will returned from his parents after New Year's, he had news he was going on a small book tour through New England and some Midwest colleges. He wouldn't be able to teach in the spring, he'd have to work on his dissertation while traveling and doing readings, but most importantly, he wasn't sure what would happen with Lily. I knew what would happen with the two of them—they would break up. He had a career ahead of him, and her life was here. What had surprised me was what happened when Will broke the news about the book tour.

Lily told Will what had happened between us. I don't know if she did because she knew this was over and didn't want to continue the relationship and continue lying to him. Maybe she was trying to manipulate him or keep him in New York. I wish I knew her real intention. All I remember was Will walking into the apartment and accusing me of being a terrible friend and person. He wasn't wrong. By the end of the week, he had moved all his belongings out of the apartment. He didn't return my phone calls. Once Will was gone, Lily and I hooked up a few more times, but eventually it fizzled out, and I stopped seeing her. She was a free spirit who couldn't be kept. She's not in love with people but the idea of things, which is why she probably left everything to find Will in Ohio, to stalk him. That's what she did, right? That's probably why she wanted to hook up with me. The idea of it.

The last time I heard from Will was before the murder. He had called me to ask if I had any idea where Lily was and if I knew whether or not she was in Ohio. He sounded a little unhinged, a little paranoid. Maybe if I would have been a better friend, maybe if he wouldn't have cut in at the party, none of this would have happened. There's such a hindsight bias when it comes to taking responsibility for the choices we make in life, but I guess even the most intelligent people are not immune to human nature.

. . . What does that have to do with my number showing up on her phone? What can I say? She called me from a blocked number, never saying where she was or what she was doing. If I had known she was stalking Will, I might have intervened in some way. Lily was so unpredictable. Unfortunately, Will got caught up in something he never really asked for. I guess, I don't know what else I could say about it. Don't go home with strangers.

Chapter 7

The sun's light crept through a gap in the window's curtains just above the sink. Miniscule silhouettes rushed like frenzied, energized atoms; tiny particles of dust suspended in the air gave the negative space texture. Will's head laid against a loose stack of papers on his kitchen table. With his mouth agape, saliva collected, soaking the paper and obscuring his scribbled notes.

The doorbell rang. A pause. Another ring roused Will slightly. Finally, the doorbell rang a third time accompanied by pounding. Will's head shot up. The soggy page stuck to his face. He removed the paper. His eyes darted to the clock on the microwave. 2:00. *A.m. or p.m.?* The knocking continued as Will hurried to the front door. "Alright, alright," he said, irritated. "I'm coming, goddamn it." He rubbed his eyes and looked through the peephole of the old door. Harvey continued to pound his fist. "Fuck," he whispered. He unlocked the deadbolt, then the knob, and opened the door a few inches. "Jesus, Harvey. What the hell?" He squinted. "What are you doing here?"

"'What the hell?'" Harvey repeated. "That's how you greet me after disappearing for an entire fucking week." Harvey made a face resembling Robert De Niro right before he kicked the shit out of the receiving party. He pointed a finger at Will. "I'll tell you what the hell. The last time I saw you, we were at Moe's, and you were quiet and acting strange. You practically left as soon as we sat down. I shouldn't have to point out how rude it was—that goes without saying. What I don't get is you not showing up to any of your classes this week, no call or email. That's pretty goddamn inconsiderate given what's happening with the department. By the way, I received nine written complaints between your two classes. You'll be lucky if those don't turn into grievances at the end of the semester. So, what the hell is going on, Will?" He crossed his arms.

"I have . . . had vertigo," he stammered.

"You have had vertigo?" Harvey asked mockingly. "Thank you for the medical history."

"No, I mean, yeah, I got verti—"

"Why are we still shouting through the door?" Harvey interrupted. "Aren't you going to invite me in?"

Will mumbled something, but Harvey had already pushed himself inside. He eyed Will. "Jesus Christ. You look like a goddamn junky. Are you on drugs because the last thing I need right now is one of my faculty on drugs?"

Will pushed the door closed and locked the knob. "Like I started to say, I had vertigo. It came out of nowhere." Will paused. "Well not out of nowhere. I had it when I was younger, and sometimes it will come back with stress or if I get a bad enough cold. I haven't been eating or sleeping much because of it."

"Or showering," Harvey said as he walked past Will and toward the kitchen. "Fine. Vertigo. Whatever. But you could've called and left some sort of message about what's going on? That's not like you. I could have found someone to sub or, at the very least, post a sign outside the classroom."

Remembering the papers on the kitchen table, Will hurried after Harvey and tried to squeeze past him and into the kitchen, but Harvey blocked the entrance.

"What the hell happened in here?"

From Will's vantage point, it looked like someone had emptied a trashcan of used and crumpled paper. "Sorry, Harvey. When I couldn't sleep, I was working or at least attempting to work on some ideas."

Harvey walked to the table. "You have the time to do new work, but you can't write me an email. Okay." He picked up a paper, frowning as he glanced at the front and then the back of it. "Work?"

"Don't touch that," Will barked as he tore the piece of paper from Harvey's grip.

Harvey glared at Will. "Seriously, Will. What the hell is wrong with you? This is not like you."

Will dropped the paper on the table. "I'm sorry, Harvey. I've just been so stressed and sleep deprived. I'm not myself. I think everything finally got to me." He paused and put a finger up as if receiving an epiphany. "Why don't I make us some coffee?" He grabbed the glass carafe from the coffee maker and filled it with water. As the liquid mixed with the burnt residue from the pot, the result was something that resembled liver-diseased urine.

Harvey cringed at Will's attempt. He leaned against the counter and then checked the surface before resting his hand. Will poured the contents into the coffee maker's reservoir. He took out an old filter full of spent grounds and discarded it onto the pile of papers in his wastebasket, the grounds scattering to the floor. Harvey shook his head.

"Normally, this wouldn't even be that big of an issue. Worse things have happened with no consequences. But I can't take any chances. Just be aware that one student is taking serious issue with your absence."

"Who?"

"Stephanie Green."

"I'm not surprised."

"I've never seen a student get so upset about not having class. What did you do to her?"

"Nothing. She's an entitled asshole," Will said, scooping new grounds from a Folgers can.

"She probably just finished reading *The Second Sex*." Harvey exhaled quick breaths, noiseless laughter at his own worthless joke. "And now she's ready to take on the patriarchy."

Will finished loading the coffee maker and turned it on. "Aren't you teaching that in your class?"

"God, no. *Ethics of Ambiguity*. We'd never get through the damn book if I had to teach it. I let Elizabeth handle feminism." Harvey paused and looked around. "You should open up a window and get some fresh air in this place." He yanked the curtains apart and opened the window over the sink. "It smells like an ashtray." He did the same to the windows on the back wall of the kitchen. "That's better."

The room seemed to be glowing with the light that filled the space. Will's eyes felt dry, and they ached. He turned the water on again and splashed some on his face. "You mind handing me a paper towel."

Harvey gave the kitchen a once over, and when he didn't see any, he began searching the cupboards.

"Never mind," said Will. He grabbed the hem of his dirty shirt and wiped the water from his face. He blinked a few times and looked at Harvey.

"Boy, you really do look like shit in this light. When was the last time you showered or changed that shirt? Have you looked at yourself?"

Will shook his head as if he couldn't fathom why he was in this condition. "I know Harvey. I'm going to straighten up everything, get dressed, and get back to life."

"With the way Seymour has been acting lately, I'm surprised he hasn't been circling the block every couple of hours."

"Jesus. I completely forgot about that. You think he'd actually—"

"I doubt it, but you never know. He's been on edge lately too, just like everyone else. This whole program reassessment thing has much of the university wondering whether or not they'll still have a job by the end of the year. There is a pretty sizeable group of people gathered outside the office of the president, protesting since Monday. Might be worth joining them at some point. Solidarity and whatnot." He put his hands in his pants' pockets. "Anyhow, it's a shame you left early. We had a good time, and Laroche seemed to be enjoying the company, but you never know how to interpret the French."

My book, thought Will. Given all his concern with finding Lily, he neglected to reach out to Laroche. "I had planned to follow up with him."

"Just do what you were doing before you went rogue."

The coffee maker beeped.

"Here, Harvey. Let me get you a cup." Will reached toward a cupboard.

"Don't bother, Will. I've got to get back to the department and meet with administration. I'll see myself out." Harvey left as Will grabbed a mug. "Take care of yourself," Harvey shouted just before he shut the door. Will ran his fingers through his greasy hair and wondered how the hell this all happened.

The moment he saw Lily in the crowd the faulty latch gave way on the rotten cellar door that held his paranoia, his despair. The clove cigarette in the ashtray, the aroma of perfume in his bedroom. But the phone call to Nick. Did he really not know where Lily was? He seemed convinced on the phone, but the piece of shit was certainly capable of lying for any number of reasons. Fucking Judas. Will hadn't spoken to Nick since he had left New York, and the guy had never attempted amends. After pressing him, Nick finally mentioned Lily's trip, but he rarely talked to her these days. Who knows? That could all be bullshit. Will had spent an entire week gathering a list of dead ends, piles of wasted paper, and hours of pointless inquiries. And for what? To compromise most of his accomplishments—New York all over again. Maybe the stress of the book and conference with Laroche had triggered a nervous breakdown. Maybe that's what he was experiencing, and Lily was just a figment of his exhausted imagination. All was not lost. He was just freaking out a little bit. Maybe some PTSD?

Will poured a cup of black coffee and sat at the table in the chair opposite the one he had "worked" in for most of the week. He lit a cigarette from the pack on the table. When the drapes had been closed, he had seen possibility and perhaps something else. Now with the curtains pulled away and the sunlight filling every inch of the room, his place and his mind were both a mess. He sipped the coffee and grabbed his laptop from underneath a loose pile of papers. He opened it and brought up his email. There was a message from Laroche dated just yesterday, which could be seen as an immediate response. Again, he felt panicked and took a drag from his cigarette, but this brought a wave of nausea. Maybe it was the black coffee on the empty stomach—*when was the last time I ate?*—or the nicotine. Hell, maybe he did have vertigo. He clicked on the subject titled *Book*:

> M. Thierry,
> I read your book on the flight home. Much of what is good about this book, I gather, is taken from or rather influenced by my book. I'm not accusing you of plagiarism, but merely claiming that you've read my book and have noted its successes. I'm sure like the last book, your second will also be a success.
> At this time, there is not a position for you at Sorbonne.

I do not mean this as an insult, but most Americans do not treat philosophy with the same regard as we do in France. It would not work. Bonne chance.

    JL

Will sat stunned. He didn't know what to think, what this meant. He placed his spent cigarette in the nearly overflowing ashtray. Of course, he knew what this meant. Will stood, forcing his chair back abruptly, and raised a balled fist to his lips. He walked in a semi-circle around the back of his chair. "Fuck." He paused for a few seconds. "Fuck, fuck, fuck, fuck." He slammed the screen of his laptop closed, a ridiculous and anticlimactic gesture. He shouted and flung the chair on its side. As he clawed the pile of papers off the table, his arm hit the rim of his mug, which sent the nearly full cup of coffee careening across the kitchen only to shatter on the linoleum floor in front of the sink. "No," he said, feeling defeated and embarrassed.

He looked at the laptop and ashtray still sitting on the table. He glanced over at the puddle of coffee speckled with pieces of white ceramic. A few papers landed in the mess and absorbed the liquid and yellowed like old newspaper. He considered salvaging the papers, but what the hell was the point? It was a meaningless pile of doodles and absurd speculations. It was waste ready to be bagged and thrown away. He left the kitchen and went upstairs to take a shower.

In the bathroom, he stared at himself in the mirror. His hair was matted and greasy. The bags under his bloodshot eyes were more pronounced than usual. A week's worth of stubble protruded from his now thin face. He took a can of shaving gel and a razor from the vanity and turned on the hot water. He squirted the gel into his hand and rubbed it into lather on what was a sad excuse for a beard. When he finished, he undressed and stepped into the shower. He turned the single handle of the faucet not bothering to let the water heat. A quick burst of cold water hit his skin, causing him to flinch and tense until it reached a comfortably hot temperature.

After showering and dressing, he went back downstairs to clean the kitchen and pull himself together. Will opened a few more windows, letting a cool, almost cold breeze cut its way through the house. He tied an overstuffed trash bag and set it at the top of the stairs leading to the backdoor. He grabbed two more bags, placing the first into the kitchen trashcan and stuffing the second with debris from the floor. A picture of Lily in a knitted red hat, sitting on a rock in front of the lake at Central Park laid amidst the papers. Will used the photo when he had questioned people around town as to her whereabouts. What a waste of time. He set the photo on the table and continued filling the bag. He found his cell phone and pressed the power button, but it was dead. He plugged it into a charger on the counter and then wiped up the spilled coffee and gathered the broken cup with a handful of paper towels. He sprayed the floor with Lysol and wiped it dry with more paper towels. He tied the bag and took both outside to his waste bins. Back inside, he immediately went to his phone and turned it on. Within a moment, the phone lit up with a list of text messages, missed calls, and voicemails, the majority of which were from Anne. He scrolled through the texts. The messages began with a concerned tone and ended in outright anger. He dialed Anne's number, and she picked up after the first ring.

"Where the hell have you been, and why haven't you called me?" She didn't give him a second to answer. "You left Moe's acting really weird, which should have been one of the biggest nights of your life, and then you don't return any of my messages. Finally, I hear from Harvey that you no-showed all of your classes this week."

"Well, here's the—"

"Seriously, where the hell have you been? I stopped by your house twice when I was out running. I couldn't tell if you were home or not. Your car was in the driveway, but all the curtains were closed, and you didn't answer the door. I knocked and rang the doorbell repeatedly. I was half tempted to break in just to make sure you hadn't killed yourself. Seriously, what the fuck is going on? This isn't like you—"

The phone jerked from his hands as he paced out of reach of its cord, and the device swung back, slamming into a cupboard door. He grabbed the dangling phone and put it back up to his ear. "Sorry, I dropped the phone. I'm not suicidal. I had vertigo. It was probably from all the stress. I didn't want to make a scene. I've been in bed most of the time because of how bad it's been. I had no idea you called until today. My phone's been dead."

"This sounds like bullshit, Will. Since when is vertigo this bad?"

"Well, I feel better now, and I want to see you. Can we please have lunch and talk?"

"It's almost three, and I'm not hungry. I'll be at the co-op until five."

"Perfect," Will said. "I'm leaving now." Will ended the call. He disconnected his phone, grabbed his keys, and headed out the back door.

Will pulled his car into an open parking spot on the street a few doors down from the Athens Wellness Co-op. He got out and looked around, expecting to see someone watching him. The usual brass bell dinged as he entered the store. The aroma of Nag Champa and vitamins bombarded his nostrils. Anne talked with a woman at the front counter but acknowledged Will with a quick glance and a hand gesture. The woman held two boxes and was too deep into her inquiry to notice him.

"I just want to know which is the better cleanse. Is it the one with kale and flaxseed or the one with acai berry?"

"Both are rich in vitamins and anti-oxidants. It just depends on what you want to get out of the cleanse. The kale will literally flush you out, making you feel lighter, while the acai berry will give you a boost of energy."

The woman shifted her weight from one hip to the other. "Well, Dr. Oz said the acai cleanse eliminates toxins, and Lord knows the way I've been feeling lately, I need to release some toxins."

Anne's irritation was obvious. "Both products are designed to remove toxins from your body, hence the word 'detox.'" She glanced at Will. "But if Dr. Oz recommends it, who am I to disagree? How much would you like?"

"I'm doing it this weekend, so however many I need for Saturday and Sunday. Also, he said that sage has cleansing powers as well. When you burn it—snuffing I think is what he called it—your aura and your living space will be cleansed. I'm really just looking to clean everything this weekend."

"Right. We do carry different kinds of *smudging* sticks in the aromatherapy section. When you burn it, take the smudging stick to every room you want to eliminate negative energy. Typically, people think about their intentions for their space."

"Honey, that sounds wonderful. I will take one of those as well. I'm ready to feel good this weekend."

"Just be sure you light the sage on a fireproof surface and extinguish the flame like you would incense."

Anne grabbed two of boxes of the cleanse, some bound white sage, and rung up the woman. She left without acknowledging Will. Anne stepped from behind the counter.

"I'm so sick of the whole Dr. Oz craze," Anne said, shaking her head. "All you have to do is get endorsed by Oprah and people believe anything you tell them. Women would start eating sand if he told them it sped up their metabolism."

"Technically, he is a real doctor, sort of."

"I'm not afraid to hit you in public. People come here with a list of crap they saw on his show. I can't even suggest anything or try to help with their selection because fucking Dr. Oz already made their decision for them. Why do I have a degree in nutrition when all I am, at this point, is a glorified cashier? They should just go to a grocery store or GNC and stop wasting my time. And that woman doesn't need a detox. She told me all about her love life before you walked in. She just needs a glass of wine and to get laid, some therapy even. Instead, she is going to shit her brains out this whole weekend and burn sage. Her house is going to smell like ass, and she will feel miserable. At work on Monday, she'll brag about what a wonderful 'cleansing experience' she had. So nurturing and spiritual. Just kill me, please."

Will laughed. "I'm sorry."

"You owe me more than an apology. One second." Anne looked to an open doorway, most likely to a back room. "Joan, I'm going to take a walk outside. I'll be back in a few minutes." Anne led Will out the front door and to a bench on the sidewalk near the storefront. She sat on the bench, while Will looked around. He didn't notice anyone he knew or a lingering eye. Soon this part of town would be bustling with the Friday evening crowd. He sat next to her.

"What's really going on?" she asked. Her head tilted slightly and eyes wide.

"Like I said on the phone, the vertigo is mainly to blame. I suppose another part to this is the email I received from Laroche." He lowered his head and then looked back at Anne. "He likes the book, but there's no position available. He said his hands are tied. I guess the combination is what kept me in bed for most of the week. I still feel like shit about it." He paused not knowing where else to navigate this lie.

"You'll get a position at another university in Paris or maybe England. That might be nice. There are plenty of universities in California, and the weather there is so much nicer too." She softened her stare, anticipating his response. "When this book comes out, I'm sure you'll get a bunch of job offers. I know it's going to do well. We'll be able to leave this shithole. I mean, there'll be nothing keeping us here." Despite her optimism, her eyes appeared glassy as if she might cry at any moment. Then again it could have been the breeze.

Will faked a smile just as he had faked the excuses, half-assed. "You're right. It'll be fine. This is just a minor setback. I don't even know why I thought Sorbonne was an option. Laroche hates me. I should have tried harder at the conference to get in his good graces."

Anne made a few more consolatory remarks and even placed her hand on his arm. Then she got up, claiming she needed to get back inside. Before she walked into the co-op, she turned to Will and said, "I'm still mad at you. Please don't do that again. We are doing this together." With the ding of the bell, she was inside, and Will was alone, kind of. Always accompanied by his thoughts, he couldn't shake Lily and where she was and what she was doing. Why couldn't he just tell Anne the real reason? She'd understand. He scanned the faces of as many people as he could see before getting into his car and driving to the university to see if he couldn't clear the air among his colleagues. As Will entered the philosophy department, he didn't hear or see anyone aside from Sylvie who sat behind a computer screen. It felt like a Friday afternoon, kind of. Sylvie briefly glanced at Will with little expression, but then looked with full attention. "Will, where have you been? I thought something terrible had happened."

He smiled sheepishly. Sylvie's "hellos" were so genuine and welcoming, despite the overenthusiasm. She was too good for this place. "Yeah, I don't know how it happened, but I came down with vertigo."

"Vertigo?" she said, confused.

"It's an inner ear thing," Will said, pointing to his ear and shrugging. "I first had an episode of it in college. Ever since, if I get sick or too stressed, it comes on kind of hard."

"Aw." Sylvie hugged Will, catching him off guard. She continued holding him.

He couldn't tell if she was slightly nuzzling his neck. It seemed she pushed her pelvis close to his. What exactly was this woman thinking? He knew what she was thinking. He backed away enough to not seem rude, while holding her arms in a mock-caressing sort of way. "You're too sweet, Sylvie." He smiled. "Thank you for caring."

"You feel thin, Will. When was the last time you ate?"

"You know, I just ate." He let her go and headed to the department mailboxes. "I stopped by to check my mail and make sure I didn't cause too much inconvenience." He stuck his hand inside the wooden box labeled THIERRY. "I heard I received nine complaints?"

"Yeah, to put it lightly, Harvey was not thrilled," she said, walking back to her desk, fiddling with something on her blouse. "I tried to discourage them from doing so, but they were dead set. It happened yesterday afternoon."

Will shuffled through the very small stack of papers and envelopes from the mailbox, keeping the important things, placing them in his bag, and discarding the rest in the recycling. He turned around, but before he began to say anything, he thought he noticed the opening of Sylvie's blouse had one more button undone revealing some cleavage and the edge of a beige bra. "I need to ask you a question." He looked around.

"Everybody's left except for Dr. Harlowe, and Harvey will be back any moment."

He leaned close to her and put a hand on her back particularly out of privacy, but he figured he would use the apparent sexual tension to his advantage. "Do you think Seymour had anything to do with the complaints?"

"Not that I know of." She leaned in a little closer. Will could feel her breath as she talked. "However, he has been complaining and asking about you and Laroche when he was here."

The department door opened, and Will immediately straightened his posture. Harvey stepped in.

"Will," he said, clearly surprised. "I didn't expect to see you until Monday."

"I took what you said to heart, and I'm trying to get things together for next week. Sylvie was catching me up on everything I've missed."

"You look better already." Harvey walked toward his office as if catching up with something himself.

"Thanks. What are your plans for tonight?"

Harvey stopped and turned toward Will. "I'm supposed to meet Elli," Harvey said trying to conceal an expression that somewhat resembled surprise or maybe confusion.

Sylvie and Will had similarly confused looks.

For the briefest moment Will thought Harvey had said Lily. "Lily?" asked Will.

"Lily? No. Who's that? What I meant to say was Elizabeth. I've got a lot on my mind. I'm meeting with Elizabeth and then going to dinner with Anne. Just a typical Friday evening."

"She's still in her office, Harvey."

"I know."

"Anyhow, I'm heading out. Sylvie knows I'm alive, and I have my mail." Will smiled at Sylvie, and she grinned as she returned to her previous task, whatever that was.

"Take care, Will," said Sylvie looking at the papers on her desk. "I'm glad to know you're okay."

Will left the department and walked through Gordon Hall, making the usual twists and turns that the old semi-labyrinthian building held, every corner looking like the last. *Why hasn't anyone thought to color code this building to make it easier to navigate?* he thought. *I'm sure Sylvie knows why.* He left through the back entrance. Once in his car, rather than driving home or to some restaurant for an overdue meal, he pulled onto the bordering street and parked in a spot shaded by some oak trees and waited.

Jacques Laroche
At his home in Paris, telephone interview

APRIL 2010

No. No. Nothing struck me as particularly awful about the town of Athens or its university. I have not visited many public institutions in America, but it certainly met my expectations of the American University: very little focus on scholarship and academic rigor, an obsession with athletics, an entire culture in and of itself, much like a town within a town. I only spent a few days there, but I could see the students rarely viewed themselves as scholars but more so as members of a club, some of whom barely meet the qualifications. There was a lack of an intellectual community despite the faculty's best efforts. Having arrived the weekend of the university's homecoming, this sentiment was very apparent. Throngs of students dressed in the school's colors, some even with paint on their bodies. Along with a parade and other events, the culmination was with a football game. This seems to me to be very indicative of the American way of life, more focus on capitalism and entertainment. Having never traveled to the Midwest, I had the feeling that if one was not in some way connected to one of these universities, then one was the other, an outsider, even as a citizen of the town in which the school resides. And in this way, the university functions much in a utilitarian manner. You would not see this in France's public university system, not to this extent.

So, it is a wonder to me that Thierry would leave an institution like New York University only to come to this place. The city life, the academics—such brilliant individuals who teach there—and the general milieu of that place is in no way comparable to Athens. No? Perhaps this is why he approached me as he did. Not at the conference but through email. I am truly surprised that we had the correspondence we did during these last few months. Having been the main critic of his singular work, one would assume he viewed me as an adversary. But to be clear, I never intended to respond to Thierry's ideas, let alone contribute to the discussion of the death of philosophy. I only discovered who this man was one day by way of my colleagues at the Sorbonne a few years ago. One of them had received copies from the publisher, the same university press that published his works, and the book was what you call a hot topic. It became a conversation piece among other groups with whom I associate. And yes, I read it. I needed to know why they were all so fascinated with this book.

It was in no way a philosophical treatise as most debut works are. The book was a catalogue of sorts: part statistics, part literature review, and part narrative. Broken down into three sections, the first was a history of the philosophers who had claimed philosophy was either dead or dying. Kant. Nietzsche. Heidegger. Foucault. Rorty. Derrida. The list goes on. The second section was a collection of statistical data and case studies regarding philosophy majors in universities and professions, consisting of enrollment, graduation and retention rates, post-baccalaureate education, department closures, employment rates in the field, and other aspects. Sure, it showed a significant trend, perhaps, but that was really all it was. The third and final section was an attempt at theorizing, in a clichéd narrative form, the "inevitable" death of philosophy. Thierry gave philosophy the feminine pronoun "she" and essentially wrote how *she would eventually wither away and die*. Again, not an unusual metaphor for reason and the study of our discipline: "she" is his Lady Philosophy.

The book was a three-part fallacy. Lifting random quotes and fragmented theories out of context from some of philosophy's greatest minds and then re-contextualizing them may have appeared to give his argument, if you want to call it that, some substance or validity.

However, merely stringing together similar ideas and stating something does not make it true or imminent. There needs to be pragmatic analysis and reason to support it. This was a hackneyed style of discourse, the utilization of metaphor as a substitution for an actual theoretical framework.

Coming from some no name American, I discarded the book and paid very little attention to what others said. But as his popularity grew in the realm of philosophy and his book sold more and more copies, I decided I must write a review, which later developed into a critique that revealed his mistakes. I carefully wrote an argument discrediting his proposition for the *death of philosophy*. By explaining philosophy's continued progress of elucidating life's problems, essentially bastardizing and orphaning each sub-field, eventually what we call philosophy will be nothing more than the self-help section at—what is that store?—Borders. Philosophy thrives through its foundations, and if those are discarded, then philosophy becomes shallow, superficial, or transforms into one or more of the other disciplines such as physics, mathematics, psychology, etc. As long as people possess the desire to explore and understand the world and the self, philosophy will flourish. The progress of philosophy is that it continues to not make progress. Rather, its ideas are explored and expressed with more intricate and sophisticated language; this is its development. The essential questions explored by the ancients are still being discussed today. What is the meaning of life? What is reality? How is the conscious mind connected to the body? I did not want to romanticize this the way Thierry had. My book was published, the critics and remote public discussed the controversy, and it seemed that people became more aware of the present situation.

It was not until Dr. Buchanan invited me to speak at their small conference that I had any prior communication with William Thierry. Once I had critiqued his book and had written a more precise and logical theory around the idea, I moved on. I may have done a few speaking engagements or interviews, mostly in Europe, some in New York. What philosophy professors are concerned with is the miasma of philosophy itself and rarely with what is occurring in the culture. They are constantly discussing Philosophy with a capital "P" and in the past tense. They regurgitate the words of so many others with great repetition but rarely invent their own ideas. Fine. They are educators who know their subjects well, but disciplines cannot survive on education alone. The disciplines must progress and continue to develop and grow. The death of philosophy affects very few and is the worst kind of theory: metaphilosophy. It is a hall of mirrors or a set of Russian dolls, labyrinthine in nature. Yet it masquerades as the Apocalypse for philosophy, the eschatology of philosophy, something that Derrida addressed when discussing Kant. It satisfies the inherent need for the finite. Maybe the death wish as Freud theorized the concept of Thanatos. Maybe entropy. Maybe the American idea of "going out with a bang." If this is indeed an apocalyptic set of ideas, then Thierry is intent on being St. John of Self-Reference.

Nevertheless, William Thierry is like many philosophers of the past who seemingly dedicate most of their life's work to unpacking, extending, and redefining a given topic or theory. I would say that is a large portion of twentieth century thought. I came to this realization when we began the aforementioned correspondence upon committing to speak at the conference. His first email had discussed his completion of a second book about the same subject, one that repudiates and re-contextualizes his ideas to the degree of being something completely different. He likened himself to Wittgenstein saying, "Like Wittgenstein, I have written a book that completely negates my first. I believe this will serve as my *Philosophical Investigations*."

It was rather absurd to compare oneself to one of the greatest minds of the twentieth century. Wittgenstein's works were written thirty years apart from one another, where Thierry had maybe three years at most. Wittgenstein showed us what language could be, whereas Thierry is showing us what happens when a snake eats its own tail. He claimed that his first book was a reaction to research he had conducted in graduate school. He confessed he had written with a mixture of uncertainty and haste. Uncertainty is necessary for enlightenment and intellectual struggle, but one should be remiss to record every act of aporia and publish it, let alone label it as philosophy.

I read his book on the flight back to Paris. It was better, much better, but it felt as if he had written it for me. I may not linger long on a particular subject, as I have said, but I know what I have written. This book stole, if I may be so bold, many of my ideas and attempted to recast them in a way where philosophy is not dying in essence, but we are intentionally killing it. I should have felt flattered, but flattery is not a philosophy. I considered reviewing the book, suggesting plagiarism, but I am not a literary critic, I do not have time for that, and there would be plenty of reviews in other publications, especially since the murder of that woman. I cannot remember exactly where I read the article, perhaps the *New York Times*. My initial thought was, 'there goes his career,' but then there is a certain celebrity that often accompanies a man of ideas who has killed someone, particularly an intimate partner—a kind of mythos is born. Given the nature of the relationship with the woman and Dr. Buchanan, this is a situation one might observe in literature or film or some crime documentary. Madness has often accompanied a great many individuals who lived a life of either profound creativity or intellectual rigor, but of those, few have taken the lives of their spouses and have later profited off the actual incident. The writer William Burroughs comes to mind, having shot his wife while under the influence of alcohol during a dubious game of William Tell. He went on to have a successful literary career and was labeled a genius and revered as an iconoclast for his influence. But perhaps more analogous was the Marxist philosopher Louis Althusser who strangled his wife. After the murder, an incident he immediately reported to the authorities, the man then spent a few years in a psychiatric hospital where he wrote a memoir recounting the event, which later became a bestseller in France. And when we talk about these men, we rarely discuss them as murderers, for their dead wives are mere footnotes in their lives and legacies, byproducts of their madness, whether psychiatric or drug-induced. The ideas and genius of these individuals are what matter and are celebrated and studied, rarely the indiscretions of their behavior. And despite Derrida having said he wished the great philosophers would have written about their sex lives to see the kind of role it played in their philosophy or influence it had on their work, what would we learn about them from that information? That really seems secondary to me. Their work is what lives on long after they are gone, not their domestic affairs.

Jack Ballard
In his apartment in Athens

NOVEMBER 2009

Before everything happened, I really looked up to the guy. He was kind of the reason why I went back to school. Prior to getting into the philosophy program at Athens University, I felt like I didn't have much going for me. I had failed out of this small liberal arts college in Indiana on an academic scholarship. I loved talking about ideas at the time, but I guess I just didn't have the discipline or motivation. I pretty much did what most eighteen-year-olds do right out of high school: party and try to get laid. When that didn't work out, I moved back to Athens to live with my mom and help her pay the bills. I worked with my mom's friend, this contractor, doing trade work: carpentry, painting, and some electrical. The money was fine, but it wasn't what I wanted to do with my life. I was also working Friday and Saturday nights at the coffee shop downstairs, which is my only job now that I'm in school. Many of my friends hang out there or at least they did a few years back. They've either moved on or don't come around much anymore. We spent most nights talking about art, music, books, and philosophy. It wasn't anything too highbrow; we were just excited about what seemed new to us and were still full of dreams and aspirations. When you love ideas and you work with your hands, like most of us did (some of them were landscapers, factory workers, or would work with me from time to time), you tend to read a lot of books or watch arthouse because it feels like you're wrestling with something intellectual, and you're part of the larger ongoing conversation. I would read the things that were popular with my friends or reminiscent of the art or movies we were into, stuff like Baudrillard, Derrida, Zizek, DeLillo, Philip K. Dick, *House of Leaves* and *Infinite Jest*—the postmodern stuff. At some point, I knew I wanted to get back into school, so I enrolled at Athens University. It felt so weird. I was probably the only twenty-five-year-old in a group of seventeen- and eighteen-year-olds going on a campus tour that I had first taken nearly a decade ago. It was a déjà vu sort of experience, but it also felt insincere because I told myself I wouldn't settle like all the other people I knew from Athens who just enrolled because it was in their back yard and the next thing to do. The joke about Athens University was, and still is, that the only score required for your acceptance was your pulse. The philosophy department was hyping, as much as they could, William Thierry, a new professor who would join them in the fall as a visiting philosopher. I had never heard of him, nor had I read any of his work. I remember stopping by the campus bookstore at the end of the visit to pick up his book. I literally couldn't put it down. I had never read anything like it. He talked about philosophy in ways that resembled the postmodern stuff I had read. The death and transformation of philosophy—all really self-referential stuff—seemed to go against the status quo. It made me want to study philosophy even more.

Needless to say, I've become pretty close with Will over the last two years. He's taught me so much and encouraged me to look deeper and push myself, things I should have realized already but just didn't. He'd talked about the possibility of NYU, his alma mater, for grad school, and I know at least two people who are in grad school there because of him. I figured opportunities like that weren't available for someone like me. Will was a great guy, and I still think he is great for the most part. Prior to what had happened with that woman, there's nothing about Will you could really find fault with. He was a good professor who spent a lot of time on his writing and was easy to relate to. But then there was that week he disappeared after the conference, and from there on, things just sort of spiraled, I guess. I mean, I still feel bad for putting in a complaint to the department. I didn't really want to do it, but Stephanie made a pretty convincing case. As a professor, you can't just not show up to classes without any notice. It's unprofessional, and you should be held accountable, at the very least, because we are paying for you to be there. Part of the reason I wrote a complaint was, and this is just between you and me, Stephanie and I are kind of dating, and I didn't want her and her friends to ostracize me. And thinking back, they were just complaints. It's not like he would be fired over something like that. And honestly, the complaints don't really bother me that much. What still doesn't sit right is what Will asked me to help him do. I figure this is probably important to mention.

It was Friday of the week Will didn't show for class, and I got a call from him sometime in the afternoon, maybe three or four o'clock. I was surprised and a little nervous because I hadn't seen him all week and had just submitted that complaint the day before. I didn't anticipate a confrontation and figured that's why he was calling. Instead, he asked me if I wanted to get dinner at Xeno's Akropolis. What was I going to say, no? It's cool when your professor makes plans to hang out. Like, you want to have that kind of relationship.

When I got there, probably ten or fifteen minutes later, he was standing in the parking lot looking kind of agitated or whatever. As I was getting ready to lock my bike and go inside, he asked if I knew my way around Graybeard Suites, the apartments across the street. Of course, I did. I have friends who live there. The place is basically student housing, aside from some low-income tenants and month-to-month renters. It's not really a great place to live at all. Then again, none of the places around that part of town are. It's mostly slumlord student rentals. As he approached me, he quickly began talking about wanting to know if there were certain people staying in the place. I suggested we go to the office to ask, but it was closed. Realistically, the office is always closed. I think I've seen the owner downtown more times than I have seen him at those apartments, unless there's a party he's decided to crash. And who wants your weird, old landlord at the party? Any time I do see him downtown, he looks like he's trying to avoid people or he's with a few other old hippie friends, some of whom are also Athens business owners. They come into the coffee shop almost every morning and talk about how they hate the way the town has changed.

Typical white guy paranoia. It's probably their generation and the pot.

Anyway, Will made it clear he wanted to basically spy on whoever was in one of the apartments. I think it was the second floor, second apartment over or maybe the third one. It was whichever one they found her in. I told him there were windows in the back, so we walked around. He had the idea to hoist me up so I could look into the apartment's window and catch a glimpse of whoever was in there. The whole situation sounded weird, especially given his absence from class, but the weirdest part was that he wouldn't tell me who he was looking for. He just wanted to know who I saw when I looked in. So, who did I see? There wasn't like a perfect view of the whole room so I'm not completely sure like what was happening, but Dr. Buchanan and the dead woman—I mean, she wasn't dead at the time—were talking and then they kissed. It was just so weird being there and seeing that. I was struggling to stand on Will to look through the window, and I didn't want them to see my face like I was some perv. I lost my balance and then fell, practically broke my ankle in the process. That's really all I remember.

Chapter 8

When Will reached Main Street, he turned left, making out Harvey's Volvo in the distance. He followed slowly, never losing sight: past the co-op, over the bridge, and into south Athens. The Volvo's left turn signal blinked a few yards before the entrance of the Graybeard Suites. Will slowed and pulled his car into the parking lot of the Greek diner across the street. Xeno's Akropolis was the only Greek restaurant in town, and the locals and college kids alike adored the place for its cheap coffee and killer spanakopita. The place was always busy, so it wasn't difficult for Will to camouflage himself. He sat in the idling beamer, waiting for Harvey's next move.

Harvey got out of his vehicle and zig-zagged his way around parked cars to the building's outside stairwell, keeping his head down the whole way. He took the stairs to the second floor, and walked past the first door, the second, and finally stopping at the third. Without a knock or apparent hesitation, Harvey entered the apartment.

Will sat for a moment wondering what he should do. He skimmed the cars in the parking lot of the Graybeard. He didn't see Elizabeth's wagon, but that didn't mean she wasn't already there. Will might have missed her getting into Harvey's vehicle when he had left the building. Will shook the idea from his mind. The sleep deprivation alone had him questioning his awareness and his logic. Why would Harvey drive all the way down here? Was he having an affair with a student? That had to be it. There's no real reason for a professor to be at the Graybeard. It was unofficial student housing as far as he knew. And since Will had been to Xeno's plenty of times, he had seen students walk over in sweatpants, looking hungover, and ready to eat something greasy.

But how would he figure out what Harvey was up to?

Maybe he could pay one of the residents to knock on the door and try to catch a glimpse that way. Give a college kid twenty bucks for beer and he'll practically do anything. Then again this wasn't a place that rented rooms hourly or even daily. He grabbed his phone and scrolled through his list of contacts, landing on Jack Ballard. He put the phone to his ear.

"Yeah, Jack? It's Will, your professor. Yeah, I'm fine. Wanna grab a bite to eat? How quickly can you get to Xeno's? Great, see you in ten."

Will leaned against his car as Jack rolled up to Xeno's on the same orange road bike he rode all over town. Will didn't even know if the guy actually owned a vehicle. Jack was still youngish and also lived locally, but there were times when Will had seen him riding that same bike in the snow during winter, one pantleg up and wearing a large parka and matching orange helmet. Did he so adamantly desire to save the environment that he'd ride a bike in inclement weather or was it hipster cred that had him pedaling through slush and zero degree wind chill no doubt eating shit from time to time on a patch of black ice? When Jack caught sight of Will, he quickly dismounted and walked the bike the last few yards.

"Hey, Will. It's been a minute. Where have you been?"

"Long week, Jack. I was a little under the weather, to say the least, but I'm feeling better. I had a nasty case of vertigo," said Will.

"That sucks. I had a friend with vertigo. He took the semester off because he was constantly dizzy. It seemed like he was at the doctor every other month. Turned out to be some kind of chronic inner ear infection."

"Before we grab a bite to eat, I need a favor. Are you familiar with this place?"

"Yeah, I've eaten here my whole life."

"No," said Will. He pointed across the street. "Graybeard Suites."

"Sure. I have friends who live there, and I've been to some parties. The dude that owns the place is alright. He tried to sell me weed a few times."

"I need to know who is staying in the third apartment over on the second floor, but I don't want whoever is in there to know I'm asking."

Jack made a face, unable to hide his suspicion. "I could ask my friends to keep an eye out for you."

"I need to know now. It's very important." Will looked at the apartments for a few seconds. "Are there windows in the back of the place?"

"You're not suggesting we break into the apartment, are you?"

"Of course not. I'm suggesting we attempt to see who's inside." Will was already heading toward the building.

"Wait up."

Will rounded the side stairwell to the building's rear. Given the landscape, it was only about ten feet from the ground to the second story window. Dense pine trees bordered the lot, and the ground floor windows all had curtains. The second-story windows were mostly curtainless. Will was already eyeing the third window when Jack appeared with his bike. Will made a face that implied "what the hell took you so long?"

"I'm not about to leave the bike out front. Someone tried to steal it one time when it was locked outside of Moe's. Asshole fucked up the paint."

Will looked back at the window while Jack set his bike against a tree.

"What I'll do," said Will, "is hoist you up so you can look in the window and tell me who's there. Just don't let anyone inside see you."

"Wait. Are there people inside? I don't know about this, man." Jack eyed the window. "What if we just get a window table at Xeno's? Then we'll see whoever leaves."

"Don't be stupid. We're already here. It'll be quick. If anyone asks, we'll say we're locked out or something." Will squatted against the brick building with his arms hanging in front of him, fingers locked together ready to grip the sole of Jack's shoe. He nodded at his hands. "It will only take a minute."

Jack worked up the nerve to shimmy Will. He backed up a couple yards and then took a few quick steps forward for momentum. Placing one foot in Will's hands, he sprung upward toward the window. Will lifted with all he could as Jack pushed off the ground. Rather than the awkward shuffling and pawing, the two moved in perfect unison. Instead of gripping the window's ledge, however, Jack smacked the pane of glass with two open palms, resulting in a loud, hollow *thump*.

"Fuck," Jack shouted.

"Jesus," Will whisper screamed. "I should have had you hoist me. Can you see anything?"

"Hold on, man. They're going to see me." Jack lifted himself to the point where his forehead and eyes were over the horizon of the windowsill. He could see Dr. Buchanan? Yes, Dr. Naked-ass Buchanan had his hand around some young, equally naked woman, with dark hair. They stood next to a bed, kissing. Dr. Buchanan pulled away slowly as the woman sat on the very edge of the bed, which was visible from Jack's vantage point. The woman glanced at the window.

Jack froze.

Something jumped inside of him. His heart raced. He couldn't break eye contact. She slid off the bed and got down on her knees in a way that seemed artificial, choreographed. She looked up at the professor who looked down at her, his hand clasped on her shoulder, and she mouthed something. He immediately closed his eyes and grabbed her head. She took his penis into her mouth. She looked at Jack as her head slowly bobbed. She gripped the professor's ass. Her stare was unflinching, and Jack had the strange feeling, given the window's frame and the aspect of what he saw, that he was watching pornography where the "actress" knew every cue, especially the part where she stares into the camera simulating desire for the viewer, a faux connection. He felt an erection stir.

"What are they doing?" Will asked, breaking Jack's concentration and causing him to lose his balance.

"Let me down."

Will did his best to lower the student, but Jack, unsettled by the scene, quickly let go of the window's ledge causing Will to teeter, holding all of Jack's weight. Jack jumped and landed at an awkward angle, which sent a sharp pain through his leg.

"Shit," yelled Jack as he fell to the ground.

"What happened?" asked Will.

Jack sat up and rubbed his right ankle with both hands. "I think I broke my fucking ankle."

"No, I mean what did you see inside?"

"Jesus, dude. Give me fucking second," Jack said. He continued to rub his ankle that was already swelling. "They were . . . kissing."

"Kissing? Who was kissing?" asked Will, leaning closer to Jack.

"Dr. Buchanan and some woman."

"Was it Elizabeth?"

"Who?"

"Dr. Harlowe from the department." His voice was getting louder. "Was he kissing her?"

"Whoa, man. Chill. I don't know who he was kissing, but it wasn't her or his wife."

"Of course, it wasn't his wife," said Will, shaking his head. "Who the hell takes their wife to a shitty apartment complex in town to fuck?"

"I don't know. People do strange things." Jack stood. "Fuck."

"What?"

"I'm pretty sure it's sprained, maybe broken." He limped to his bike and reached into the small messenger bag that hung from his seat. "I need a cigarette."

"So, what did she look like?" asked Will, unconcerned with Jack's predicament.

"I don't know. Thin. Long, dark brown hair. Attractive?" He pulled a pouch of American Spirit tobacco out of his bag. He took out a rolling paper and pinched some tobacco onto the paper. "Why the hell do you care so much?"

Unprepared for the question, Will's face went blank. "You wanted me to look into the Dr. Buchanan issue, didn't you?"

"Seriously? This is how you're doing it?" Jack licked the edge of the thinly rolled cigarette. "What the fuck does this have to do with his alcoholism and teaching style?"

"You can't mention this to anyone."

Jack placed the cigarette at the corner of his lips. "I won't," he said out of the side of his mouth. "First of all, this is shady as hell. We look like we're either trying to break in or, at the very least, pervs." He lit the cigarette and inhaled. "I hang out here. If anyone sees me," he exhaled, "I'll be known as the creepy guy who looks into everyone's windows. I don't need that shit."

Will considered asking Jack to hoist him up so he could identify the woman. But why push his luck? This was not going at all how he had anticipated. Somehow Will would have to come up with some explanation that didn't make him sound psychotic. Then again, he was the guy who missed an entire week of work because of his mysterious case of vertigo. "Alright, let's go." He took a pack of Camels from his pocket, pulled one out, and put it between his lips. Jack handed him a lighter, and he lit the cigarette.

Will led the way, reemerging from the back of the building. Jack slung his small bag over his shoulder and walked his bike, or rather limped while using his bike as support. Will turned back to Jack but refrained from saying anything more about the incident. "I'm sorry about your ankle, Jack. I didn't mean for this to happen."

"It's definitely swelling. I just need to put ice on it."

"You still want to eat?"

"Dude, I lost my appetite."

"Can I at least give you a ride back to your apartment or wherever you need to be?"

"I'm fine. I don't have anywhere to be at the moment." He took a long hit and exhaled. "I'll just take it easy and coast back to my place." He put his right leg carefully over the bike.

"Uphill?"

"Really, it's fine."

"Again, I'm sorry about your ankle. I'll make it up to you." He exhaled smoke.

Jack held the expression of a wounded animal: affectionately pitiful. "Yeah, sounds good." He put his rolled cigarette back to his lips, this time clenching it in his mouth. It looked like a joint. He pushed off with his good foot and then swiped the ground a few more times with the same foot like a little kid learning to ride. He didn't look back.

Will stood in the complex's parking lot, cigarette in hand. He looked yet again to the third apartment door on the second floor. He walked across the parking lot to the other end of the building where the Graybeard office was located. Numerous sun-bleached flyers and pieces of paper were taped to the inside of office's large pane glass window. The office door had a faded OPEN sign. He stood outside and took a few more hits of his cigarette before he flicked it into a bucket half full of caked sand, soggy butts, and some wads of gum. He tried the handle. Locked. *So much for signs*, he thought. He put his face close to the large window and cupped his hands around his eyes, trying to block out enough light to see into the place. The lights were off, and there was clearly no one inside. He considered telling Anne about Harvey, but what was the point. As fucked up as things seemed, he didn't need one more situation that would explicitly involve him, let alone one where he coerced a student into being a peeping Tom. There was nothing really left to do but return to his car and drive home. So much for a typical Friday evening.

Anne Buchanan
In the living room of her home

NOVEMBER 2009

If it wasn't for my piece-of-shit husband who can't keep his dick in his pants, none of this would have happened. I don't actually care about him fucking around, not at this point. I was going to leave him for Will, but that's not happening, not now. I just don't understand. It's not like she was drop-dead gorgeous. She was thin, pale, and sickly looking, in my opinion. But, apparently, she was a slut, and I suppose some guys like that kind of thing. What guy doesn't want a woman with no self-respect or boundaries? She probably let them do whatever they wanted to her. I just can't believe it.

Like, who in their right mind comes all this way after what—two years!—and rents a room so they can spy on an ex-boyfriend? A fucking stalker, that's who. And who knows how long this had been happening. I just can't wrap my head around it. Then she seduces my husband. Why him? What lies did she tell that were so enticing? No woman in her right mind would do something like that. Normal people don't do that. They just don't.

And now everything is ruined. With Will. With Harvey. With my life. Sure, I was unhappy and feeling stagnant, but what marriage doesn't have it peaks and valleys. When I think back to when I met Harvey, he was exactly what I needed at the time. He was smart, successful, handsome, and talked a lot about Paris and philosophy. It was charming. Then again, that's his schtick, but it was new and sexy and made me believe we'd do exciting things together. I instantly fell for him, and in a year and a half, we were married. I soon realized I was secondary to his work. The talk about Paris was just talk. We never went anywhere, actually. He preferred to read about it in books and talk about Sartre and watch French New Wave movies. It's like he wished he lived in another era, but he wanted to experience those things as a spectator. It was so pathetic. I realized that even though I basically had everything I could ask for, I was married to someone whose only excitement came from work, bourbon, and some bullshit version of "the life of the mind." I had not signed up for that.

When Will arrived sometime in the second year of our marriage, I realized I had made a mistake. Everyone else saw Will's obvious traits: skill, youth, and good looks. But I could see what Harvey saw. Will was a savior of sorts. Harvey was sure that he would save the department. And as stupid as it sounds, I thought Will would save me. How dramatic and naïve, right? Realistically, what was he really saving me from? A life of financial comfort and occasional boredom? Harvey was stable, charming, powerful in his own right, and he, for the most part, took care of me. The sex was fine. He was a confident but selfish lover. He took control, which I liked, but it was always more about him and less about me. At times, I felt like I was married to Ernest Hemingway, given his drinking and occasional misogyny. Other people have endured much worse in relationships. But the excessive drinking and working and middle-of-fucking-nowhere Ohio just all of a sudden felt so depressing when I met Will. I could tell Will and I shared a longing for something else, and it was clear my relationship with Harvey had an expiration date. There's no doubt in my mind he could have bought me my own yoga studio and funded whatever kind of endeavor I wanted, but eventually, I would find myself attracted to someone else and have some pathetic affair with a guy in one of my classes who isn't really all that attractive or interesting out of the sake of convenience or necessity or just plain boredom, and I didn't want that. That sounds miserable, but it's how I felt. And that's when I knew I wanted Will.

I didn't show any interest in Will at first, and in fact, I even avoided him. When Will was at our home twice a week for dinner or drinks,

I'd stay in the kitchen or watch television or say I was meeting a friend for lunch, always making a point not to linger or make too much eye contact. I came to more events and played the devoted show wife to Harvey, only speaking a few words to Will when we were together. This way Harvey felt like he could trust Will.

In late spring of Will's first year, Harvey attended a conference in Boston for a long weekend. I casually invited Will over for a nice fire in the backyard and a beer. I thought having a beer was friendly and fun. It gave the impression we were just two pals "shooting the shit." Nothing sexy about it. If I had said a fire and wine, well, that could have been seen as seductive. Wine implies romance or passion and usually you share a bottle of wine with another person, which is somewhat intimate. I didn't want to suggest too much and run the risk of him not coming over. When he arrived, we built a small fire in the back and had a few beers and made small talk. We talked about all the places each of us had been, how I moved here after a bad breakup to stay with my aunt, how I couldn't seem to stay in one place for too long. Being here for the last four years was the longest I'd stayed anywhere since college, and even in college I would spend most of the summers traveling. It was the privilege of having a father who was a doctor. At some point I switched to red wine and offered Will a glass. He took it and began talking about his time in New York, something he had only alluded to previously. I suppose I had pushed him to talk about it by bringing up the year I had lived in New York.

We were onto the second bottle when he brought up Lily. He told me how they met and what life was like when they dated. He kept looking off and pausing during parts of the story. I figured it was the wine finally getting to him. Then he brought up the stuff about how she basically ruined his life in New York.

She fucked his roommate Nick who was supposedly his best friend at the time. Don't get me wrong. I'm no stranger to infidelity, but if you're someone's best friend, you don't do something like that. You just don't. You respect boundaries. When Will found out, he ended up leaving for a small book tour. Just took what he needed, put the rest in storage, and left.

That's when Lily began spreading lies about him. She'd hang around the NYU Philosophy building and tell students he'd been dismissed for sleeping with his students, some even high school age. She started rumors that he was bad-mouthing the faculty. They took away his teaching assistantship and suggested Will only return to campus when he was to defend his dissertation. Did you know they can dismiss you from your graduate program for something like that? The thought of spending two, three, four years working towards something only to be told you can no longer continue due to salacious hearsay. You would think they'd need evidence but no. They can just deem you unfit to continue. It's such bullshit. But that wasn't even the worst part.

They had an incident in Central Park. Yeah, she had taken him there to confess about the stuff with Nick. They weren't sitting on a bench or in a somewhat private area. They were just in the middle of one of the walking paths, people all around them. She and Will began arguing, of course, like any couple in this very situation. According to Will, at some point, she told him off and turned to walk away, but Will grabbed her. That's when she flipped out. I don't believe force is ever necessary, but that was far from aggressive. What do you do with something you don't want to lose? What are we presumed to do as people? We hold on to the things we love or care about, so we don't lose them. We don't want to let them go. Once he grabbed her, she screamed something like, "Don't touch me. Let go of me." From what Will said, she didn't have trouble making a scene. The argument, if you can call it that, drew a lot of attention, which was probably the last thing Will wanted. Two larger guys approached them and asked if everything was alright. She told them Will had just slept with her best friend and wouldn't let go of her or leave her alone. He told them she was a liar, and they were only having a conversation. Apparently, one of them hit Will without warning, which immediately turned into the both of them kicking the shit out of him. From what Will remembers before he was knocked unconscious was Lily standing and watching with no inherent look of concern. Nothing. She just turned and walked away. Luckily there were park cops nearby who broke up the fight. They arrested the two men and sent Will to the ER. He's lucky they stopped the two when they did. It could have been so much worse. But she stood there with no expression and watched two strangers hit and kick her boyfriend. And then she just walked away like it didn't even matter. Who does that? I would never do that to anyone, especially someone I loved. She was so fucked up.

At this point in our conversation, I had no words. It seemed like this was the first time he had talked about it with anyone. I held his hand and rubbed his arm. It felt like the right thing to do at that moment. When he finished the story, he just sort of stared off. I still wasn't sure how to respond other than maybe to say how awful that was, but the silence seemed sufficient. Silence and wine. I remember getting up and grabbing the bottle of wine that was half gone, moving my seat closer to Will, and just sitting there in the dark in front of the fire in silence. I poured him some wine, and he put his hand on mine. I set my glass on the ground and turned to kiss him on the cheek. Instead, I grabbed his face and kissed him on the mouth slowly. He didn't stop me. We went inside and slept together in the guest bedroom. I could tell that's what he needed, maybe not logically but that's what I felt. When we were done, he insisted on leaving which I thought was the right move. However, given how late it was and how much alcohol we had had, we drifted off and the next thing I knew, it was morning. It seemed so negligent. I knew Harvey wouldn't be back until Monday morning, but what if he had come back unexpectedly? Also, how many neighbors saw Will come over or the small fire in the backyard but then didn't see him leave? There were so many variables. Instead of Will leaving once he awoke, I made him something to eat, and he left around noon. You don't know who's watching. We didn't talk about it like it was a drunken mistake. It wasn't. It was the beginning of our relationship, one we couldn't see to its end.

What makes me the saddest, though, is knowing all our plans will never happen. God, we had so many plans. We were going to leave this place together once his contract was up. We had hoped for Paris. Who knows? Maybe we'd be traveling all over. Will would have certainly been invited to all sorts of events and lectures. We could have left this shitty fucking place. What infuriates me is Harvey brought that woman into our lives and destroyed everything we had. He was supposed to be this smart fucking guy too. If he had just chosen any other woman, none of this would have happened. Then he could have been like all those other academics who sleep around or fuck their students to no consequence. Sure, higher education. Elevating minds. The only things that are being elevated are their dicks or their fucking egos. I've never seen a more dysfunctional group of people in my entire life, and I've spent time with all kinds of people. You have a PhD and have written all these seemingly intelligent articles or books, but you mean to tell me you can't tell a crazy bitch when you see her. Goddamn it. Fucking bastard—I'm sorry . . . I don't mean to cry. I don't know. I just can't at this point. One minute I'm enraged by the whole situation and the next I'm sobbing and feeling this overwhelming sadness. I guess I just know I will always have this aching feeling that my life could have been so much more. I could have been with someone who made me feel alive, and that's just never going to happen. What Will did changed us. It changed everything. None of us will ever be the same after this. Will might go to prison for the rest of his life, for the rest of mine. I could wait for him, but it wouldn't be the same. The thought of being with someone who killed another person with his bare hands is too difficult to endure. I might as well go back to home to Pittsburgh, back to my parents because this place is dead. My life as I know it is dead. I feel like a ghost. And what do the dead do? They return to familiar haunts only to moan and echo past lives.

Chapter 9

Will awoke early Monday morning a little before six, already distracted. All he thought about was what his students would say concerning his weeklong hiatus. The Philosophy Club President would undoubtedly put him on trial, demanding an explanation for her inconsiderate professor's absence and a damn good one, too. In this educational economy, students wanted what they paid for, which happened to be the equivalent to an "A for effort." Anything less was grounds for a grievance. Isn't that how capitalism worked? Could he blame them? There weren't really discounts in this market unless you count scholarships or grants. And a refund? Unheard of, unless your terrible or delinquent professor somehow failed to cruise under the radar. Then they'd prorate it.

And then there was poor Jack who would limp into class with an over-animated expression of pain, seeking sympathy for his misfortune. The students would ask what happened, and he'd probably lie about some near serious but minor bike injury where some oblivious motorist nearly sideswiped him. Among these scenarios was the one where Will would yet again have to continue the façade of having crippling "vertigo," rendering him incapable of normal human function. What a stupid fucking excuse that was, but an excuse he intended to use with the utmost confidence because any ounce of weakness or uncertainty shown in this line of work, and you'd never shake the reputation of being a pushover.

As he poured a cup of coffee, Will still felt like he had gained zero clarity on the whole Lily situation, if you could even call it that. Wasn't that the point? Leave the Graybeard, clear your head, and get back to life, your real life. Yes, it was time to get back to his life but seeing her—it was her—had left him with the desire to see her again. It was Lily. The way she looked at him like she knew him, knew exactly what she was doing. Showing off even. Unless she had a doppelganger with an uncanny smile living in the middle of Ohio, which wouldn't be too unlikely given the 22,000 students who currently resided in Athens. Was anything really out of the realm of possibility? She had locked eyes with him. He didn't physically touch or speak to her that night, but an observation of phenomena (*i.e.,* Lily's presence) was evidence enough. However, the cliché "seeing is believing" didn't account for visual hallucinations and faulty memory reconstruction; research has shown that eyewitness testimony is one of the most unreliable forms of evidence in existence. He felt himself spiraling again. Will had the pressing feeling to scavenge through the garbage.

He left his coffee on the kitchen table and walked out the back door to the trash bin. He lifted the lid and ripped a hole into the side of the thin, white plastic bag. The lack of sunlight made viewing the bag's contents difficult. He dug through it until he found a black notebook covered in coffee grounds and smelling like a damp cigarette.

Back at the kitchen table, he sipped his coffee and opened the notebook. If it made no sense at this point, he'd throw it away, burn it even, and forget the whole thing. He leafed through the pages, finally landing on one:

FACTS
-Djarum Black cigarette butt in ashtray on porch – Lily's brand
-Overwhelming smell of perfume in bedroom, reminiscent (unmistakably) of Lily's perfume from small NYC shop (name?)
-Nick doesn't know Lily's whereabouts
-Night of symposium: Lily sat in the back of Burns Theatre
-Ray from Moe's gave me a weird look when I showed him a picture of Lily and asked if he'd seen her—he hadn't
-There are Zephyrs (surname) living in Ohio—they have no knowledge of being related to Lily

-Professor in the biology department refused to run DNA test of cigarette butt

<u>*UNCONFIRMED THEORIES*</u>
-Lily lives in Athens
-Lily knows where I live
-She has communicated with one or more of the department faculty/staff:
>*(a) She and Seymour are working together. Seymour's sad excuse for surveillance and intimidation*
>*(b) ~~She is a student at Athens U~~ CONFIRMED- she is not enrolled or living in student housing*
>*(c) She gained access to the house from university staff*

-She watches me at home and perhaps at work as well (possibly thanks to Seymour)
-Staying at one of the local hotels, but managers would neither confirm nor deny
-Nick is lying and knows where she is and might be with her. Could he be the reason she's here?

What he needed and what he wanted, as it was with most people, were not the same. Reading the notebook left him with an unsettling feeling he could not push from his mind. It didn't matter how rational he tried to be; past experience told him that she was literally capable of anything. If she wanted to be here, she would come. If she wanted to fuck up his life, she would find a way. But with all the time that had passed, why now? Or was he the one creating this implausible incident and circumstances that were in the process of derailing his sanity and his life? What if the facts were not facts at all but a curated list of unrelated phenomena that he collected, organized, and gave a theme? Again, the follow-up question was why now? He put the notebook in his messenger bag instead of returning it to the garbage where it belonged. He rubbed his eyes and cheeks before finishing off the last of his lukewarm coffee. The whole situation felt like Nietzsche's *eternal recurrence.* He went upstairs to shower.

It took a half second longer to start Will's car. The morning was cold, colder than normal near the end of October. With global warming and weather patterns changing, an early winter might be exactly what the meteorologists predicted. Then again, this was the land of unpredictable weather, where a single week could begin with temperatures in the eighties and then drop to below freezing, where sunshine and clear skies welcome you on Monday and by Friday there'd be an inch of snow. Will took his usual two-and-a-half-minute drive to Gordon Hall and shivered every second of it. A thicker coat would have been wise.

The parking lot wasn't as full as it usually was at nine-thirty on a Monday morning, an indication some students either dropped their morning classes or failed to see a reason to show. It beat the crowded parking lots and students walking around in baggy sweatpants and greasy hair as if they were part of some campus-wide pajama party. Will noticed Seymour's red Audi. It was best to avoid the man, given his weeklong absence.

Once inside the department, Will hoped to make it to his office without contact from anyone. Unfortunately, that would not be the case. The moment the door closed, Sylvie glanced up from her work and greeted him as enthusiastically as ever.

"Will, I'm so glad to see you."

"Morning, Sylvie. Back to the swing of things."

"Over the weekend I did a little research into your vertigo," she said, beaming.

Was that really necessary? he thought. "That was so nice of you, but you shouldn't have. I'm sure the worst has passed."

"Nonsense. I can't not do this. You know what it's like to get a little obsessed and gather as much information about something as possible. Let me show you what I found." She reached into a drawer behind her desk and pulled out a stack of papers thicker than anything Will had ever handed his students. "The first section of this explains the symptoms, but I'm sure you're aware of most of those since this isn't your first time. The second section is treatment and exercises you can do to help prevent reoccurrence. The third part is a collection of testimonials from people who live with vertigo. Finally, the fourth section talks about vertigo through the years. I thought it all very helpful and interesting. Did you know that an old nickname for vertigo was Watchmaker's Disease? Apparently, people who had to focus or concentrate on small tasks for extended periods of time were susceptible to bouts of vertigo. What an interesting fact?"

"I didn't know that." Will reluctantly took the stack of papers.

"And when you're finished with that," Harvey said, walking out of his office, "I'll bring you a copy of Hitchcock's *Vertigo*, so you can see what happens when it goes untreated." He grinned.

"You know," Sylvie cut in, "I almost included the film in here for him to watch, even though it's not really applicable. I do love James Stewart. But it's such an unusual role to see him obsessively following that girl, the ex-fiancée secretary, and trying to overcome his fear of heights." She looked at Harvey. "What's that called again?"

"Acrophobia," said Harvey.

"Right. You don't have acrophobia, do you Will?"

"No," said Will, feeling anxious. "I don't have a fear of heights, and I've seen *Vertigo*."

"Then you're familiar with the part where Jimmy Stewart drives himself crazy with his obsessions and chases after things he probably shouldn't," said Harvey. "And he inadvertently gets a woman killed because of it. It's a terrible thing to let your obsessions get the best of you."

Does he know about Anne? Lily? Will wondered. "Of course not, Harvey." He glanced at Sylvie who looked a little confused as if she were missing some deeper meaning, a vague reference, most likely the same thing Will was also not quite understanding. "Well, thanks again, Sylvie. I'll take a look at this stuff later today." Without acknowledging Harvey, Will left.

He passed Elizabeth's office. Her door was shut, but the light was on. He passed Seymour's office, relieved that the door was also closed, but the light was off. Once in front of his office, Will shifted the awkward stack of loose papers to one hand, took out his keys, and unlocked the door. Inside, he set his bag and the papers on his desk, a pitstop on the way to the class. He sat on the edge of his desk and crossed his arms. *What was that about?* "I just want a normal day."

His eyes wandered around the room, trying to clear his head, taking a few deep breaths, attentive to the negative space—bare white walls, the area around each book or shelf of books, the carpet. The absence of identifying objects on the walls and shelves were characteristic of who he seemed to be: a visitor. Maybe if he had just hung more pictures, then people wouldn't have to be so presumptuous, skeptical even. Maybe it was his fault for not making this place more of a residence than a waiting room. Seymour, or anyone for that matter, wouldn't have to invent their own narrative about who he was. But objects can be false signifiers, creating baseless inferences. Whatever the matter, people only cared about their own interpretation of things.

His eyes continued along the books on the shelves. Some were his and some were there when he arrived, and even the combination of books was a kind of red herring to getting inside William Thierry's head. He noticed a book lying flat on an otherwise barren shelf and walked over to put it with the others. *Flowers of Evil.* "Weird." He grabbed it. *I don't remember this,* he thought as he opened the cover to see something scrawled in black ink.

* * *

"One second," she said, leaning off the bed, reaching in her purse.

Will glanced at her naked back and the shape of her hips protruding from under the covers. Flawless. She came back with a book.

"Here," she said, handing it to him. "Read something from it."

"Did you really take the book from the party?"

"I borrowed it, kind of. I just wanted you to read something out of it like you did the other night. You can return it if you want, but I doubt he'll ever miss it." She looked at him as if she were letting him in on some lighthearted secret.

"Of course, he won't miss it." He leafed through the book and landed on "Her Hair."

When he finished, she took a black pen from his nightstand. "Write something to me."

"I'm not going to just write in someone else's antique book."

She snatched it from him. "Fine. Then I'll write something in it."

She thought for a moment and then said the words as she wrote them:

To Lily,
You're not so evil though you may be poisonous to cats.
Love,
Will

* * *

Will shut the book. "There's no way." He made an obligatory examination of the book for its authenticity, turning it from cover to spine to cover, as if there would be some clue to indicate how it materialized in his office. It was the same brown hardcover with gold script and edging. He opened it again and read the writing, her handwriting. "How the fuck did this get here?" *How did she get in here?* There was no mistaking that the book arrived sometime during Will's hiatus, but he should have seen it when he came to the department on Friday. Was he really that unobservant, distracted? Wait, no, he actually didn't go into his office that day what with Sylvie paying him more attention than usual. Had Sylvie let her in? Harvey? Seymour? Maybe she had given the book to someone else to put in here. There have been plenty of times students have entered his office unannounced, unnoticed, and often unwanted, but the door was always unlocked in those cases.

He glanced at the clock on the wall. Ten minutes until class. He took the notebook from his bag, opened it to the next blank page, and wrote the following:

Lily's copy of Flowers of Evil *on the bookshelf in my office. Either Lily was in here, or she had contact with someone who could have placed the book in here. Question office worker and maintenance personnel?*

Will placed both the notebook and the copy of Baudelaire in his bag and slung it over his shoulder. He turned the lights off, shut the door, and then checked to make sure the door was locked. The key slot and casing didn't appear to have signs of tampering. Will fiddled with the knob, turning it quickly, and then vigorously shaking it. He even added a few solid blows with his shoulder, trying to get the thing to budge. No luck. He turned to leave and saw Elizabeth standing outside her office, staring at him.

"You lock yourself out?"

"Um. No. Just making sure the lock isn't faulty. It felt like it was slipping or something. You know this old building."

"You alright?"

"I just think someone might have been in my office while I was away."

"I'm pretty sure someone was in your office," she said, plainly.

"Wait, what?" He let go of the knob and approached her. "Who was in my office?"

"I figured you knew. Something about needing notes or whatever for your students. I'd ask Harvey. Is something missing?"

Will was about to ask her more questions but stopped. "Thanks, Elizabeth." He headed for Harvey's office, passing Sylvie. He stopped in Harvey's doorway, neither bothering to address him nor knock. Harvey stood at his desk, looking through some papers.

"Why was someone in my office?"

He glanced at Will.

"Who exactly was in there?" He asked before Harvey could answer the first question.

"I had Sylvie scour your office for some kind of agenda, so we could have someone fill in for you during your absence, but you barely have anything in there."

"I never said it was—"

"You would have known this," Harvey cut him off, "if you had listened to your voicemail or answered your goddamn phone at all last week."

Will stopped and took a deep breath. "Sorry, Harvey. You're right. I'm going to make that up, like I said. I'm heading to my first class now, and I plan to get everyone caught up."

"I'd never just go into someone's office without first notifying them."

"Right." Will almost turned to leave but then asked, "So then no one else was in there, like possibly a student or, I don't know, Seymour?"

"Other than general maintenance, no."

Will acknowledged with a nod and left the office.

Most of the students were in attendance as Will unpacked his bag next to the podium in the front of the room. He did his best to avoid eye contact like it was his first day teaching. Too many apologies would make him look like he owed them something. Stephanie walked through the door with the usual entourage. Jack was nowhere in sight, which didn't set right with Will.

"Before I begin," Will said, "I just want to apologize for last week." He looked around the room, making eye contact with Stephanie at each pass. "I became ill after the conference, and it was difficult for me to do much. If anything like this occurs again, I promise to provide you with a substitute or at the very least notify everyone and email notes."

Stephanie whispered something to Patrick, and then he asked, "What exactly did you have, Professor Thierry?" A legitimate question.

I deserve this, Will thought. "I had an extreme case of vertigo, accompanied with flu-like symptoms."

"I heard it's a lot like the spins," said one girl.

"That's one way of looking at it, and in some respect, it is. I had issues with balance and walking. And like I said, flu symptoms."

"God, I hate the spins," said another. "I always end up throwing up."

"How do you get vertigo?" asked Patrick.

Will could not think of his name, ever. "In college, I think I got an ear infection and it just sort of happened for a while, months in fact, on and off." He lied. "I had to leave school for a semester." He shuffled through the papers in his bag and found a list of causes that Sylvie had provided him. "Here's a list of what causes it: Meniere's disease, vestibular migraines, labyrinthitis—"

"Labyrinthitis?" blurted Stephanie. "What does that even mean?"

"Watching David Bowie's performance in the *Labyrinth* might give you vertigo," said Patrick, smirking. "Do you really have a fact sheet about this?" he asked.

Classroom control, Will thought, as he felt his body flushing. "You know, Patrick, it wouldn't hurt for you to carry around a fact sheet. You might see your grade improve."

Half the class laughed, which silenced the student.

"If you must know, Mrs. Shepard in the philosophy department pulled together some information because of her concern. She's very considerate. But you spend enough time walking around this building, and you'd probably develop vertigo, too," said Will. No one laughed. "Anyhow, enough with that. Let's get back to where we left off, and we should finish the semester as intended." Will took out a copy of Derrida's *Writing and Difference*. "Turn to page 178 in your packet." As he leafed through the pages to the marker in his book, he noticed something move in the doorway. He looked up. It was Jack, limping pathetically into the classroom. Will tried to acknowledge him with a half-smile, but Jack avoided eye contact. The way he moved seemed exaggerated. His expression more pained than Will remembered, and the limp seemed kind of jerky like he was dragging a bullet wound. It was as if the guy had rehearsed his entrance.

"Derrida asserted, 'That philosophy died yesterday, since Hegel or Marx, Nietzsche, or Heidegger—and philosophy should still wander toward the meaning of its death—'"

A cell phone went off. Will looked up along with some of the students. Quickly realizing it was his, he walked to his bag and fished around until he silenced it. "Sorry everyone. Where was I?" He looked back at the book. "'Or that it has always lived knowing itself to be dying . . . that philosophy died one day, within history, or that it has always fed on its own agony, on the violent way it opens history by opposing itself to nonphilosophy, which is its past and its concern, its death and wellspring; that beyond the death, or dying nature, of philosophy, perhaps even because of it, thought still has a future, or even, as is said today, is still entirely to come because of what philosophy has held in store; or, more strangely still, that the future itself has a future—all these are unanswerable questions. By right of birth, and for one time at least, these are problems put to philosophy as problems philosophy cannot resolve.' What exactly is Derrida saying about the limits of philosophy?"

Will gathered his things as the class left. It felt good to be in the classroom again. Jack lingered as usual, which meant a lengthy conversation was to follow. Seemed like things were back to normal. Usually, this would have bothered Will, but he was glad the student's routine had not been hindered by the incident at the apartments.

"Will, can I talk to you?" asked Jack.

Will felt slightly panicked, anticipating the conversation. "What is it Jack?"

"The stuff over the weekend really fucked me up."

"This isn't the best place to talk about it. Why don't we go to my office?"

Jack, still sitting at the desk, lifted his leg and pointed at his foot. "I can't really make the hike, Will. I sprained my ankle when we were spying on—"

"Shh," Will motioned, finger to lips, walking to the door and closing it. "Okay, Jack. What do you want to talk about?"

"I had Dr. Buchanan's Existentialism class before this, and I just couldn't pay attention to a word he was saying. All I could think about was that woman. Jack looked down. "The look on her face was unflinching. She saw me, and I feel like Buchanan knows." He stood, readying himself to leave, but upon putting weight on his sprained ankle, he winced. "Sorry I brought it up." He slung his bag over his shoulder.

"That woman didn't recognize you, and Dr. Buchanan doesn't know anything. I'm sorry I asked you to do it. I didn't realize what we were getting ourselves into. But Jack, I think we should be able to deal with this like adults."

"Really? Since when is it a requirement as an adult to," using finger quotes, "'deal with' spying on people having sex. That's some weird fetish shit or whatever. I didn't sign up for that. I'll see you later." Jack opened the door and quickly limped out of the room.

Will didn't bother to chase him or apologize. He'd get over it eventually. Will reached for his phone to check the time. A new voicemail. He pressed the notification and listened.

"Will. Hi. It's uh . . . well, it's Lily. This is so weird, but I'm in Athens and wanted to see you. I'd leave you my number to call me back, but I'm sure that would give you all the more reason not to. I'm at the Graybeard Suites in Athens. My room is 203 if you want to catch up. If not, that's fine, but I think it would be good to see you. Bye."

At that moment, Will didn't feel like himself. All he could hear was a buzzing, something inaudible. He held the phone, but it didn't feel like it was in his hand. He was right. He was fucking right. And then it hit him. *The third room on the second floor. Harvey. There's no way.* His thoughts trailed off. He took out his wallet and grabbed the picture of Lily. He rushed out of the room and down the hall, quickly realizing he ran the wrong direction, turned around and headed to the front entrance. "Stupid fucking maze."

Jack wasn't in the building's entrance. Will pushed through the front door. The cold hit him. He immediately shivered. Groups of students moved from place to place but no Jack. Then in the distance, maybe a hundred feet away or so, he saw his student limping. "Jack," he shouted, running to catch him. He grabbed Jack's shoulder. Jack turned around.

"I'm really sorry," said Will. "I'll make it up to you, I promise. First, I just need one last favor."

"Seriously?"

Will held out the picture of Lily. "Is this the woman you saw in the room?"

Jacked looked at the picture. Unable to hide his surprise, he gave Will a suspicious look. "How do you have a picture of her? Do you know her or something?"

"Is this the woman you saw?"

"Yeah, but how—"

"Thanks," Will said as he turned and ran back toward Gordon Hall. "We'll have a beer soon," he shouted.

Larry Welch
In the Graybeard Suites, room 203

SEPTEMBER 2010

People give me shit for turning this room into a tourist attraction, but I don't see it that way. It's not like I'm doing anything wrong. It's my place, and I'm just charging a small fee to show people a room where something happened. Not so different from any other place, if you ask me. Who doesn't want to see room 217 when they visit the Stanley Hotel in Estes Park? You know, the one from *The Shining*? To be a business in this town, you need a gimmick or else how would you ever make any money? This is small town America. I've seen plenty of ambitious people open restaurants and shops and then close within a year or two. They didn't know their customer base or didn't have something unique to offer. You gotta appeal to your clientele, as they say, know what people want, and push what you got. Hell, Moe's had Guy Fieri stop by their place because one of the owners had gone to high school with him. And because of it, they showed up on an episode of *Drive-ins, Diners, and Dives* promoting their "Damn Near Famous Burger." People love hamburgers and celebrity endorsements. That's the dream. And don't get me started on Xeno's Akropolis. Nobody really went there until *My Big Fat Greek Wedding* came out. I should know. You can see the place if you just look over your shoulder. Yeah, across the street. And the owner isn't even Greek. He married in. But that's all it took.

So why can't I make the best of a bad situation. It's not like I wanted this to happen. I'm just trying to run a business and provide people an affordable place to stay. Nobody wants a person murdered on their property. It lowers the value. It makes people think they aren't safe. They start moving out or to another part of town, and sure enough, I could go out of business just like that. I got lucky, really. Things could have been much worse. The place could have been trashed. If the kill wasn't so clean, there could have been blood and who knows what all over the place. After the police finished the investigation and it wasn't deemed a crime scene anymore, I sort of left everything as it was. But no sooner than I locked the door, people started coming around asking about the incident or wanting to look at the room. People got no shame. First, it was the tenants that lived here, then it was the students who had heard about the murder. I wasn't in the room when it happened, but you don't have to be James Patterson to envision it. I was there when the professor called in the murder and then later when he was questioned by the police. I had to identify the body since I had her information and knew who she was. I mean, she had lived here for like three months at this point. I would say that makes me pretty damn credible. I even snapped a photo of her when I was in the room. You know, when the cops weren't looking. So lifeless and precious there on the floor. What a waste. She was so young and pretty. Such a tragedy. And believe it or not, at some point, people from different parts of the country were asking about the place. I was getting phone calls as far away as California. Who knew? They wanted to see what it looked like. They wanted to know where the murder took place, what the woman had done during her time here, if she was your typical stalker. They are worse than reporters. Did you know there is like a network of people who do crime and murder tours? Yeah, neither did I, but they follow serial killers and different kinds of murders and then visit the places where it happened. Pretty self-explanatory, I guess.

That gave me the idea to open up the room as a kind of tour, about a few months or so after it had happened. I left the layout in generally the same way, like I said. It didn't seem necessary to make any kind of renovations. I had it cleaned like any of the other rooms when tenants leave. I added a few framed pictures of lilies, as you can see, set a few vases of lilies around the room, and dubbed it "The Lily Suite." It's a nice touch, right? Thought it would really make it official and add a little ambiance to the place. I tripled the price of the room and made it either a nightly or weekly stay. You would not believe how many people want to visit. In case you're wondering, the room's booked until the end of the year. And you want to know why? People are curious about death, and they love a good murder story. They wanna be close enough but not too close. They don't wanna die, and they don't want their friends or loved ones to die. But give them a good murder story, and they eat that shit up. There's like encyclopedias and shit about this. Why do you think those true crime movies and books sell so well, even the shitty ones? Why does it seem like there's no end to serial killer documentaries, shows about men and women who killed their spouses, seasons of *Law and Order*? People want to know the details and the motives, man. The who, what, where, when, why, and how about it. And when it's in your hometown, even more so. Everyone says the Midwest is such a quaint place full of people with good morals. If it were, you probably wouldn't need a church on every other goddamn corner. So, I tell them as many details as I know, kind of tell them stories about her and what she did while she was here—embellish it a tad—and ask them if they want to see the photo for an extra couple bucks. And guess what? They ask to see the photo every single time. This is even a stop on this year's tour of Haunted Athens. One of those group tours led by some of our town's clairvoyants around Halloween. I know them all, and they're the real deal. I've had a few of them to the room, and they've said there's a lot of strange energy in there, man, in the whole place actually. I'm not surprised. This building has seen some things. If you only knew the people who had stayed here. Bands like Jefferson Airplane and Buffalo Springfield stayed here when they played in town in the late 60s. There's even a rumor that the Zodiac killer stayed in this very room. Recently, I had a writer come rent the room for a week. He said he was writing a true crime book about the whole incident called *The Death of Lily*.

As you can see, I also like to offer some related town history, man. I guess that's the benefit of being a townie. What's eerie about this whole situation is how this isn't the first Athens U professor to kill someone. People may not really know about it or remember, but it was in the paper from the day he was discovered, then through the trial, and finally his conviction and sentencing. I was just a teenager when it happened, but having lived here all my life, I remember it well. The guy killed his pregnant wife by suffocating her—or maybe he strangled her? I can't really remember which one. Either way, he squeezed the life out of her and their unborn child. Then he crammed her into a barrel and threw her in a lake just at the edge of town. I don't know how someone can do something like that, but it really shook people. Every time there was something new about it in the paper, my mother would just go on and on about how awful the whole thing was. How such a beautiful place like Athens, Ohio would have something like this happen. How some outsider came in and killed one of our own. At that time, the town was a little smaller, tighter knit. The part about her being pregnant was probably what set my mother off—people really hate it any time there's children involved, you know. But because he was a transplant and someone who educated the next generation, that really affected people. He was teaching their kids and should have been a little more high-minded. Not some degenerate who would just kill his pregnant wife because he was screwing some other woman. That's something that people don't forget, well, until they do. Man, it's funny how small towns will have that kind of selective amnesia. I'll probably have to start charging a lower rate for the room as time goes on. But I figure you gotta make hay while the sun's shining. People won't even remember her name in a few years. No one ever remembers the names of the victims unless we're talking like Sharon Tate who, coincidentally, was also pregnant. Hell, they barely remember the names of the killers unless they're high profile and have a real following, like Manson, Bundy, Dahmer, or John Wayne Gacy. Otherwise, you're stuck with some nickname that just basically describes who, where, or how you killed. The Boston Strangler. BTK (bind-torture-kill) Killer. The Acid Bath Murderer. Lady Killer (how original). Or recently, the Cleveland Strangler. That one kind of hit home being so close. They found eleven bodies decomposing inside the guy's house and basement, all women who had been raped and strangled. The smell was so bad the neighbors thought that something foul was going on at the sausage factory nearby. They even called the health inspector on the place. You can't make this shit up. It almost sounds like a joke. My point is, if I asked you to name the Cleveland Strangler, could you do it? Would you know his actual name? Probably not. But you'd most likely be able to tell me how he lured them in and killed them. What about any of his victims? You might know the types of victims: addicts and prostitutes. But do you know their names or the kind of lives they lived? The people they were before they were his victims? Could you honestly answer any one of those questions? I doubt it. No one cares about or remembers those details. And like this one, they are all just a bunch of dead girls.

Autumn Zephyr
In the Athens Police Station

OCTOBER 2009

I never met Will Thierry, Lily's murderer, who erased her from our lives, plucked her from existence. What made him think he was so special that he could just force himself onto her and determine her fate? Did he feel a sense of entitlement like so many men do when it comes to women and their agency, their bodies? Did he feel threatened? Did he lose control? There's a part of me that wants to know, demands to know. Maybe I want closure, but I don't think that's it. I'll never have closure, not with something like this. Then there's that part of me that already knows. The answer is always so banal, so predictable, so flimsy. It's always the same: men want to dominate women's bodies and minds, control the narrative. The insecurity and fear they feel when they realize it isn't possible is so pathetic. If he had thought of her as a living, breathing person with blood coursing through her veins who had thoughts and dreams and people who cared about her, how her life was braided together with so many other lives and that her life and now death affects them, maybe he would have resisted. But the piece of shit murdered my sister. My mother is a mess, basically in total denial. She used to call me every week and ask how Lily was because she was too afraid to ask her herself. She would tell me to make sure that Lily was making good choices and staying out of trouble. What do I tell her? The girl is nearing thirty, and she has to make her own choices and live with them. I was just there to listen and try to give her whatever I could. That's why I chose to come here and identify her and take her body back so we can make the funeral arrangements. I refuse to stay for any trial, and I certainly don't intend to ever return to Ohio. There's no doubt in my mind he'll defend his actions and deny any kind of responsibility. His lawyer will find a way to twist the facts and the situations, defend his character and make it seem like it was her fault. If she wouldn't have put herself in such a questionable situation with its strange and risky circumstances, then she wouldn't have died. How about if he hadn't have put his hands around her neck and squeezed the life out of her, she would still be alive. I couldn't stomach them putting a dead woman on trial, recklessly speculating about her motives, intent, character, and what she was thinking at the time. Blaming the real victim while the perpetrator is portrayed as some innocent, upstanding educator coerced into a situation like that. He was either defending himself or it was a crime of passion or provocation. I'm just so angry about this. No one deserves to have their life taken from them, especially by a person she considered to be the best thing to have ever happened to her. Yes, that's what Lily had said. She had come to my apartment a few times during their relationship a few years ago. The first time was to tell me she had met some guy who wasn't like any other guy she had ever been with. He was a professor and intelligent and just nice to be around. Then maybe six months later she had stopped by again and talked about how she fucked it up. Apparently, she had done something she shouldn't have and ruined things with him and everything was a mess. She was sobbing and frantic, which was unusual for her. She wouldn't tell me what had happened. She was always kind of vague on the details with her dating life unless she was bragging or something. So, this wasn't all that unusual. Lily would stop by, when my husband was at work, and kind of update me on her life. It was never anything huge or surprising. She'd talk about new jobs, things she was doing with her friends, new guys she was dating, plans she had, her dreams and ideas, or whatever else was going on. She might have been kind of flaky or someone who drifted from thing to thing, but she was young. Who isn't trying to figure out their lives in their twenties? Eventually, it seemed like she had gotten over him or whatever. He had moved on, and I thought she had too. But here I am finding out she had borrowed a friend's car, drove to Ohio, and had been living in what looks like a motel room for three months. I don't even know what to think. That's not the type of family or lifestyle we came from. I get that it was for this guy, but if he was so great, then why the hell did he kill her? Tell me that. I just don't understand how anything got to where it is at this moment. And the news says she was part of some love triangle with another professor from this college. She had her issues, but she was a good person. I don't know how she got herself mixed up in something like this. Did he manipulate her into it? Did he promise her something? This shouldn't have happened. Lily didn't deserve to die. It's all so strange and surreal. These people will go on living their lives and eventually forget about it, but I won't. I have to live with this void for the rest of my life. And all she'll ever be, at this point, is a photo on a website or an entry in a database. Another victim, another tragedy.

Chapter 10

Will arrived not more than ten minutes after leaving the university, but he sat in his car for nearly a half hour contemplating his new situation. *How did I not see this?* he thought. It was so clear now that hindsight took Will's paranoid coincidences and used it to power the neon sign pointing to Lily's room. It was the writing on the bathroom stall. However, sane people don't conspire, or, at least, they don't act on conspiratorial notions, hunches some people would call them. If he were going to confront her, he needed to do it now. She had been in his office and his home. Who knows who she had spoken to or what else she had done? If history tends to repeat itself, and she was capable of anything, then this wasn't going to end well, if it even would end. She might have talked to Anne and told her something so disturbing that Anne wouldn't even bring it up. What if Anne allowed that information to carve away at her insides, slowly changing the way she felt and acted toward him until one day she just blew up over something like making the coffee too strong or grabbing the wrong grocery item? Lily might be the whole reason why Seymour was acting this way. Will stopped there. The whole barrage of thoughts was overwhelming and nauseating. He felt the urge to vomit, then again, he may have only imagined it, hoping to expel the despair and angst he felt. Either way, he needed to alleviate all doubt. He had tangible proof and even a voicemail. What he truly needed was her physical manifestation, her animated flesh, some material act of confirmation.

He grabbed the book from his bag and left his car. Secrecy didn't matter at this point. He walked with such determination he felt like a caricature of himself, too confident and too serious, like there should be a soundtrack playing behind him. What would he do once inside? Seriously, *Will, what will you do once you get inside?* He stopped at the bottom of the steps. *Could this be another setup? Blackmail?* He proceeded up the stairwell that smelled a little like piss, probably compliments of a few drunken college students. Will glanced in every direction and even scanned the parking lot a third and fourth time as he walked along the second floor. He put his hand up to the sun-faded door to knock, but instead grabbed the doorknob and turned it. Unlocked. Of course, it was. He slowly opened it and stepped in.

Lily sat reclined on a bed with her knees to her chest. She was looking at her phone. There was nothing very significant about what she was doing or how she was dressed. It all seemed so casual. Jeans and a sweatshirt. She glanced up, and though she didn't seem surprised, she was clearly stifling her excitement. Something about her face.

"I didn't think you'd actually come."

"You knew I would, what with all of your subtle hints."

"I don't know what you're talking about," she said, now sitting up with her legs crossed lotus style.

"You don't?" Will stepped closer to the end of the bed. He was serious, almost too serious, like everything he had been doing was theater. "I don't know how or when you broke into my house and office, but I don't want you here." He tossed the book on the bed.

She glanced at the cover and looked back at Will, her stare energized despite his lack of response. It was like she refused to act the way that was expected of her. "I'm not sure what—"

"So, you didn't come to the conference," he interrupted, "and you didn't break into my house or spray perfume in my room or leave one of your goddamn cigarette butts in the ashtray on my porch."

Her face softened. "I can explain the conference and the book." She paused, but Will just made a face that implied *go on*. "I read about the conference and wanted to see you. I was just too afraid to actually tell you I was coming for fear you wouldn't let me in or something. I tried to sit in the back, unnoticed, but I knew you saw me, which is why I left so quickly. And the book. Well, I gave it to the office administrator and told her I had borrowed it one day and to just return it to your bookshelf. I guess I wanted you to find it at some point." She had teared up.

Will felt something remotely like affection for what she was saying, but the rational part of him knew how she could spin a story, how she could pull people in. "And the perfume and cigarette?"

She squinted with a look of confusion. "I seriously have no idea what you're talking about."

"You're not the only one keeping an eye on people. You need to leave before you do something you can't take back. Before you fuck up what I have here."

Lily began to cry, though it hardly affected the timbre of her voice. "I don't know what you're talking about, but I came here to be closer to you. I'm here because I love you, and I'm sorry for what happened with us. I know you still love me."

"I haven't loved you in years."

"That's not true. I know you still think about me."

"Please, just go back to New York. At least you still have that option. Back to Nick and all your shitty friends before you ruin things. Leave me and everyone in my life the hell alone."

"I can't do that, Will. There's something about you that's always stuck with me. There's still something between us. We're meant—"

"Stop it. This whole thing is fucking crazy. It's been two and a half years. There's nothing between us."

"But there is. There's always been a deeper connection. I feel it, and I know you do too. It's why you can't forget about me. It's why we're meant to be together."

"Just stop. It'll never happen. You're so parasitic." He paused. "I don't even know why I'm here. I just needed to know that I wasn't losing my mind. That I wasn't fucking crazy."

She slid to the edge of the bed and stepped to the floor. "I've done so much to get you here, standing in front of me. We can be together. Nothing else matters. If you're worried about Harvey's wife or your time left here, I'll tell him what you two have done while he's been working. It's so scandalous, Will."

"Fuck you."

"I would do anything to be with you. And if you think New York was bad, just imagine what these nice, small-town folks will think."

Will didn't know what to say. But there was that old feeling quickly resurfacing. Lily walked close enough to Will that he could feel her breath. He didn't move. It all felt so delicate.

"Just tell me you love me, and this will all be over. We'll go back to New York." She put her hand out, grazing Will's arm. "I know you still think about me."

He let her hand rest on his arm, her skin touching his. It felt so familiar. Her lips touched his. He lurched back and jerked his arm away. "No. I'm not doing this again." He turned and walked to the door. "Please. Just leave me alone."

"Fine. When Harvey finds out, you'll lose your job and then what? Where will you go? As long as you're alive, I'll find you. And someday we'll be together no matter what I have to do. You can't deny it forever. I will be the last thing you have in your life."

He had opened the door, but quietly shut it. He turned and walked toward her, his face void of expression. She half smiled as he approached her. Without a word of warning, he placed his hands on her neck as if going in for a kiss. Instead, he squeezed hard, forcing his thumbs onto her windpipe. Her eyes went wide and small gasps of staccatoed words came out but nothing intelligible. She tried to pull back, but with his momentum and her weak footing, they clipped the corner of the bed and fell to the floor. Now on his knees, he straddled her and squeezed harder than he'd possibly ever gripped anything before. She was erratic motion, grabbing at his hands. The grabbing turned into clawing. He didn't let up. Her face reddened. She kicked, her bare feet slamming into the carpet. She scratched at his hands and wrists, intermittently swiping at his face, only creating red marks. By the time she had even drawn blood, she was fading. Her movement slowed and finally stopped. Her body went limp, staring all the time at Will.

Will loosened his grip and slumped onto the floor next to her, slouched against the bed. He heaved, trying to catch his breath, not realizing how worn out he felt. His hands tingled and throbbed, the blood pumping hard. Thumping was all he felt through his entire body. He closed his eyes and leaned his head against the side of the mattress. Pounding in his ears. He opened his eyes, stood, and looked at Lily's lifeless body, her eyes vacant and bruises already forming around her throat. *This isn't real,* he thought. *This didn't happen.* He stared at his hands for what felt like an eternity. And then he fled.

Elizabeth Harlowe
In her office in the Department of Philosophy, James A. Gordon Hall

AUGUST 2011

Do you want to know why our program is still alive and functioning? It's not because the administration suddenly realized our department had inherent value as the core of a liberal arts education. The university kept our program as a direct result of the murder. Of course, they didn't quite express that as such, but it's obvious. It received national attention. The headlines were embarrassing: "Deconstructing Murder" and "Philosophy is not the only thing dying in Athens" or even "Professor kills ex-lover, philosophy enrollment spikes." This was not the kind of influence or reputation I wanted our department to have. It made us look like a bunch of crazy eccentrics. Rather than academic success and intellectual rigor, our program gained publicity through people's absurd and negligent behavior. But as acting chair, I want to shift the focus back to education and develop a reputation for turning out philosophically adept students, instead of sexually deviant faculty. The life of the mind is often a romanticized one, but it's neither sexy nor a violent one. However, that doesn't change what happened.

When they discovered the woman strangled inside the apartment, there was so much attention. Nothing like that had ever happened in this town. The type of violence that tends to permeate our campus is usually theft, alcohol related, or sexual assault, but never has a faculty member of the college killed someone. This was no ordinary occurrence, and the weeks that followed were tense. Reporters and questions. The police dissected Thierry's life. We were all questioned again and again. The only people who knew anything turned out to be Dr. Buchanan and his wife Anne. The administration told us to respond with the appropriate action to avoid further scandal or a perceived cover up. Now that Thierry is in custody, and the headlines have died down some, at least the national ones, I can talk about the department.

We finished the fall semester, some of us taking a partial overload by teaching the remainder of Thierry's courses. We cancelled the Death of Philosophy course and awarded students full credit. We also provided counseling services in our department for the students, if needed. Near the end of winter break, the department met with Dean Murphy and the university president. He laid out the path for the rest of the academic year, which included several meetings that would decide the future of our department.

They made the following recommendations for a course of action. First, Dr. Buchanan was to be removed from his position as chair, and I was named interim chair for the time being. Dr. Buchanan would still be allowed to teach, but he would have to teach his full load. The philosophy conference would be postponed the following academic year. Due to Thierry's absence and the unexpected increase in spring enrollment (twenty-five percent!), we hired a few more adjuncts and gave a current part-time instructor a temporary full-time appointment. With the additional influx of students for the spring semester, our program was seeing numbers it hadn't seen since the eighties, due in part to the scandal. Despite this strange celebrity our department gained, there seemed to be genuine hope and direction for our program. In May, the administration again met with our department, and I was made acting chair. Dr. Buchanan was put on leave, and we were given three full-time positions: one visiting lectureship, one full-time NTT appointment, and one tenure-track appointment. The dean expressed his desire for "world-class faculty," so we needed to find the best. Dr. Dylan was in line to retire but agreed to stay on one more year to help with the transition. The final implementation, as the dean put it, was to allocate more funding to our department in order to do more for our students. Better faculty means better students means a better program, which leads to more enrollment. We went from being a program on the edge of closure to being valued and invested in. I hate to say it, but this was the best thing that could have happened to the philosophy program, maybe even the university.

We are in a position for our program to develop into something distinguished and notable. We've laid out a new plan to better engage students and prepare them for either jobs after undergrad or graduate degrees. We're more involved with other philosophy associations and programs. We've developed a lecture series that allows for contemporary philosophers to connect with our students. We've also partnered with Freie Universität Berlin for study abroad opportunities. These measures could mean Athens University will turn out the next great minds of this generation, encouraging more women to study philosophy. No longer will we have to tolerate old white men dominating the intellectual playing field, men whose ideas relegate women to lesser roles. There seems to be a bright future ahead for not only our program but our discipline as well. Perhaps the days of death and decline are past.

Thomas Dylan
In the Campus Reading Room, Manasseh Cox Memorial Library

OCTOBER 2011

I used to come here almost every day during my tenure as a professor of philosophy. The university added this observation area where we stand, a kind of cozy reading room for students, sometime in the mid-nineties when it began the first phase of the campus-wide renovations to increase enrollment. This room is rather gratuitous, considering the floor, ceiling, and walls are cherry wood, not something less expensive like pine or poplar with a cherry stain or even wood paneling, and there are over two dozen plush armchairs at five hundred dollars a pop like it's a presidential study. I'm not saying the students don't appreciate or deserve that kind of luxury, but the crumbs in the cushions and the drink stains on the upholstery may prove otherwise. It's truly one of the better additions provided by the university, a room that could potentially draw more students to the library. What a thought. Granted, they also added a Starbucks on the first floor, the fourth one on this damn campus. As you can see this building is massive, the tallest building on campus and the highest point in Athens County. The founders clearly had the American notion of a "city upon a hill," or college rather, seeing as the university predates the town's establishment. In this reading room, you can see everything in the surrounding area, and undoubtedly, one can see the Cox Library from nearly any point in town. It's our beacon, what people should be looking to, thinking about, seeking out. This place is where knowledge is unearthed, a kind of potential energy. And so, I would get my coffee and an éclair, walk from the Gordon Hall parking lot, take the elevator up fifteen floors, sit in one of those cushy armchairs and stare out at the campus. The untold possibility, so still, so serene, just waiting for something important to happen. I'd have a momentary sense of pride as I'd sit here able to see everything as the sun rose on a new day, thinking of what could be discovered. But let's be real, that barely happens here or at any public university in the country for that matter, at least among the general student population. These kids are just out of high school and don't know how to handle their newfound freedom in any other way than trying to get laid and binge drinking cheap alcohol. So many of them are just barely managing their coursework, nursing hangovers, daydreaming, or are so full of anxiety they can barely produce a reasonable thought in their brains that even mirrors critical thinking let alone innovation. Whose fault is that? Grade schools don't prepare students for college, so the bastards are already starting this race with their shoes untied. Students blame faculty for low grades, difficult material, inflexible deadlines, or chafing personalities. Faculty blame coddling or negligent parents, parents complain to administration that their children are treated unfairly, and the administration reprimands faculty for having any standards whatsoever. All the while, banks are giving out loans so great that these kids could, in theory, pay tuition, cover all their amenities, buy a new wardrobe, and even lease a car with the money left over. And why is that? Because even though we value education, we value comfort more, despite the cost and unreliability of both. Comfort is the last thing that will get them anywhere, especially when it comes to their education. As an educator, you try to push them and present them with challenging material, and they complain. They aren't ready to contemplate their insignificance, especially in an era where everything is paradoxically mundane and amazing, where they've spent most of their lives receiving rewards for doing what is expected of them. And all of that is done with a mixture of sincerity and ironic detachment. They truly think they are going to be well off with their degree. Once they do graduate and realize securing an entry-level job is difficult and a dream job nearly impossible, their future looks abysmal. Maybe they were poorly advised because we want them to succeed, but we don't want to crush their dreams by showing them job market statistics.

I taught for forty years in the philosophy department, and I do believe in the intrinsic value of the humanities. But let's face it, the majority of these students will not go on to do great things. Many of the students I've taught in undergrad were using this as a means for self-discovery and finding their place in the world. That's fine in one respect. People should be using the humanities as they were intended: to explore the depths of humanity. Yet that seems like a high price just to figure out who you are. A stack of books, some traveling, and a set of challenging circumstances could facilitate that. What's funny is, again, so many of my students thought they were going to be the next great writer or philosopher and that their thoughts were completely unique and awe-inspiring. What most of them couldn't see, due to inexperience and a lack of self-awareness, was their perspectives amounted to a watered-down version of existentialism—*Sartre Lite, Diet de Beauvoir, Camus Zero*. It's rather pathetic, but you look at them like cute little puppies you fostered and trained. You hope for the best, but you don't know how they will be with someone else. You pray or hope they don't turn into the asshole that constantly barks at every little thing and jumps on everyone, the one you can't take for a walk because he might bite a child. And again, I ask, whose fault is that? Well, in the department there was, and I imagine there still is because I haven't been gone that long, a poster to the left of the door as you entered the department titled, "Who Has a Degree in Philosophy?" Below the heading are about fifty portraits of famous and successful people ranging from Angela Davis to Steve Martin to Alex Trebek to David Foster Wallace, one of the greatest minds in American Letters. You know what I think about that poster? Horseshit. Absolute horseshit. First, a philosophy degree even twenty years ago had more currency than it does today. Second, to think that any of my past students could hold a candle to any of the individuals on that poster because they received a four-year philosophy degree from Athens University is absurd and delusional. What job exactly does this degree prepare or qualify them for other than "Bachelor's degree required"? There is no job as a philosopher waiting to be filled once they graduate. There's no aptitude test to rate their level of profundity unless you take a "Which Philosopher Are You?" quiz online. Hell. There are so few teaching positions in philosophy that no one in their right mind would ever bother with a graduate degree in the field. And whether it's a bachelors, masters, or even a doctoral degree, most of them end up working as bartenders or in the service industry. I had a student who graduated a few years back, and he still works at the bagel shop in town. When I see him, he tends to give me that look of shame shrugged and talks about having a flexible schedule and being able to do what he wants, which gives him time to read, write, and think. He's a smart kid with no ambition because you should be doing those things regardless of the schedule you have. But I'm sure he thought he would get a job and do great things and was unique and profound. They all do. Another student guilty of bad faith.

Every year we feed them this message at commencement, the culmination of academic horseshit. The modestly rehearsed university orchestra plays as the procession of distinguished faculty advance down the aisle, each in his or her respective alma mater's garb, some more colorful and elaborate than others, while the president greets and admonishes a captive crowd eager to hear their child's name read aloud and watch their student walk across the stage to receive that hard earned diploma after a speaker, typically a white-collar professional whom the president praises with accolades because they're friends, gives a speech about the power of perseverance and accomplishment of a college degree, and the families laugh and cry and congratulate everyone in a large group hug, lighting cigars and wooing. We all know this event, and if you've been to one, you've been to them all. For the students and parents, this is a milestone event, one marked with pride, prestige, and symbolism. And why shouldn't they look at it like that? For some, this is a major accomplishment and well deserved. However, for the faculty, it's really just one last annoying event they have to attend before they can post grades and check out for the summer.

As each year went by during my tenure, this event felt less

distinguished and more like a dog and pony show. "Pomp and Circumstance" sounded more like "Entry of the Gladiators." This senile, stubborn, and undignified group of brightly colored circus clowns shuffled to the beat, rubber necking everyone in the room, eating up the attention or better yet not acknowledging anyone, as if they were royalty and no one was worthy to touch their garments. Just a group of geriatrics in colorful bathrobes with a lifetime full of flaws. Did you know that one of the professors, whom I will leave unnamed, used to wear a witch's hat with a long peacock feather in its brim? She didn't like that her original, accompanying cap was so plain and simple. You better believe people complained because no one wants to be outdone. And their excuse? She was defiling the sanctity of the ceremony. I still laugh about that fucking hat, and part of me wishes she would continue to defy decorum and wear it anyway. Stir up the pot a little. And the speakers got worse and worse every year. It was like sticking a ventriloquist dummy in an expensive suit at the podium and playing a recording. Every message was the same. Now, I don't encourage paying exorbitant amounts of money for celebrity speakers, but if I hear another businessperson relate an expensive summer excursion to these students' career paths or even the journey of life, I may run around the auditorium, screaming like a stark-raving lunatic before committing seppuku on stage. The luxury of "hiking" the Swiss Alps should not be a metaphor for the failure and success of young people's lives and careers. How do you reconcile that image with the surmounting student loan debt? The oversaturated job market? The economic recession? *Just keep climbing!* And finally, the students at this point get called up in droves, quickly herded across the stage, names mispronounced despite the supposed safeguard of phonetic spelling—god forbid you're a person of color, an international student, or your name just has some ethnic flair—and then handed a dummy diploma that isn't worth a goddamn. It's truly disgraceful.

But it's been two years since I really had to be part of that, two years since Thierry killed that woman. You'd think an event like that would shake a university, having a faculty member murder someone in cold blood. All it did was bring more national attention to this place, which meant more students, more funding, and the renovations continue undisturbed. The philosophy department had a spike in enrollment, which basically guaranteed the viability of the program and the faculty and staff. We were actually able to hire some full-time positions and a handful of adjuncts, the wheel horses of any institution of post-secondary learning, once Harvey and I left. I'm certain that with Thierry's reputation he could have had a permanent position here if it weren't for the legal issues. He became a celebrity of sorts. The man was accused of murder but is being tried for manslaughter. The most he can get is ten years in prison, but because of his insanity plea, he'll likely serve it at a psychiatric facility. It's a shame but not surprising. Any person is capable of any kind of vice or virtue providing the right circumstances.

Even with all that has passed, nothing really feels much different than before, I suppose. From up here, you can see that the university has not slowed its pace with the renovations. There's something troublesome about how people can mistake remodeling for prosperity and greatness. Sure, the campus looks nicer and more people will want to be here but the same could be said for gentrification: there is always a group who will be disparaged and displaced. In the latter, it's the impoverished, usually non-white, inhabitants who are forced out and then can't afford to enjoy whatever becomes of the area, usually hip stores and restaurants and high-priced condos. And no one seems to mind because the place looks better, and the burden has been moved. In this instance with the university, it's always the students. They are the only way this model works. But there has to be an end goal, and it's certainly not improving the education of the students, despite what the top says. The aesthetics do not change the way the place is operated, and it sure as hell doesn't improve the quality of educational instruction, which is in the most disrepair.

We believed it at first, when the renovations began with the library, again, where we stand in this very room. We praised the administration for wanting to attract students to the place that could provide them with the most knowledge, the most appropriate place to study. But it was merely sleight of hand, a bait and switch. I cannot tell you how many times I've seen members of the Office of Institutional Advancement bring donors and developers here to survey the campus and talk about the changes that could and would inevitably be made and how they would better integrate the university and the town. This reading room was merely a fancy observation deck for them to have a full panoramic view of what the university could be, and all the while, never once mentioning the building that facilitates this surveying, all these books on every subject in so many languages. Athens' Tower of Babel. Sometimes I would leave the library, envisioning the weight of all that it contains, its relative size to mine, to other buildings on campus or in town, how it contains multitudes.

In front of the library is a large patch of grass known as the Quad. The university uses it for festivals or events. Students will sit in the grass and study or just socialize with other students like these are the best years of their lives. But when that area is full of people for any number of reasons, I've envisioned the library falling on the masses of people gathered, crushing and killing them. I understand how morbid that sounds, and I'm not in any way encouraging or wishing a kind of terrorist attack or literal disaster, but it's something I think about every time I'm here. The image is forever embedded in my mind—not the weight of the building materials or the force of the building's collapse but all those books toppling to the ground, the intrinsic weight of those words and ideas from all points in time, so heavy that these human bodies couldn't withstand the impact but only, maybe their minds. And once the dust settles, people would know what ideas can do, the power that language and knowledge truly possess.

Acknowledgments

I have enormous gratitude for so many people.

This book would not have seen the light of day if it weren't for Anthony Tamburri, Fred Gardaphé, and Paolo Giordano; Nicholas Grosso's expert editorial guidance; and the support of Bordighera Press.

To my parents, Paul and Joyce Meduri, for your love, strength, and support over the years that helped fuel my creativity. I am indebted to my wife and first reader, Amber, whose love inspires me every day and to my children, Lil and Milo, who make each day challenging and meaningful—thank you for understanding when I need to write. To my brother and fellow armchair philosopher, Jeremy, for encouraging, antagonizing, and collaborating with me for most of our lives—we've kept each other sane all these years. To the Meduri family and Anderson family alike who always cheered on my creative endeavors. To Bryan and Lori Gray for the support, the dinners, the walks, and the conversations.

I'm grateful to the collaborators:

To the NEOMFA for cultivating my writing, for critiquing early chapters, and for the many late-night beers. To David Giffels for your generous insight and support. To the Kent State University English Department for invaluable teaching and academic experience. To Chris Prosser and Ben Zushin for being gracious yet critical readers of early drafts. To Korey Kunze for the talent, artistry, and vision that went into your cover artwork. To the word nerds in the Tooling U-SME Content Department for making work enjoyable. To Rodney and Carla Wilson for the countless cups of coffee, conversations, hospitality, and friendship—believe it or not, I wrote the first draft of a short story that would later become this novel in the back of Scribbles. To Mike Sanders for introducing me to the postmodernists and for pushing me to write even when I didn't know what the hell I was doing. To Patrick Davis, Peter Campion, and Cory Firestone at Unbound Edition Press for first publishing "Down the Garden Path" in the anthology *The Experiment Will Not Be Bound.*

And without the support, direction, mentorship, and encouragement from Varley O'Connor, there would be no book. You dedicated so much of your time to nurture this work from its inception.

Thank you.

About the Author

MATTHEW MEDURI is a writer and educator living in the Midwest. His writing has appeared in *Belt Magazine*, *Catamaran*, *Chautauqua*, *Gastronomica*, *Story*, and others. He was twice listed in "Other Distinguished Food Writing" in *Best American Food Writing* and is the recipient of an Individual Excellence Award from the Ohio Arts Council. *Collegiate Gothic* is his first novel.

VIA Folios

A refereed book series dedicated to the culture of Italians and Italian Americans.

KATHY CURTO. *Not for Nothing*. Vol. 134. Memoir.
JENNIFER MARTELLI. *My Tarantella*. Vol. 133. Poetry.
MARIA TERRONE. *At Home in the New World*. Vol. 132. Essays.
GIL FAGIANI. *Missing Madonnas*. Vol. 131. Poetry.
LEWIS TURCO. *The Sonnetarium*. Vol. 130. Poetry.
JOE AMATO. *Samuel Taylor's Hollywood Adventure*. Vol. 129. Novel.
BEA TUSIANI. *Con Amore*. Vol. 128. Memoir.
MARIA GIURA. *What My Father Taught Me*. Vol. 127. Poetry.
STANISLAO PUGLIESE. *A Century of Sinatra*. Vol. 126. Popular Culture.
TONY ARDIZZONE. *The Arab's Ox*. Vol. 125. Novel.
PHYLLIS CAPELLO. *Packs Small Plays Big*. Vol. 124. Literature.
FRED GARDAPHÉ. *Read 'em and Reap*. Vol. 123. Criticism.
JOSEPH A. AMATO. *Diagnostics*. Vol 122. Literature.
DENNIS BARONE. *Second Thoughts*. Vol 121. Poetry.
OLIVIA K. CERRONE. *The Hunger Saint*. Vol 120. Novella.
GARIBLADI M. LAPOLLA. *Miss Rollins in Love*. Vol 119. Novel.
JOSEPH TUSIANI. *A Clarion Call*. Vol 118. Poetry.
JOSEPH A. AMATO. *My Three Sicilies*. Vol 117. Poetry & Prose.
MARGHERITA COSTA. *Voice of a Virtuosa and Coutesan*. Vol 116. Poetry.
NICOLE SANTALUCIA. *Because I Did Not Die*. Vol 115. Poetry.
MARK CIABATTARI. *Preludes to History*. Vol 114. Poetry.
HELEN BAROLINI. *Visits*. Vol 113. Novel.
ERNESTO LIVORNI. *The Fathers' America*. Vol 112. Poetry.
MARIO B. MIGNONE. *The Story of My People*. Vol 111. Non-fiction.
GEORGE GUIDA. *The Sleeping Gulf*. Vol 110. Poetry.
JOEY NICOLETTI. *Reverse Graffiti*. Vol 109. Poetry.
GIOSE RIMANELLI. *Il mestiere del furbo*. Vol 108. Criticism.
LEWIS TURCO. *The Hero Enkidu*. Vol 107. Poetry.
AL TACCONELLI. *Perhaps Fly*. Vol 106. Poetry.
RACHEL GUIDO DEVRIES. *A Woman Unknown in Her Bones*. Vol 105. Poetry.
BERNARD BRUNO. *A Tear and a Tear in My Heart*. Vol 104. Non-fiction.
FELIX STEFANILE. *Songs of the Sparrow*. Vol 103. Poetry.
FRANK POLIZZI. *A New Life with Bianca*. Vol 102. Poetry.
GIL FAGIANI. *Stone Walls*. Vol 101. Poetry.
LOUISE DESALVO. *Casting Off*. Vol 100. Fiction.
MARY JO BONA. *I Stop Waiting for You*. Vol 99. Poetry.
RACHEL GUIDO DEVRIES. *Stati zitt, Josie*. Vol 98. Children's Literature. $8
GRACE CAVALIERI. *The Mandate of Heaven*. Vol 97. Poetry.
MARISA FRASCA. *Via incanto*. Vol 96. Poetry.
DOUGLAS GLADSTONE. *Carving a Niche for Himself*. Vol 95. History.
MARIA TERRONE. *Eye to Eye*. Vol 94. Poetry.
CONSTANCE SANCETTA. *Here in Cerchio*. Vol 93. Local History.

www.ingramcontent.com/pod-product-compliance
Lightning Source LLC
Chambersburg PA
CBHW020400030726
47496CB00007B/2232